# The Flower Man's Daughter

# The Flower Man's Daughter

## Jack Sobel

3/25/2010

To My Long Time Friend Dave —

Thanks for reading this story — I hope you enjoy it!

Jack

**To order additional copies of this book, contact:**
Xlibris Corporation
1-888-795-4274
www.Xlibris.com
Orders@Xlibris.com
50344

To Debbie, for all she does,
and all she is.

Heartfelt thanks to
editor extraordinaire, Alexis Richland,
and artist, Dennis Wheeler.
To Amber and Sami,
Faye, Lou, Gary and Stu,
Gary H. and Marty,
TJ, Frank and Tom,
Donna and Denis,
Glenn the gun collector,
Lee the storytelling sailor,
Duane the photographer,

and especially to Roberto, Dora and Andrea.

# PROLOGUE

Tony Gannon's sleep was interrupted by the sound of an air force jet streaking overhead. Unusual. Downtown Santiago wasn't in a military fly zone. *I must be dreaming*, he thought. He kept his eyes closed. But then crackling noises came from several different directions, the reports of automatic rifle fire. And then the vibrating bass tones of the tanks joined the chorus. Their engines roared in a deep throaty chant, like a hundred monsters growling in harmony as their treads rumbled across the cobblestone streets. From the sounds of it, they were working their way toward the Presidential residence, *El Palacio de la Moneda.* Tony's bed vibrated and shook, and he came fully awake. Then the phone rang.

"Stephens?" It took Tony a second to recognize the voice on the other end: John Colson, the head of CIA Branch 5 operations, which included Uruguay, Paraguay, Argentina, and Chile. Tony had only seen him at a couple of briefings and had never spoken to him directly. When Mr. Colson addressed an assembly of field officers, they listened carefully. He gave out information and instructions with particular authority, always involving especially important or sensitive issues. He didn't repeat himself, and he rarely answered questions. His involvement signaled "priority" with a capital P. Tony knew he was about to receive a varsity assignment.

"Yes, sir. This is Andre A. Stephens." Tony tried to sound alert and ready.

"You going to sleep through this goddamned party, rookie?" Mr. Colson barked.

"No, sir, Mr. Happ." Tony was careful to address Colson by his code name.

"Well then, get in the white Volvo waiting in front of your building. The driver will take you to the palace. You'll be meeting a guy there. Name of Mongoose. Bring your briefcase."

Tony had an official tool kit comprised of a false identification card, some cash, a pack of local cigarettes, and some disguise materials including fake eyeglasses. But the reference to his "briefcase" meant he was to bring his gun. He was not authorized to carry it unless specifically instructed, which hadn't yet occurred in his short career. This would be the first time. It was now unmistakable. Something serious was happening.

Tony bounced out of bed and was dressed in an instant. His "briefcase" was always ready, loaded and tucked in its ankle holster. He grabbed it and strapped it on. A glance at his watch told him it was 10:00 AM. He scurried down through the lobby and flew out the front door of the building. The presidential palace was exactly two kilometers to the northwest. Outside, the roar of the tanks was eclipsed only by the occasional sound of an explosion bursting somewhere in the distance, and the sound of small arms fire. The morning sky to the northwest was lit up, as if by lightning, but there were no clouds and no rain, and in between flashes, the sky was blue and clear. It was man-made fire, the kind that accompanied regime change in South America.

# CHAPTER 1

In Monday's barrage of new mail, phone calls, conferences, and meetings, a telephone message at the prestigious Miami law office of Ginsberg, Simon, Dunphey, Gamble and Graham could easily have been overlooked. A young woman about to graduate the University of Miami School of Law was inquiring about employment. No reason for it to stand out—most of the partners were Miami alumni and the firm kept regular contact with the school's placement office, hiring several new lawyers every summer. But this candidate had asked for Anthony Gannon by name.

Tony brought the pink message slip to his secretary. The firm's offices were on the thirtieth floor of the Intercontinental Building, with a view eastward across the blue-green expanse of Biscayne Bay to Miami Beach and the Atlantic, and Deborah Thomas often watched the big cruise ships make their way out to sea. "Ms. Thomas, shouldn't this go to Heinemann for the recruitment committee?"

Ms. Thomas looked up. "Oh, yes, Mr. Gannon. I told her about our hiring committee, but she said you'd want to talk to her. About Carlos and Diana Gonzales. That's all she said. We were interrupted, I guess. Do you want me to call her back?"

Tony felt goose bumps rise. He was a senior partner in a prestigious law firm, a veteran attorney not to be trifled with—feared, even. He was married, happily, and no longer had a thirst for extracurricular flings. His dark hair had thinned considerably and what was left was half gray. More than a few pounds of softness had gathered around his middle. *Carlos and Diana Gonzalez.* Thirty years earlier he had witnessed incredible chaos in Chile, chaos to which he himself had secretly contributed, and about which he had not spoken since. For thirty years he had protected the secrets of those times, but he had never forgotten them.

Tony ran his hand over his mouth and then stroked his beard, his mind drifting back. The Gonzalez's story began in 1973, in Santiago, the capital of Chile, during the whirlwind of revolution. Actually, it had started the year before that, in America, on the Ivy League campus of Yale University.

# CHAPTER 2

Tony felt more than a little out of place entering Yale as a freshmen in 1968. Other than some sons of powerful families whose acceptance had been predicated more on the strength of their family's wealth and power than on their academic abilities, Yale students were the brightest applicants from preparatory schools around the world. Tony Gannon, in contrast, was a happy-go-lucky fellow from a rough-and-tumble neighborhood in the suburbs of Philadelphia. But he was bright and adventurous, and by the time he entered his senior year of high school, his academic and extracurricular record had been impressive enough for his guidance counselor to believe Tony could qualify for a scholarship wherever he chose to go. So Tony had set his sights high. Why not think Ivy League?

Harvard's application called for him to list every book he had read in the preceding ten years (which meant going back to age seven) and required several essays. Though he wouldn't have admitted it, he was intimidated. And it was too much work; not exactly Tony's cup of tea. Yale's application was shorter. Straightforward with no essays to write. So Tony chose Yale.

He filled the application out without involving his parents. They hadn't gone to college and couldn't have offered much help. Frank Gannon thought a man should take no guff from anyone, that sometimes he needed to earn respect with his fists. Angela Gannon preached the opposite—that displays of anger and violence showed a lack of class—that intelligence and civility were what people respected and what true manhood was really about. Tony made sure that no one ever took him for a coward, but at the same time, he didn't bully anyone or start fights. If on occasion, his father and mother simultaneously congratulated and chastised him for his involvement in a schoolyard skirmish, that was all right. And both his parents had always stressed the value of education. In fact, Tony had gotten sick of hearing that it was the best way to avoid a lifetime of backbreaking labor.

All first year students lived in Welch Hall. Each floor held two residential suites, along with a large bathroom and shower. The suites consisted of a common living room and two double bedrooms, housing four boys. Tony shared one bedroom with Henry Harper, a quiet fellow from Syracuse, New York. Alex Liggio, a laid-back Californian, and J. Curtis Pierpont shared the other. Although all three were "bluebloods", Henry and Alex were good guys, and Tony liked them. Pierpont was another story.

J. Curtis Pierpont's future had been well assured by the trust fund his parents established for him when he was still in the cradle. He had been educated at one of the finest boarding schools on "the Continent," which is where he had learned his manners, and fluent French. Pierpont knew which fork to use to eat his salad at a formal dinner and actually owned a custom-fitted tuxedo. He spent more time at the squash courts than the library. On weekends he liked to take the train from New Haven down to New York City to hobnob with the "in crowd." His family's main residence was in Palm Beach, Florida, but they also had a twenty-second floor apartment in Manhattan at the luxurious Hanover House. "Quite a satisfactory view of Central Park," Pierpont carefully observed, with appropriate reserve, around anyone worth impressing.

But what galled Tony, what really stuck in his craw, was Pierpont's pipe. He had an entire rack, in fact, displayed on the mantle, containing an assortment of elegant burl and briar masterpieces with names like Dunhill and Churchill. To Tony it looked ridiculous, an eighteen-year-old boy puffing away with his nose in the air and his eyebrows knitted contemplatively in the unmistakable posture of a junior aristocrat. Tony could have tolerated him, but for the disdainful attitude J. Curtis displayed for anyone boorish enough not to have inherited big money and upper class refinement. J. Curtis regarded such commoners as barely above street urchins. Low-class hooligans, the lot of them. Hardly civilized, to be sure.

Tony tried to stay away from him, but that was difficult in the modest Welch Hall quarters. So he decided to have a little fun with the guy. Maybe loosen him up. He began calling him Curt, even after Pierpont pointed out that family and friends always called him J. Curtis. That spurred Tony on to even greater displays of familiarity, like reaching across the table in the dining hall to take a forkful of Pierpont's mashed potatoes. "Let me try them spuds, Curt," Tony would say. "Thanks, ol' buddy!" J. Curtis wouldn't eat another bite, but he was too polite to protest, and instead carried his tray back to the kitchen and put it on the bus table.

For several weeks, Tony Gannon and J. Curtis Pierpont managed to coexist. Then Pierpont did something he shouldn't have done, and Tony reacted by doing something he shouldn't have done either.

Tony had gotten a job at the Yale student laundry. He would spend one night a week dumping dirty sheets from pull-string blue laundry sacks into large canvas carts, and delivering them to the massive washing machines. The pay was minimal, but there was one perk: free linen service. Once a week, another student working for the laundry would come to his room, pick up the sack stuffed with his dirty bed sheet, pillowcases, and towels, and leave clean replacements in the common room.

J. Curtis had come back from a brisk squash match and was preparing to enjoy a smoke. But the tar in his pipe had accumulated a bit, and needed to be cleaned. He pulled the stem from the bowl and looked around for something to wipe off the thick black resin. Tony's clean towels were lying across the back of the sofa. J. Curtis Pierpont had grown up with maids. There was never a shortage of clean anything in his house. If one needed a towel, well, one simply asked and a fresh one was provided. So he didn't understand Tony's anger when Tony returned to the rooms and found tarry black streaks down the middle of his clean towel.

"It's only a towel, for heaven's sake," J. Curtis said when Tony questioned him. The condescension in his tone pushed a button. Tony cut off the debate and reacted. The next sounds heard in the room were moans coming from the crumpled heap that was J. Curtis Pierpont. "You hit me," he said incredulously, clutching the sore spot in his chest that Tony's fist had just created. He was amazed.

"Yes, my good man, I did," Tony responded in his best British butler's accent. "And if you would be so kind as to stand, I will look forward to completing the exercise." His fists were clenched. If Pierpont was man enough to get up, Tony intended to knock him down again.

"You're insane," J. Curtis said before sprinting out the door. The next day, Tony heard that upon his parents' insistence, Pierpont had been reassigned to a single room. Henry and Alex laughed about the peasant's revolt, as they called it, and thanked Tony. Their suite would be a much friendlier place for the rest of the year.

# CHAPTER 3

Tony and Steve Frazier were best buddies throughout their time at Yale, but their friendship was truly cemented one bizarre night in their junior year. They had been at a party and had drunk their share of beer. Actually, they had drunk more than their share. At about 2:00 AM, they decided to get some fresh air. It was a cold night, drizzling a little, and the streets of downtown New Haven were deserted. Each boy stashed a couple of beers in the pockets of his overcoat. As they walked along Chapel Street, in front of a bar and grill named Johnny's Tavern, Frazier reached over and snapped the radio antenna off a parked car. No reason for it. Pretty stupid, but that's what he did.

Before either of them had time to laugh, a police car turned the corner. The boys froze, not sure if the two cops in it had seen what Steve had done. But the car pulled up and stopped. The cop in the passenger seat climbed out, scratching an impressive belly. "Hey, you two! Either you're the dumbest kids I've ever seen or you're drunk. So which is it, you been drinkin' or are you just stupid?"

Steve Frazier was known in Tony's circle of friends as "Ironman" because he could continue drinking long after the rest of the group had gotten sick or passed out. He was tall and apparently had a "hollow leg" or maybe two. More than once, Tony had fallen into an alcohol-induced nap and when he awoke, there was Ironman,

15

smiling, offering a freshly opened can. "You don't look good, man. Here, have a beer. You'll feel better."

On that cold New England night, in response to the cop's question, Ironman dropped the car antenna so he could reach into his coat pocket and pull out a beer. "Sure, officer, we've had a few brewskis," he replied. With the bleary-eyed smile of a drunken teenager, he held the can up. "Even got a couple left. And they're still cold. Want one?"

It didn't take long for the big-bellied cop to have Tony and Frazier leaning over the hood of the police car while he dug in their pockets and confiscated the beer. After that, he opened the back door and ordered, "Okay, you clowns. Get in. You're coming downtown with us."

Frazier was still smiling that *Mad* magazine, Alfred E. Neuman, *what—me worry?* smile, but Tony was stunned. Were they being arrested? They flopped into the back of the police car, and by the time Tony's butt hit the seat, he was sober. His mind raced. He had never been arrested. What kind of trouble was he in? He had heard of Yalies getting scolded for public drunkenness—nothing more than that. But this was a New Haven police car he was in, which was a lot different than Yale's own campus police. Different in a bad way. Some locals regarded Yalies as rich, spoiled, and needing to be put in their place. Would they spend the night in jail? Would they get kicked out of school? What would he tell his parents? Frazier was the dumbass who snapped the antenna. Really it was his problem—not Tony's. *Maybe I'll just wait and see what happens,* he thought. *I'm not the one in trouble.* Then he looked over at Frazier, whose face had lost its beer-buzz smile. Now there was a worried look, not quite panic but close. It had apparently dawned on him that the situation wasn't funny. Certainly the cops didn't seem to be joking. Tony knew he couldn't leave his friend on his own. He started thinking harder.

The cops hadn't asked their names or taken their ID cards, Tony realized. A plan took shape. He whispered to Frazier, "follow me."

Frazier nodded, moving his head just enough to show he had heard. The car stopped at the curb in front of the police station. When the passenger cop opened the back door, Tony stepped out and waited. As soon as he saw Frazier was out of the car and had his feet on the ground, Tony exploded into a dead run. Frazier followed. The boys were off in a desperate sprint.

"Hey, you jokers, stop right there!"

But Tony and Frazier kept running. Something whizzed past Tony's right ear: a full can of beer. The fat cop was too lazy to chase them and too smart to shoot them. So he just hurled the can and nearly took Tony's head off with it. Tony and Frazier didn't let up running until they were inside the dorm. Then they waited until almost sunrise, fearing the cops would come for them. But they didn't. Tony never spoke of it again; Frazier told him that he had mentioned it to his father, but no one else. Tony didn't understand why Frazier would have wanted his old man to know. Certainly he wasn't going to tell his. But there were a lot of things about Ironman that Tony didn't get, so he let it go. The boys had been damn lucky.

# CHAPTER 4

Carrie Barber and six of her girlfriends went to a party at Tammy Weston's house because they had been told that boys from Yale would be attending, not just the same New Haven boys Carrie had known since the first grade, who she'd pummeled—when they deserved it—as an elementary school tomboy, the same boys who had begun paying attention to her when she was fourteen and her hips had taken shape and her breasts had blossomed, seemingly overnight. Now her hair was golden and straight and her eyes clear and blue. She may not have been as popular as her friend Tammy, but when boys looked at her they kept looking. Although her face didn't betray it, whenever that happened, mixed with the twinge of embarrassment she'd also begun to feel something new and strange, something frightening and exciting at the same time.

At the party, Carrie stood with her friends, talking and laughing. When a good song played, they danced. The Yale boys introduced themselves, engaged in conversation and, after a while, some even asked for a dance. But Carrie kept looking at one in particular. He wasn't the most handsome, but there was something strong and masculine about him. He was well built and obviously fit. His hair was wavy and dark brown, almost black. His blue eyes were alert and full of mischief. His nose was bent a little to the side, giving him a rugged look. His naturally straight teeth were very white. A slight dimple in his right cheek amplified his electric smile. His skin was dark, as if he spent a lot of time in the sun. When he was introduced to her, she couldn't help fidgeting self-consciously.

Whatever he said during their brief, awkward moments together sounded intelligent. He looked like a jock, but didn't act like one. He asked her questions and listened to her answers. He seemed genuinely interested in what she had to say despite the trouble she had expressing herself. After a few minutes, though, some other boys arrived at the party and called out to him. He told her it was nice to meet her. Then, before he went off to greet his friends, he looked deep into her eyes. His look penetrated and resonated. Definitely special.

Out of the corner of her eye, she watched how he gestured with his hands as he interacted with his friends. She heard them laugh out loud more than once. When he looked her way, Carrie noticed his smile. And those eyes. He didn't stare, always returning quickly to the conversation with his buddies, but she felt his awareness. She tried to act like she didn't notice, but she was tickled.

Tony came back and asked Carrie to dance. It was a slow song, and Tony really didn't know how to dance, but he took her in his arms and it was magic. Before that first song was over, she had agreed to another and then another. The hours flew by; they were learning everything about each other.

After they finished dancing, they were winding their way through the crowd back to their seats, Carrie a few steps ahead while Tony followed. When they passed a table where some guys were sitting, one boy reached out and wrapped a meaty arm around Carrie's waist. "Hey there," he announced, to the amusement of his friends at the table, "You're quite a tomato. What's your name?" Carrie tried to push him away, but she was helpless. The guy was built like a linebacker, and drunk. He had a grip on her like a lion on a fawn. But only for a moment. Tony quickly pulled the guy's arm loose and got in between them. "Back off," he said quietly. But his face was close enough for the other man to hear every syllable. "She's with me." The low volume of his voice amplified its menace.

The drunk looked at Tony and saw Tony looking right back at him. His glare was unmistakable, and the message was clear. It said, "I will fight you right here and right now." Tony was only 5'7, but his hard-edged fury had amplified him dramatically, like a switch on his adrenaline valve had been flipped, releasing a burst of "fight or flight" energy to his muscles. It occurred to the drunk that this whole thing might not be worth the trouble. There were plenty of babes at the dance, and this guy was crazy.

The drunk chuckled. "Okay, tiger, she's with you." The tension had been broken but he continued, "For tonight, anyway." He looked back at his buddies, who were smiling and enjoying the show. "Let me know when you get tired of little Mr. Macho here," he said to Carrie, carefully eyeing Tony, "and when you're ready to step up to the varsity."

Carrie grabbed Tony's arm and pulled him away before he could react. "Come on, let's go." Carrie hated violence and thought that fighting was stupidly juvenile. But she couldn't help feeling proud, almost gushy. Tony had rescued her. He had been courageous and valiant. What girl wouldn't love that? And to Tony, it was the natural order of the universe. From now on, it would be his duty to take care of her and make her happy. He was Carrie's king, and he would protect his queen.

Of course, that didn't prevent Tony from being a scoundrel whenever the opportunity arose. He had a powerful, ever-present sex drive. And Carrie trusted him, and presumed he was satisfied with their physical relationship. It never occurred to her that her boyfriend had a wandering eye, the adventurous spirit to follow through, and the secretive nature needed to keep it from her.

For the most part, Tony kept his affairs to himself. Never bragging, not even to his friends. And before he took a chance, he considered the risks and calculated his strategies with control. As friendly as he was, he still had a basic distrust of people. "The only person you can really trust in this world," his father had told him, "is yourself." So he stayed deliberate. He didn't rush into situations that could come back to haunt him. He liked his relationship with Carrie and didn't want to upset it. Part of that was making sure not to take foolish chances with her heart. He was careful to avoid giving her reason to be jealous or suspicious. He trained himself to ignore other girls when he was with Carrie, and he never complimented another girl's looks, not even when Carrie asked him obliquely. More than once she called his attention to a girl with a remarkable figure or an especially lovely face and asked him what he thought. He always acted surprised, like he hadn't noticed. "Oh, she's all right, I suppose," he would answer. "But she can't hold a candle to you."

But in truth, Tony didn't miss much. He was always alert and quick to spot pretty girls. Nonetheless, he taught himself to sweep with his eyes, not stare. Carrie never caught him "checking out" another female. But he saw them, all right, and often enough they saw him too. Tony was constantly on the prowl, and when Carrie wasn't around, like when she went with her family on summer vacation, Tony was ready. He almost always had something lined up, something casual and convenient. Someone willing to help him work off that relentless sex drive of his. Carrie never had a clue.

# CHAPTER 5

The companies listed on the interview sign-up sheets in Yale's placement office had names like General Electric and Westinghouse. Tony had signed up for an interview, as a graduating senior, with the Continental Electric Company. He presumed it would be just another stiffly pleasant chat with a low-level executive from a big corporation that had openings for young engineers. Recruiters from all major industries came to campus. It was Ivy League, after all, and Yale graduates were much sought after. Tony had already been to "meet and greets" with representatives of several big engineering companies, including Motorola, Boeing, and Hughes Aircraft.

The Continental Electric interviewer was named Osvaldo Padron. He was a compact man with serious eyes and thick hands, too muscular for his clothes and several pounds overweight, like an athlete who had let himself go. The beefy ex-athlete in his ill-fitting gray suit opened the door to the waiting area and stood looking at Tony. Tony put down the magazine he had been reading, got up, and smiled. Mr. Stiff-and-Starchy stared back like he'd never seen a smile and didn't know what to make of it. Tony reached out, and the man took his hand and shook it once. "Ola, Senor Gannon," he said. "Yo soy Osvaldo Padron. Por favor, pasa."

Tony was surprised to hear the man speak Spanish. But he had no trouble understanding or responding. "Mucho gusto a conocerle,

Senor Padron," he said. The equivalent of "Nice to meet you, Mr. Padron." Tony walked through the door, and Padron followed. Still speaking rapidly in Spanish, he asked Tony to move a particular chair from across the room to a table in the center. Tony complied. The man continued, "Puede sentarse alla," he said, motioning for Tony to sit. Tony said, "Gracias," and sat down. For several minutes the conversation was conducted entirely in Spanish. Tony thought it was cute. He was being given a little test. Which, as far as he was concerned, he was passing quite adequately. Tony's ability to speak Spanish started with a summer job in a Puerto Rican grocery, a bodega, close to his high school in Pennsylvania. He mostly took the job because a good-looking classmate named Maria Elena worked there. He had his share of fun that summer and learned more than a little Spanish in the process.

But Padron's next words were in English, "Do you think you can follow orders?" he asked. "Maintain your discipline? Control your temper—even if you get angry? We don't want any loose cannons working for us."

Tony switched back to English, too. "Well, sir, I guess so. I don't have a problem behaving myself . . ."

"Baloney," Padron hissed suddenly. "What about at O'Brien's? Now come on, there's no use pretending. You remember the night. I'm sure that big lug does. Probably wishes he could forget it, but I bet he can't. What was his name? Dowling, right? No, no, it was Downing, wasn't it? He ended up missing two football games because of the right hand you landed. Your temper really took him by surprise, didn't it?"

Tony stared. The muscles around his mouth tightened, and the smile he came in with was gone. *Who is this guy?*

Then Padron continued. "We have a, shall I say, 'a mutual acquaintance.'"

Tony heard the words but didn't respond. He was still thinking about Brian Downing, and "the punch." On that night, two months earlier, Downing had thoroughly deserved what he had gotten. He and a couple of his teammates on the Yale varsity football team had drunk too much beer and were getting loud. "This is my bar," he was bellowing. "Any of you pussies got a problem with that?" No one responded and the bartender just shook his head. "What's the matter, no one wanna get his ass kicked?" he added, looking around the room. "I didn't think so." Then he laughed and stumbled toward the bar to retrieve another pitcher, making sure to push aside any guy in his path and grab for any waitress within reach. Tim Downing, six-foot, five-inch, three-hundred-pound offensive tackle, had become a poster child for the Obnoxious Louts of America.

Tony had had a couple of drinks himself and was feeling ornery. *Somebody ought to put an end to this loudmouth's irritating show,* he thought, and since no one else seemed up to it, Tony decided to volunteer. He called out, loud enough for everybody to hear. "Hey tiny, your mama called. She said you've had too much to drink. You need to go home and let her put you to bed." Slowly, Downing turned to see where the voice was coming from. He blinked a few times in the slow, comical way that drunks blink. When he saw Tony, all of 165 pounds, staring at him from across the room, he formed a sloppy but distinctly unfriendly grin that said, *this is going to be fun.*

"You talking to me, midget?"

"Go home, pal," Tony said.

"I ain't your pal, shrimp," Downing said and began lumbering toward Tony. As he did, his friends began lifting their bulky frames out of their chairs. Tony looked around at his own buddies, who were eyeing the exit door like panicked deer searching for a way to escape an approaching pride of lions. From what Tony could see, they weren't going to stand with him to face these jerks. He knew he would have to act swiftly or else catch a beating from Yale's offensive line.

The last thing big Tim Downing would remember was the blur of Tony uncoiling from a crouch, right arm bursting forward with a fist like a brick at the end, rocketing straight toward his face. He would not recall the actual impact of fist to cheekbone or the loud thudding sound it made. Or the backward flight of his entire body or its crash onto a table full of beer bottles or the table's splintering collapse onto the floor. No, Tim Downing wouldn't remember any of that. But he would remember the black eye and the ringing in his ears and the headache that persisted for days. Chances were pretty good he would think twice before bullying a stranger again. In all his battles on the football field, going back to the peewee leagues, Downing had never suffered such a swift and punishing blow.

Tony couldn't dwell on the memory of it. He pulled himself back to where he was, sitting in a little room interviewing for a job. "Forgive me, Mr. Padron, but I don't understand. Who is this mutual acquaintance of ours?"

"We are always on the lookout for a particular kind of fellow. You should be pleased to know that someone thinks you might have what it takes to work for a company like ours."

"Mr. Padron, it seems you have a rough opinion of me. If I've got a bad temper, and if I'm so rowdy, what kind of engineer does Continental expect me to make?"

"Mr. Gannon, sometimes we can appreciate rowdy."

"Okay, now I really need help," Tony said. "What are we talking about? Why are we having this interview?"

"Let me be candid with you, Mr. Gannon. We don't expect you to be an engineer at all. But we do expect to trust you. Can you be trusted?"

"I don't know," Tony said. "This is getting pretty mysterious. If you're not interested in engineers, why are you here?"

"How do you feel about America, Mr. Gannon?" Padron asked.

"Just fine, Mr. Padron. I love my country. We may not be perfect, but we're still the best in the world. But what does that have to do with designing electrical circuits for Continental Electric?"

"National security, Mr. Gannon. My associates and I also love America. And we serve it in ways and in places other people don't even think about. Would you like to do that, Mr. Gannon? Would you like to serve your country overseas?"

"Like in the army?" Tony said. "I don't think so." In 1972, victory in Vietnam was nowhere in sight. Few understood the purpose of the war. Fewer still strongly supported the effort, and hardly any young men were happy about the idea of going there to fight. Among Tony's college friends, being drafted was a disaster to be avoided. But Congress had instituted a selective service lottery based purely on dates of birth, and it was a simple system. If your birth date matched a call-up number, you were drafted—and there were no student deferments. A young man could be taken even though he was enrolled in college full-time; and the lower his number, the more likely it was, sooner or later, he would be called. Some felt strongly enough that they were willing to flee to Canada to dodge the draft, although Tony wouldn't ever consider doing that. If he was called, he planned on going. That's what his parents would expect. But during the national lottery his birthday was assigned number 231 out of 365. They'd have to take a lot of fellows around the country before they'd get to him. He wasn't going to give up that good fortune now by volunteering, and he saw no reason to apologize for feeling that way. "I don't see myself as a soldier," he said.

"No, Mr. Gannon, we don't see you as a soldier either."

"All right, I came here expecting to interview for an engineering job, and it sure doesn't seem like that's what you're here for. Isn't it time you told me?"

"Yes, Mr. Gannon, I think it is. But before I go any further, I need your assurance that you will respect what we are about to discuss. That you'll keep it between us. Whether you're interested in my offer or not." Padron's eyes narrowed, the furrows in his brow deepening.

Tony looked at Padron's face. The words he had just heard sounded so melodramatic, so Hollywood, that Tony felt himself starting to smile but he stifled it when his search of Padron's eyes revealed only their intensity. The man was completely serious. "I give you my word, sir."

"Thank you. And let me mention that I appreciate your suspicion. That's a healthy trait in our business. Now let me tell you the truth. I am not here to hire an engineer. I represent The Central Intelligence Agency of the United States government. Perhaps you've heard of us. We look out for America all around the world. How would you feel about a career looking out for America, Tony?" Padron leaned forward, his eyes now searching Tony's.

"I already told you I love my country, Mr. Padron," Tony answered, returning Padron's stare. The intensity of the moment was palpable. "But I am not sure I know what this all means."

"Intelligence. You know, looking, listening, finding things out. Sometimes taking action. Covert. Clandestine. Secret. The world is a threatening place. Communism's goal is to destroy our way of life. We can't let that happen. We gather information from dangerous places, places where we aren't welcome, that don't broadcast their real agendas. We need to keep tabs on our enemies so our politicians can try to persuade them to our point of view. And if they don't want to listen and won't get with the program, then we need to be there to stop them, if we can. So we look for young men like you. Independent fellows with suspicious natures who can keep a secret. Men with confidence and toughness. Self-reliant and clever. The kind of guy who can keep his wits in stressful situations. It doesn't hurt if they can speak another language like you do. And then we give them the best training in the world. We teach them how to meet people, how to fit in, how to be observant without being noticed, and how to look beneath the surfaces, beyond the appearances. How to get at the truth. And how to take care of themselves. Then we put them to work overseas. It's risky, going places where you're not supposed to be and seeing or hearing things you're not supposed to see or hear. So it takes nerve too. And loyalty. But it's important work, Tony. Very important. We protect America by finding out things other guys want to keep secret. A lot of people around the world are jealous of America, and some of 'em are downright hostile. So it takes courage to do this kind of work. You need to be able to keep secrets from everyone, even your own family. You need to be in control of yourself. To feel comfortable operating on your own. To follow orders and think for yourself at the same time. To stay cool if things get hot. Not everyone can handle it. But we pay those who can very well. And there are other rewards. It will keep you out of Vietnam, no matter where you stand in the draft lottery. So how does all that sound? Think you might be interested?"

Tony tried to contain his enthusiasm, "Who wouldn't be interested? You'd have to be a real loser to pass on an opportunity like this. But you already know I'm no saint, and you must know there are guys here at Yale much smarter than me and more polished, that's for sure."

"We're not looking for bookworms or choir boys," Padron answered. "The FBI loves straight arrows. And there's a lot to be said for that. But we prefer a little moxy. We want 'em curious. And suspicious. And sneaky. You know, risk takers with brains. Which is why we liked things we learned about you. We admired your nerve, that you took chances but didn't lose control. And we like it very much that you speak Spanish. And the fact that you're an engineer. Well, we liked it all."

"Okay." Tony said. "I've kept a few secrets. I'd say I've taken a few chances too. Small stuff, by your standards, I know, but I think I can get to the level you're talking about. And I'll need a job pretty soon, if I don't get drafted. My lottery number is pretty good, but who knows how high they'll go? I sure don't want to end up carrying a rifle through the jungles of Southeast Asia. And getting paid well—I don't have a problem with that. Not a bit. So that's a start."

"Yes, Anthony," Padron said, "That's an excellent start."

A couple of weeks after the interview with Mr. Padron, Tony received a telephone call. "Anthony Gannon?" the voice inquired. "This is George Sweet from the Continental Electric Company."

"Hello, Mr. Sweet," Tony said.

"We received a very favorable report from Mr. Padron after your interview. He said you're an impressive young man."

"That was kind of him," Tony offered. "Please thank him for me."

"We'd like to move to the next step in the hiring process. Are you still interested?"

"Yes, very much," said Tony, and he meant it. Mr. Padron had told him he would be hearing from someone, but then a couple of weeks passed without anything. Tony's anxiety increased each day. He kept reviewing his conversation with Mr. Padron. More and more he wondered if maybe he had botched it. Why else hadn't they called? One subject in particular made him squirm. At the end of the interview, Padron had outlined the process for becoming a field officer, and Tony had expressed disappointment with the length of it. The path for a brand-new college graduate like Tony, one who had no military background, ordinarily took several years. First, the young candidate would be required to enlist in a branch of the military. Padron had suggested the navy. "Not nearly as tough as the army or the marines," he said. But whatever recruitment office the candidate chose, special arrangements would be made in advance so that his status as a future intelligence officer was known to those that needed to know. The candidate would sign up for a five-year enlistment. He would then be sent for basic training just like any other recruit. Afterward, he would receive a special appointment from the Secretary of the Navy to Officer Candidate School. He would be in with about three hundred other naval cadets—mostly noncommissioned types. OCS could take a year or more. Depending on his class rank, he could earn a regular commission—instead of a reserve commission—and come out as a second lieutenant. He would then be transferred to a military installation, probably a submarine base, since it provided the best cover. He would have to serve a year or so there. Then he would be sent back to Washington DC for Junior Officer Training, consisting of a couple of years of specialized training and technical instruction, including rotations through various secret CIA facilities around the country, whichever were most appropriate for the kind of work he was being prepared to do. Finally he would be assigned to a job at CIA headquarters in Langley, Virginia. Only after all of that would he be considered for an assignment overseas. The entire process could take five or six years, Padron had explained.

When Tony had heard that, he felt deflated. He had just finished four years of college, and five or six more years seemed like an eternity. Besides, how would he explain to Carrie and his parents that he was enlisting in the navy? Wouldn't they be confused and disappointed? Why waste an Ivy League education by joining the military?

Tony had tried not to show his disappointment, but Padron had seen it and said something about not worrying in advance. Tony had thought that maybe that end-of-interview exchange soured Mr. Padron on him. So when Tony was offered a couple of engineering jobs, one with Harris Semiconductors in Florida and another with Westinghouse Electric in Pennsylvania, he was pleased enough. Both offers included good beginning salaries and benefits. They were great jobs. But he had not stopped thinking about the glamour and mystique of working for the CIA since his interview, and now Mr. Sweet's call had him almost giddy.

Sweet explained that the CIA's hiring process was meant to be deliberate, thorough, and foolproof. Not only did they want to recruit the best and most effective people, they also wanted to avoid potential problems, from unreliable mistake-prone candidates or those with personal weaknesses and vulnerabilities, all the way up to the worst-case scenario, the planted moles, or double agents. The communist bloc equivalents of the CIA, most notably the Russian

KGB and the Soviet-influenced East German STASI, were constantly trying to infiltrate the American intelligence services, just as the CIA was constantly trying to develop "assets" within their communist counterparts. Tony, never having traveled outside the United States, and having no discernible link to any hostile foreign country, was not a high security risk. Nonetheless, every potential new hire was given a preliminary review. Public records were checked, and a little basic snooping was carried out. Even assuming no red flags, the entire process, from initial interview to the granting of a top-secret security clearance, could take many months. As it progressed to the more in-depth phases, extensive and thorough background checks would be conducted. Candidates were repeatedly "fluttered"—the CIA term for polygraph or lie detector testing. And it could be years before a new officer would be trusted with even the lowest level clandestine or covert assignment. In the meanwhile, there would be work for the candidate to do as he waited to pass the CIA's basic thresholds, and later more sensitive instruction, extensive foreign language training, lectures from experts on an array of subjects—both political and cultural—followed by intense training and special operations practice. And all along the way, the candidate would be tested and retested.

Sweet told Tony to expect a letter, which would contain an application and some forms. "You'll also need a copy of your college transcript and a passport photograph," he added. "Bring everything to our meeting." He asked Tony to meet him a week later at a diner close to the expressway. Tony knew the place and quickly agreed. He was so happy he wanted to shout, but he also wanted to show the restraint he felt appropriate for an intelligence officer. "Yes," was all he said. He hung up the phone and pumped his fist.

The envelope arrived the next day. It contained several pages, including a cover letter without letterhead, signed by Mr. George Sweet. The first paragraph thanked Tony for his interest in the agency's career training program. Then it gave a list of titles available at "your local library or bookstore," including *The Craft of Intelligence* by Allen Dulles, *A Short Course in the Secret War* by Christopher Felix, and several others on espionage, counterespionage and covert action. References were given to the more important chapters. It was "strongly recommended" that Tony read as much as possible, noting that "the interview process is always more rewarding for the applicant who is well prepared." Also enclosed was Applicant Information Sheet No. 1, which described the kinds of screening the agency would conduct before making a hiring decision, including loyalty and security checks and evaluations of competence and physical and emotional fitness. Applicant Information Sheet No. 2 listed transgressions that would disqualify an applicant, including "any behavior, activities or associations which tend to show that the individual is of questionable character, discretion, integrity or trustworthiness; any deliberate misrepresentations, falsifications, or omissions of material facts; any criminal, infamous, dishonest, immoral, or notoriously disgraceful conduct, habitual use of intoxicants to excess, drug use or abuse or sexual perversion; and membership in, or affiliation or sympathetic association with, any foreign or domestic organization, movement, group, or combination of persons which is totalitarian, Fascist, Communist or subversive." Next came a multipage employment application with instruction sheet. Tony was required to sign and date all the documents. Finally, there was a document entitled "Secrecy Agreement" with the word *sample* printed diagonally across it.

The papers amplified Tony's excitement. By the time he met Mr. Sweet at the diner, he had read almost of all of the books, signed the applicant information sheets, and filled out the application. He really wanted the job and had resolved to accept the long, slow journey required to become an officer. But he needn't have worried. One of the first things Sweet told him after taking the papers was that there were positions that needed to be filled right away, including many requiring particular language skills. Tony would be "hired" by Continental Electric and sent directly to a CIA screening and orientation facility in Massachusetts. There he would be tested on a variety of subjects, including his ability to speak and understand Spanish, while the FBI did a thorough background investigation. Mr. Sweet explained that he would need to pass all the psychological and proficiency exams, and that his scores would need to be pretty damned high. But Tony was delighted. If he received his security clearance, he would move on to the next step—the intensive training needed to prepare him for the real thing, an assignment in the field.

At the meeting, Mr. Sweet gave Tony the address for Continental Electric's ordnance systems regional office in Pittsfield, an aptly named small town in Western Massachusetts, about three hours' drive from New Haven. He was to report to the main entrance on Monday by 9:00 AM sharp. That didn't give Tony a lot of time to make arrangements, but he was happy to do whatever he needed to do to get ready.

"I'll be there, Mr. Sweet," Tony bubbled.

"Good," came Sweet's reply. "Very good."

# CHAPTER 6

The ordnance systems office was part of a Continental Electric mini-city, with more than a dozen enormous buildings spread across five entire square blocks, containing several huge plants, including the entire plastics and synthetic materials division, turbine and electric motor factories, electronic systems plant and the ordnance or weapons systems complex. A high, barbed wire fence surrounded the ordnance systems complex, which was accessed through a well-guarded gate. Tony showed his identification to the guard, who checked a list on his clipboard. The guard wrote down the tag number from the rear of Tony's car, and then instructed Tony to park in a space close to the guardhouse doors.

Inside, he was greeted by a stern-looking, heavyset woman seated behind a desk. She asked him to sign a visitor's roster and handed him a temporary badge. Then she advised that he would need to wait for his escort to come out from the administration offices.

"If you tell me where to go, I can let myself in."

"This is a secure installation," she scolded. "Visitors aren't allowed to just stroll around. Your escort will be down in a moment. You can have a seat."

While he was waiting in a set of well-worn plastic chairs, Tony examined the name badge she had given him. Limited Access, Escort

Required. The lady at the desk saw him looking and reminded him that his badge was to be displayed at all times.

After a few minutes, a tall, slender man entered. He was wearing a white shirt with a narrow dark tie. The legs of his trousers were too short and revealed an inch or two of white sock above black shoes. With his eyeglasses, he reminded Tony of a goofy-looking teaching assistant from Yale's theoretical physics department.

"Hi," he offered. "I'm Henry. Henry Johnston. You must be Anthony Gannon?"

"Yes, sir, that's me," Tony answered, perhaps a bit too cheerfully, but he was excited and having trouble hiding it.

"Good," said Johnston. "Pleased to meet you. I'll be taking you to the training office. Ready to go?"

Tony got up, and the two of them walked down a long hall with doors on both sides, identical except for the number painted on each. At the end of the hall, they came to a set of double doors. A small red sign over the right door indicated "Secured Area." A little box above the doorknob had a keyhole in it. Johnson pulled out a large key ring and inserted one of its many keys into the box. He motioned for Tony to pass through and then followed.

Tony was startled by the view. They were on a metallic catwalk which ran along the wall. Thirty feet below was the factory floor. Huge partially built machines moved slowly along a conveyor belt as workers tended to them. Scaffolding was everywhere, and technicians used it to climb onto, crawl over, and reach inside the great metal structures. They looked like ants swarming over the fallen bodies of much larger insects. Tony and Mr. Johnston passed above another enormous factory floor and then another. The rooms were like airplane hangars, with the capacity to house manufacturing operations for large component parts for jumbo military application. Engines as big as trucks, turbines, compressors, and other machines. Tony didn't recognize any of them and Johnston noticed. "We manufacture weapons systems for the government. Those guys are assembling turbines for submarine engines," he said, pointing to a group of workers dressed in orange coveralls and wearing white gloves. "Pretty impressive, eh?"

"Wow," was Tony's response.

"One of those babies can weigh eighty tons or more." Johnston said. "And they're built to the tiniest tolerances, too. Reliable as hell. We don't want anything to go wrong on a nuclear boat."

"No, I guess not."

"We're very proud of this plant," Johnston continued. "We build a lot of sophisticated equipment here. Mostly for the navy, you know." Tony nodded although he really didn't have any idea about it. Later he would learn that the U.S. military worked hand in glove with several big contractors to develop state-of-the-art weapons systems. A lot of technology that eventually found its way into the civilian world was initially designed for strategic, military application.

Eventually, Tony and Mr. Johnston arrived at another set of double doors, again marked "Secured Area". Johnston pulled out yet another key and opened the door. On the other side a pleasant-looking woman handed Johnston a clipboard and a pen. He signed it and handed it back to her. "Molly, this here's Anthony Gannon. One of the new guys. He's going to be a technician on one of our big navy contracts. Anthony, say hello to Molly Morgan. She runs this place. Unofficially, of course."

Molly looked up at Tony and smiled. "Welcome," she said, looking him over like a tailor measuring a customer for a new suit. Tony squirmed. Finally, she smiled again and said to Johnston, "Nice-looking young man. Where'd you say he was from?"

"He just graduated Yale, if you must know," Johnston replied.

"Oh, I'm impressed. Are you married?"

"No, ma'am," Tony answered. *Is she flirting?* he wondered.

"I know they'll be keeping you busy," Molly said, tilting her head towards the cubicles behind her, "but come and visit. Better yet,

I take my lunch in the cafeteria every day at noon. Maybe you can join me for a sandwich one day soon. I'll tell you what's good."

"That would be nice," Tony said. Molly was attractive, in a dignified way. And her flashing eyes were sending a message, no doubt. Tony wondered what her hair looked like out of its tight bun. She was older than he was used to, but still, no need to rule anything out. He looked at Johnston. The man was just standing there.

But Molly was more perceptive. She said, "I see you're anxious to get going. It was nice to meet you, Anthony."

"Nice to meet you, too," Tony replied.

"Good luck," she added. "I think you'll fit in just fine." Tony thanked her and looked again at Johnston, who finally took the cue.

"Okay, Anthony," Johnston said. "Why don't we continue on?"

Mr. Johnston escorted Tony through the cubicles to an office at the end of a long corridor. A glass window was covered by white Venetian blinds. The door was open. Tony read the letters on it—Director of Orientation. At the threshold, Mr. Johnston waited for the gentleman seated at the desk inside to look up. When he did, Johnston said, "Good morning, Albert. This is Anthony Gannon. The new tech trainee. Anthony, this is Albert Koslow, our orientation director. He'll be in charge of you for the next few weeks." Mr. Koslow got up from his chair and approached. He held out his hand and said, "Hello, Mr. Gannon. I'm Albert Koslow. I'm the orientation director. I'll be in charge of you for the next few weeks." Tony looked at him, then at Johnston. Was this guy serious? Johnston's expression was stern, but just for a second. Then he and Mr. Koslow broke into smiles. Mr. Koslow's way of breaking the tension, Tony surmised. I bet they do the same thing with each new guy. He smiled, too. "Hello, Mr. Koslow," he said. "Nice to meet you."

"Actually, I'd prefer you call me Albert. You'll have a lot of serious stuff to learn in the coming days, from a lot of serious people.

No question about that. But I want you to think of me as family. I'll be your mama and your papa while you're here. You have a problem, you come to me. You need help with something, my door is open. You pay attention, do what you're supposed to do, learn your lessons and you'll get along just fine. How does that sound, Anthony?"

"Sounds great, Mr. Koslow. I mean, Albert. And from now on, it's only fair you call me Tony."

Tony was assigned his own workspace, a cubicle not far from Koslow's office. He would be given materials to read and would meet with various people for interviews. He would have access to the language lab. He would participate in calisthenics, and was expected to keep in shape. Also, he would submit to periodic lie detector testing while investigators worked on his security clearances. If all went well, in a couple of months he would be sent to Camp Peary, near Richmond, Virginia—"the farm," as Mr. Koslow referred to it—for the more intense "stuff." Assuming he was still in the company's good graces, he'd then become eligible for further assignment.

# CHAPTER 7

Over the next few weeks, Tony was interviewed and tested almost daily. The reminders of the need to tell people only that he was being trained for an engineering job with the Continental Electric Company were incessant. Which meant he was going to have to lie professionally. Secrets were going to be his business. At the same time, his new employer would allow him none. Officers needed to be as transparent as glass; there could be no privacy as between officer and Company. Tony had to sign a stack of authorization forms allowing the government to review his entire scholastic record, including high school and college, medical records and employment and personnel records for any work he had ever done, including part-time and summer jobs.

Occasionally, he was given feedback by Mr. Koslow or one of the other training officers, but usually he was alone in his little cubicle, almost buried by the volume of material he had been given to review: lengthy papers on the CIA's internal structure and organization, guide maps through its various divisions and departments, and an introduction to the terminology of its bureaucracy. The CIA sure loved its acronyms and abbreviations. It was like having to learn a new language. And essays criticizing international communism, which seemed like course materials for graduate level world history and politics classes. Koslow asked him to sign confidentiality agreements under oath, and then the documents started to get more interesting. Papers describing fairly recent events in Chile and the contemporary political environment there were so current and so detailed that Tony wondered if they had been given to him by mistake.

Tony was given a battery of psychological and personality exams and then a series of lie detector tests. For the first, he was told to report early in the morning to a room in building 14. He introduced himself to the receptionist and took a seat along the wall. The receptionist paid no further attention to him. After a few minutes, he was greeted by a man in what was clearly the standard uniform—short-sleeved white shirt, narrow tie, and black trousers and shoes. He was short, shorter even than Tony, and had the red hair and freckled, ruddy complexion of a leprechaun. He was, like everyone else, clean-cut and clean-shaven, but he wore thick eyeglasses, which made his eyes look huge.

He led Tony into a small room. Tony was uncomfortable, though he wasn't sure why. He had nothing to hide. He glanced around the room. The walls and ceiling were covered by acoustical tile. A leather easy chair had been placed in front of a desk, which was dominated by a large apparatus with dials, graph paper, and long, narrow pens. The man, who hadn't introduced himself, directed Tony to sit in the easy chair, which faced away from the machine. He pulled a straight chair from behind the desk and sat down in front of Tony.

He explained matter-of-factly that Tony had passed the preliminary psychological profiles and had reached the phase of the security clearance process necessary for access to top secret material and, of course, for employment with the Company. All employees, even the director of the CIA, the Honorable Richard H. Helms himself, had to submit to the polygraph, and not just when they were hired, but periodically and without advance notice throughout their careers. Then he gave Tony a prepared statement to sign, acknowledging that Tony was submitting voluntarily to the test, and that he would make no claim against anyone no matter what the outcome. Tony signed that form, and another one pledging that he would not to speak to anyone about the specific questions or the testing in general.

Then the man reviewed the questions with Tony, all of which were to be answered either yes or no, starting with simple ones: "Is your real name Anthony Gannon?" "Is your birthday June 15, 1950?" Then they would get more interesting. "Have you been honest on your job application?" "Have you ever been a communist or belonged to any communist organization?" "Have you ever visited a foreign country?" "Have you ever visited a communist country?" "Have you ever known any officials of a foreign government?" "Have you ever known an intelligence officer of a foreign government?" "Have you ever worked for a foreign government?" "Have you been asked by anyone to apply for employment with the CIA?" "Have you told anyone outside the CIA of your efforts to obtain employment?" Then would come a series of personal questions like, "Have you ever engaged in any homosexual activities?" "Have you ever performed any deviant sexual acts?" "Have you ever taken tranquilizers?" "Have you ever smoked marijuana?" "Have you taken any drugs today to help you take the test?" As the interrogator went through the list of questions, Tony found himself losing his bravado, which he would later learn was exactly its purpose. The key to a successful lie detector exam was putting a person with something to lose in position to be nervous.

The pretest interview took more than an hour, and Tony was feeling uneasy. The interrogator started to connect the apparatus, speaking as he worked. He said that the lie detector was used exclusively in the Company by the Office of Security, which kept the results confidential, regardless of whether he was selected for employment or not. For this reason, he explained, Tony should be perfectly honest. He reminded Tony that each question called for only a yes or a no, and that if the interrogator perceived that Tony was having a problem with a question or series of questions, he would interrupt the test so they could discuss it. Tony was even more uncomfortable as he realized that some questions didn't really lend themselves to yes or no answers. *No matter*, he reassured himself. *I'll do the best I can and if they don't accept me because of my answers, it just wasn't meant to be.*

The polygraph equipment consisted of three devices that were attached to Tony's body. Each of them was connected by tubes or cords to the assembly on the desk. The interrogator explained that each measured a different physiological response, and the changes were marked, in real time, by three pens on moving graph paper. A blood pressure cuff was wrapped around Tony's upper arm, and a two-inch-thick corrugated rubber tube was placed snugly around Tony's chest and fastened in the back. A handheld device was secured against Tony's palm by stretching springs across the back of his hand. The cuff measured changes in pulse and blood pressure, the chest tube measured changes in breathing rhythm, and the hand instrument detected changes in skin moisture caused by perspiration. Tony was told to look straight ahead at the wall, to be very still, and reminded to answer only with a yes or a no. The interrogator sat facing the back of Tony's head, and Tony directed his answers to the wall in front of him.

During the pretest interview, Tony had found himself struggling, resenting some of the questions and the invasion of privacy they represented. He had been tempted to try to control the exercise, to beat the machine. But when the test started, he knew that would be foolish. He was not in control. Not at all. He was conscious of the increase in his pulse, the changes in his breathing, and the sweat that sprang from his palms. He tried to distract himself by counting the holes in the wall tiles. He tried to limit his anxiety by pondering whether there was a camera on him—perhaps behind one of the tiles, focused through one of the dark holes. The interrogator moved very slowly, always pausing after Tony's answer before asking the next question. Then he asked Tony some that had not been mentioned in the pretest. "Have you answered any of the questions deceptively?" "Have you been untruthful in any of your responses?" "Have you tried to hide anything?" Tony answered no to each.

The interrogator was shuffling papers. He told Tony to please remain seated. That he was almost finished, but that he thought Tony had had trouble with some of the questions. He suggested they discuss it. "What were you thinking when you answered the question about whether anyone had asked you to try and gain employment with the CIA?" Tony couldn't come up with anything. "Nothing in particular." The interrogator insisted he try harder to remember, but Tony could only reply that he had nothing on his mind but the question. The interrogator reminded Tony that his cooperation was essential for a successful test, and that there was no way he would be hired without passing it. He mentioned two or three other questions that Tony appeared to have had difficulty with. Tony suspected the interrogator was testing him. He knew that some of his answers were half-truths, but he stuck to them. The interrogator resumed his questioning, often repeating a question.

After a while, though, he told Tony he could go and unhooked him. "You will be advised of the results when the Security Office reviews your case and the charts." He sounded pessimistic. Nonetheless, Tony cheerfully thanked him and left.

Tony was summoned back to building 14 a few days later to repeat the test. He was unsettled, presuming he had failed the first one, and they were giving him another chance; but then it occurred to him that perhaps he had passed, and they were just making sure that his answers had been accurate. The first test had lasted more than two hours, and the repeat test was only slightly shorter. The questions were similar, but Tony patiently answered them again. Several times the interrogator went over questions he suggested had given Tony trouble, and just like the first time, Tony insisted he had not been deceptive.

At the end, he felt no more sure of how he had done than after the first examination. Some of the answers he had given could be construed as misleading. But he had been essentially truthful and certainly consistent. He hoped for the best. In the meanwhile, he was given odd jobs to do and plenty more to read. Other than the materials on Chile, little stimulated him. His readings covered the political system in Hungary, the history of the monarchy in Monte Carlo, how to blend in at a reception in Marseilles, the best way to dress to appear to be on holiday in Algeria. He hoped the process of getting his security clearance wouldn't take long because, to put it bluntly, he was bored.

# CHAPTER 8

One afternoon, Mr. Koslow came to Tony's cubicle and interrupted his reading of a report on the diplomatic hierarchy of Peru. Tony had been in danger of falling asleep at his desk. Mr. Koslow wanted him to accompany a senior staffer named James McCluskey on a delivery to the military airlift base at Dover, Delaware. What was being delivered was not mentioned, but Tony didn't care. The fact that he would get out of his godforsaken cubbyhole for a day was all he needed to hear. Besides, McCluskey, or Mac, as everyone called him, was a friendly sort. Rumor had it that he had been trained as a fighter pilot but got into difficulty in Vietnam when he objected to dumping exfoliates. Yes, the lush jungle forest provided cover to the enemy, so clearing the vegetation was a legitimate military strategy. But Agent Orange was supertoxic, capable of dramatically wiping out trees and bushes by the acre and nobody seemed particularly concerned about what prolonged and repeated exposure might do to innocent civilians or, more importantly, American troops. Except for Mac. He was disturbed enough that he refused to participate. Dropping poison from a plane wasn't proper work for a real pilot like James Frances McCluskey. So here he was, cooling his heels, waiting for another assignment, stuck in Pittsfield with the new hires and junior officers in training. But he didn't let it get him down. He was living with his wife in a nice apartment close to the CE plant.

He could tell a joke with the best of them and had the kind of laugh that made everyone else laugh too. Captain Jimmy McCluskey was just a really good fellow.

For this excursion, he would be "piloting" a big step van down the interstate, the package secured in the back. The trip was to take four hours each way, and they would leave in the morning, which meant Tony would escape an entire day of cubicle duty in the CE offices. Tony was instructed to be ready by 7:00 AM so McCluskey could drive him to the warehouse where the truck would be waiting. They needed to be on the road by eight so they could be home before dark.

McCluskey was somewhere in his early thirties, which made him a senior figure to Tony. He was incessantly cheerful, with a knack for finding something funny in even the most serious situation. The morning of the trip, McCluskey arrived with a container of hot coffee for Tony and a bag of doughnuts. Tony had forgotten the joys of early rising and was still a few rpm's short of wide-awake. He got into McCluskey's Chevy pickup and mumbled his thanks. McCluskey laughed and slapped Tony on the back. "Come on, kid, it's time to wakey, wakey."

Tony sipped his coffee gratefully while McCluskey launched into a story about his wife's recent trip to the department store. Apparently, Mrs. McCluskey loved to shop and didn't particularly understand the concept of budgeting. "So I see her wearing this new dress," he began, "and I says, 'That's pretty, how much did it cost?' and she gives me this look, like I'm crazy, and tells me, 'No, dear, I've had it for months.' Well, Tony, I ain't no lawyer or nuthin', but I just didn't feel like she'd answered my question. So I asks her again. 'Yes, honey, I know, I know. But how much did it cost?' So she says it was on sale, and we saved 40 percent. 'Isn't it pretty?' she asks me and then she gives me one of those looks, like I must be the biggest jerk in the world for not thanking her for saving us all that money by getting the goddamned thing on sale, like they gave her cash for the 40 percent she saved right there at the register." McCluskey chuckled and waited for Tony to respond.

Tony could only ask, "So what'd you do then?"

"I did what any red-blooded American husband would do. I told her she looked great and then I shut my mouth."

Tony shook his head and smiled. "Good for you, Mac," he said, silently promising himself that he would shoot himself right in the head if he ever even thought about getting married.

At the warehouse, the step van was ready to go, and they were soon rumbling down the turnpike in it, talking about this and that until McCluskey put on his blinker as they approached an exit. Tony noticed that they were far short of their intended exit in Delaware.

"We making a pit stop?" he asked.

"You could say that," McCluskey responded. "There's a place not too far off the highway I'd like to visit, just a little detour to look up an old friend. Take me a few minutes, tops. If I'm lucky, and I'm feelin' lucky, I can make it up to myself for the way Susan's always saving me 40 percent, if you catch my drift. Just a quick visit and *boom*, we're back on the road. You don't mind, do you?"

Tony didn't have a clue what McCluskey was up to. But he wasn't in any hurry.

"Sure, Mac, whatever you say."

McCluskey maneuvered the van through a series of turns and eventually came to a stop along the curb of a very quiet street. The buildings were all brick and grimy, like warehouses. Tony had no idea where they were and realized that he was totally dependent on McCluskey. "Stay in the van, Tony. I'll be back in a minute." McCluskey jumped down from the driver's seat, and crossed the narrow street briskly, disappearing through a windowless door underneath a neon sign that said Package Store. Tony began to squirm. Was this some kind of a test? Was he supposed to do something other than just sit there? His mind turned toward the package they were delivering. He wished he had asked McCluskey about it. Was it something valuable, something someone might try to steal? Tony didn't like being in the dark, but that's exactly where McCluskey had left him.

Tony fixed the outside mirror so he could see alongside the truck and behind it. He rolled up his window and then reached over and rolled up McCluskey's too. He was unarmed and didn't know what he would do if anyone approached, but he was damn sure going to stay alert. He knew that Mac was authorized to carry a gun, but nothing had been said about it. Tony wasn't familiar with weapons, but it would be good to have one right now, as a security blanket, so he looked in the glove box and under the front seats. The cab was empty except for the morning's coffee cups and the bag the doughnuts had come in. The dashboard clock ticked the seconds off as Tony sat for what seemed like an eternity but what his watch claimed was only five minutes. *Get hold of yourself, Gannon.* He looked up and down the street for the one-hundredth time. Nothing. Wherever they were, it sure was quiet.

Just then the door to the package store opened, and McCluskey emerged with a six-pack and a smile. Tony looked at him. *Did McCluskey bring us out here just for a couple of beers? The guy must be nuts.* McCluskey stepped around to Tony's side. Tony rolled his window back down. "What the hell, McCluskey?" Tony said, his exasperation obvious.

"Don't worry. That friend of mine is here. I haven't seen her in a while and I'd like to visit for just a few more minutes." He was still smiling like a kid on Christmas morning. "I thought you might be a little thirsty, so I brought you something." McCluskey took one of the beers and passed the rest of the six-pack to Tony who reached for them without returning McCluskey's smile.

"I'm feeling pretty stupid sitting out here with my thumb up my ass," Tony complained.

"Somebody's gotta stay with the van," McCluskey explained. "I'll tell you what, she's got a friend. Maybe I can get her to come out here and keep you company."

"Are you crazy?" Tony asked.

"Maybe, a little," McCluskey said. "But who isn't a little nuts?"

Tony was still frowning. McCluskey went on. "Look, Tony, everything is good. I don't get a chance like this too often and I want to take advantage of it. Please bear with me. Just give me a few more minutes and you'll end up thanking me. Or, if nothing else, you'll end up with a great story to tell the grandkids."

And as it turned out, McCluskey was right about having a story to remember. Years later, when Tony could hardly recall anything else about the trip to Dover with Jimmy McCluskey, he would clearly remember what happened in the front seat of that step van while it was parked on a deserted street somewhere in New Jersey. The vision of that pretty brunette, stepping out of the package store in her dark dress with that randy expression on her face—that memory would always stay sharp. And the way she looked, walking coolly toward him, her hips shifting seductively with each step—that part he would remember as well. And how she smiled as she told him how handsome he was, and asked if he would mind sliding over so she could join him, and how she looked into his eyes as she hiked her skirt up to climb onto the bench seat, and how she revealed the longest most tapered legs he had ever seen, and how his heart began pounding when he realized she wasn't wearing any panties, and how she kissed him and how she reached for him and felt his hardness, and how she unzipped his pants and bent forward to kiss him there and stroke him and how she slid herself deftly over him and on top of him until he was thrusting deep up inside her. Those things he would probably never forget, no matter how long he lived. Yep, that damned McCluskey was right. Tony would surely remember this night, though he doubted he would tell the story to his grandkids, if he ever had any.

# CHAPTER 9

After another month of reading, interviewing, and testing, Koslow told him to report to the office of the deputy director of training, Colonel Chuck Blake. Koslow wasn't smiling. Tony tried not to jump to any conclusions, but he was concerned. He wasted no time getting to the colonel's office.

As he arrived, he saw John Chambers, another new guy, coming out. His head and eyes were pointed toward the floor and he barely responded when Tony said hello. *Not good*, Tony thought. Before he could question Chambers, the Colonel's voice came out through the open door. "That you, Gannon?"

"Yes, sir," Tony answered.

"Good. C'mon in."

Blake appeared to be in his mid-50s, and was six feet four inches tall and close to three hundred pounds, which he carried with an air of dignity. He was lighting his pipe, which Tony decided was good. If the colonel was going to tell him he'd been disqualified and was being sent home, he probably would have done so promptly and directly. Bad news was delivered unceremoniously. So Tony was pleased to see the colonel linger. After a couple of puffs demonstrated the pipe had been successfully lit, the colonel turned toward Tony and shook his head. "Never easy sending a guy home."

"Sir?" Tony said.

"Breaks my heart, even after all these years." Blake added.

Tony swallowed, then waited.

"Had to let him go, you understand. Failed the most basic test we've got around here."

Tony felt a wave of relief. It didn't seem like Blake had him in the same category as Chambers. He waited for the colonel to continue.

"You know the receptionist, Molly Morgan?"

"Yes, sir," Tony replied.

"Of course you do. You had lunch with her on . . . let's see . . ." Blake was reading from a file. "Oh, yes. The 23rd. She ordered an egg salad sandwich and you had the tuna. Am I right?'

Tony searched his mind. Nothing stood out. His lunch with Molly had been pleasant. She spoke about herself and also seemed genuinely interested in what Tony had to say. Now that he thought about it, she had asked a lot of questions. At the time, he thought nothing of it. But she *had* pressed him about his work. "So tell me, Anthony, what do you really do? You don't seem like a stiff, engineer type. You're much too cool for that. C'mon, you can tell me. What's your real job?"

Tony had assured her that he was indeed an engineer, training to work on a technical project CE was doing for the Navy. "I guess it may not be that cool but I really am fascinated by electrical circuits," he had said. "Always have been."

Colonel Blake had put down the file. "Chambers flunked that exercise. Badly. I guess he wanted to impress her. Thought he was gonna get in her pants. The man just wasn't Company material. I had to let him go."

Tony nodded. He was learning.

"But, I'm glad to say, that's not a problem for you," Blake said. "You, young fellow, have passed all the tests, the personality profiles and the psychological exams, the Molly Morgan test, every last one of 'em, and, I'm pleased to tell you, you've earned your secret security clearance."

Tony was finally able to exhale. He was now eligible to move on. The colonel emphasized that this was just the beginning. Repeated psychological testing would continue. He would be taught his "tradecraft" and receive the best training the intelligence world had to offer. It would be specific and intense. But if he paid attention and gave it his maximum effort, he would never regret it. Assuming it went well, he would receive the highest security clearance—designated "top secret"—at which time he would be eligible for a field officer position with an overseas assignment. It could be anywhere in the world, the colonel said.

"Congratulations," the colonel soberly offered. Tony missed the serious tone of the Colonel's message. He was too elated. It didn't matter where they sent him, or what he'd have to do, only that they had accepted him, and that "show time" was getting closer.

The colonel reminded him that he was entering increasingly sensitive territory. More than ever, since he was headed for a field assignment in clandestine services, in partnership with many other dedicated officers, it was extremely important that he not disclose the covert nature of his prospective employment. Not to his parents, not to his friends, and not even to his girlfriend. With that, the colonel gave Tony a packet of papers containing his new orders, including where to report and when. Tony left the meeting floating on air. He was going to Camp Peary, where JOTs were trained for assignments around the world.

# CHAPTER 10

Camp Peary was just a few hours' drive from Washington DC on the road to Richmond, Virginia, but it might as well have been on another planet. "The Farm" was in the middle of nowhere, surrounded by wilderness. The CIA did a huge amount of training there—some for its own officers and some for military and paramilitary agents of allied countries. The secrecy of the place started at the entrance gate, a couple of miles from the main compound. Tony's paperwork was thoroughly inspected while a guard asked him a series of questions. Then he had to wait while the guard made a lengthy telephone call. Eventually, Tony was cleared to pass and given directions to the offices of the director of training.

In the briefing room, chairs were lined up auditorium style facing a podium and a large blackboard. A small crowd of young men were already waiting. Someone slapped Tony's shoulder and he turned. He couldn't believe his eyes. Steve Frazier stood before him. Tony's smile was almost too big for his face. "I was hoping I would see you," Frazier said.

"How did you know I'd be here? And what the hell are *you* doing here?"

Frazier looked around. There wasn't a lot of conversation going on among the individuals in the group, but nobody seemed to be paying any attention to them. "You saved my butt that night outside

Johnny's Tavern." Frazier said. "You kept me from spending the night in jail. Or worse. I might have gotten kicked out of school. I told my dad about it because I was afraid he might find out. It used to amaze me how he always seemed to know stuff. And he was pretty pissed off at me for pulling such a dumb stunt. But he really perked up when I told him how cool you were."

Frazier explained that his dad was an officer with the CIA, and that not long after that, the CIA had begun their loose surveillance of Tony. Tony thought back to the things Mr. Padron had said during the first interview—how the Company knew about him and had been watching him. Now they made sense. Frazier's father had identified him as the sort of bright kid with guts, loyalty, and the ability to keep a secret that the CIA was always on alert for.

"Remember how we took off like scared rabbits? I don't think I ever ran faster than I did that night."

Tony laughed. "We were lucky we didn't get shot. I'll never forget the sound of that beer can whistling past my ear. That cop came awfully close to planting it in the back of my head."

Training at Camp Peary was a lot more intriguing than the time Tony had spent in Pittsfield. During the first week of classroom work, the lectures were on the same subjects as the papers Tony had been reading, but their treatment was deeper. The lecturers, most of whom were current or former field officers, offered new insight, frequently incorporating personal anecdotes. And the curriculum got progressively more interesting. Tony was assigned to several smaller classes on topics like disguise, escape, photography, lock picking, using and deciphering code, surveillance and undetectable opening and resealing of correspondence. How to hide things using secret compartments in specially modified shoes or books or cans of shaving cream. How to follow people without being detected and how to avoid being followed. Trainees were sent out into the streets for exercises meant to sharpen their skills. After each one, they were debriefed, critiqued, and given constructive suggestions for correcting mistakes and improving their performance.

Some men were being groomed for special areas like counterintelligence, where the focus was on preventing enemy discovery or infiltration of Company operations. Others were taught current approaches to sabotage, including instruction and training with explosives; they were called the "burn and blow" boys. But Tony was more interested in the Foreign Intelligence division called P&P—paramilitary and psychology: extended, ongoing secret operations crucial to accomplishment of the Company's mandates. It was the most dangerous division, but also the most enticing. It included intelligence gathering and manipulation of events in foreign countries. Tradecraft was the term for the tools and techniques used by an officer to accomplish his mission and to keep secret operations secret. Psychology came into play in the recruitment and exploitation of foreign citizens, called agents, in their own countries.

Tony was taught that one of the cardinal virtues of a P&P officer was the capability for detached manipulation of human beings. Nobody made any bones about it. Successful operations depended on good, day in and day out, agent control. Permanent CIA stations and bases operated across the globe. In fact, as one instructor announced with obvious pride, the only countries without undisclosed CIA operations were the United Kingdom, Australia, New Zealand, and Canada. The scientific, military, and economic secrets of all other countries, governments, and political groups were fair game.

Junior officers were being prepared for assignments around the world. Quickly though, Tony's personal curriculum focused on South America, particularly the four countries comprising Branch 5—Uruguay, Paraguay, Argentina, and Chile. He was disappointed not to be groomed for a European assignment. CIA stations in the capital cities of Eastern Europe were considered the most important work venues because of the Cold War. But Tony rationalized that his South American slot did not reflect negatively on his ability or his standing among the junior officers. There was no mistaking his fitness, he assured himself. Instead, it was just a simple function of his relative fluency in Spanish. And so at least one lecture every day explored the history of one of those four countries and another dealt with its culture. He was often reminded that his life might depend on things he was learning here. So he paid attention like he had rarely done at Yale.

Tony's early afternoons were spent in a room resembling a gymnasium without basketball baskets, volleyball nets, or bleacher seats. Instead, the floor was covered with foam mats. Self-defense was taught by Walter Thomas Melamud. Captain Melamud was a swarthy ex-marine of Lebanese descent with a nose that had been broken so many times it looked like a lump of putty. Captain Melamud's techniques emphasized speed, balance, and precision. Strike your adversary hard enough in the right place and he would crumble. Agents were not supposed to engage in knockdown, drag-out battles. They were supposed to know how to deliver a crisp blow to the Adam's apple or solar plexus that disabled an enemy quickly. For situations calling for more force, there was always the trusty handheld weapon.

Captain Melamud began each lesson reiterating company philosophy, which was to avoid physical conflict, if possible. "Keep a low profile, gentlemen," he said, "and you'll get your work done more efficiently. Nonetheless, situations may arise where you will need to protect yourself. That is what I am here to show you. The best way, most times, will be to surprise your opponent, to overpower him quickly, and leave him lying on the floor, gasping for breath, while you slip off, back into obscurity."

Captain Melamud taught the trainees timing and leverage. "You're quick," he told Tony. "But you need to work on your balance. An awkward swing will leave you vulnerable. Good footwork makes the difference." He forced Tony to concentrate on his feet and hips and showed him how to establish positions from which he could develop maximum force.

Every day or two he would introduce another technique for disabling an adversary, including identification of the best targets on the human anatomy for each. The trainees practiced the moves, over and over, until they dropped from exhaustion. And then Melamud made them practice some more. "Proficiency may save your life, gentlemen," he shouted. "And proficiency requires muscle memory. Which only comes from repetition. So get back to work!"

Tony rapidly became one of the better students in the group. Captain Melamud often used him in demonstrations, directing Tony to attack him in one way or another. At first, Melamud's agility and quickness kept Tony off-balance and frustrated. He wasn't able to touch the captain, much less land a decent blow. Instead, he'd extend awkwardly only to be pushed or pulled completely off balance. Several times, Tony tumbled to the floor. His classmates didn't laugh because they knew they might be unlucky enough to be the captain's next victim, but Tony was nonetheless embarrassed.

After a while, though, Tony got better and more comfortable with the techniques. He could identify the targets on his opponent's body and how to strike them accurately. His speed and finesse increased by the day. But whenever he felt like he could stand up to the captain and would lash out at him, determined to deliver a solid blow, Melamud would deflect it, move quickly to the side, and thump Tony in the side or the back of his head as he tumbled to the mat. "Shift your hips and keep your feet underneath you," the captain would shout. "Stay balanced or you'll always end up on your ass."

Tony was building up a full-grown grudge against Captain Melamud. Which made him work harder and put more into every exercise. He fantasized about connecting with a kick or a punch that would send the captain reeling. Perhaps Captain Melamud purposely taunted Tony, knowing it made him learn his lessons faster and better. Then again, it was also quite possible that Captain Melamud was a sadistic bastard who enjoyed punishing young recruits. Either way, Tony took his lessons very seriously and absorbed them quicker than most. And like a boy with some new toys, he looked forward to using them.

Weapons training was given in the late afternoon at a vast indoor and outdoor shooting range. The instructor, Stanley Borges, demonstrated a variety of pistols, including several models of the popular Smith & Wesson revolver. But the company also had access to the newest semi-automatics, some of which weren't yet available on the open market. Tony had never held a gun before, but he had a steady hand and a good eye. He took target practice with the old reliable Colt .45, a weapon that had served the US armed forces for more than fifty years. Then he tried the brand-new Czech version, the CZ75. He also tried the P220, a weapon which the Swiss manufacturer, SIG, had developed in partnership with Sauer of Germany to avoid Switzerland's stringent firearms export restrictions.

Tony was shown how to clean the weapons, load and unload them in the dark, and carry them inconspicuously. Borges said he was impressed by Tony's good marksmanship, which added to his enthusiasm. He applied himself hard to the training and took extra target practice on the ranges. He fired countless rounds with the Colt, the Smith and Wesson, and the SIG-Sauer; and before long, he was comfortable and accurate with each.

But the one he liked best was the German-made Walther PPK/S. Its designers specifically intended it for undercover use by plainclothes police so its frame was streamlined and small enough to carry in an ankle holster, much less obtrusive than a belt or shoulder holster. As a result, it fit Tony's hand better than the others. It had a unique feature, a spring-loaded pin, which protruded when there was a round in the chamber, giving an instant indication, visually or by feel, that it was ready to fire. It had a seven-round magazine and could be carried with a bullet in the chamber and the safety on but the hammer down. It could then be fired by simply releasing the safety catch and pulling the trigger. No need to cock the hammer manually as was required by single-action pistols, making it faster to bring into action. Such features made the Walther PPK/S a weapon of choice among spies, including Ian Fleming's fictional creation, James Bond. Not surprisingly, several of the young trainees selected it for their agency-issued weapon.

Stan Borges was a relatively young instructor; he did not appear much older than Tony. He was thin and wiry with long fingers. When they shook hands, his index finger reached almost all the way to the crook of Tony's elbow. Borges stood about six feet tall and walked with a spring in his step that exuded athleticism. With curly brown hair and piercing blue eyes, he looked more like a tennis instructor than a weapons expert. He never spoke about himself, so the trainees learned little about his background.

However, there was a rumor circulated amongst the trainees that Borges had a pretty sister so Tony began wondering if he could wrangle a friendly introduction. The social life wasn't particularly fulfilling over these last few weeks, and Tony was feeling frisky. In their sessions at the range, he tried a couple of times to steer the conversation in that direction but always came up empty. Whenever Borges spoke, he kept it strictly about firearms. Still, Tony was nothing if not clever and, when it came to the pursuit of women, persistent. He eventually mentioned that one of his brothers, who had worked security one summer at a liquor warehouse in Philly, had to carry a revolver. From there, he was able to ask, as innocently as a kindergarten kid, whether Stanley had any siblings himself. But Borges wasn't going for it. He answered yes. And left it at that. If he'd opened a dictionary to the word *private*, Tony was sure he'd see Borges's picture. And he never did meet the man's sister.

# CHAPTER 11

One morning the junior officers assembled in the briefing room for another field test. Tony was happy to see Frazier in the group. Their paths had not crossed in weeks. "Where've you been, Ironman?" Tony asked.

"They've been teaching me how to drive, secret-agent style," said Frazier. "They've got this great course and some really hot cars. I've been loving it." Frazier always loved cars and motorcycles. Sort of how he felt about women. *Anything fast*, Tony thought.

Just then, Colonel Pace approached the podium at the front of the room. "Gentlemen," he began, "today we are going to see how much attention you've been paying. We've set up building 12. I won't burden your little minds with too much detail beforehand, but you should recognize it once you get inside. You'll be going in the front door, one at a time, and your assignment will be to make your way through the place and eventually exit out the back door. Altogether, less than a tenth of a mile. Of course, we included some activity to keep you from getting bored. We've prepared a sketch of the floor plan, and we'll show it to you before you go in. Maybe even give you a whole minute to look it over. It's not exactly an obstacle course, but you won't be able to just sprint through. Part of the drill is for you to take notice of things you see along the way and to describe them accurately when you are debriefed afterward. And, gentlemen, just to make it more fun, you will be timed. The goal is to complete the task in a reasonably rapid time while keeping your eyes open. And because we want you to try real hard, your performances will count toward your class ranking, which will help us make some decisions about assignments later on. But for the meantime, if that isn't enough to light a fire under your butts, we'll see if we can't come up with rewards for those who perform best, like extra dessert after dinner. And for those who need to improve, well, maybe they won't get any dessert at all."

Tony looked over at Frazier, who was looking back at him. They knew what Colonel Pace was saying. Everyone hated calisthenics, which were part of the daily regimen. Forty-five minutes in the morning before breakfast, and another forty-five before dinner. Conducted by a real marine drill sergeant, they could be brutal. But Colonel Pace referred to calisthenics as the most enjoyable part of the day—pure pleasure he would say. Like having dessert before the meal. None of the junior officer candidates shared his enthusiasm for exercise, and the colonel knew it. Every one of them would like nothing better than to be excused from that "pleasure" for even one day.

"We'll see you over at building 12," the colonel continued. "Any questions?"

One hand went up. Danielson, a serious fellow from the Midwest.

"Yes, Mr. Danielson. What would you like to know?"

"Equipment, sir?" Danielson asked.

"Good question," the colonel observed. "But the answer is no. No cameras. No tape recorders. No pens. Not even a watch. Just hustle your ass through the building and keep your eyes open. Simple." Pace was smiling. "Any other questions? If not, you ladies report to building 12 on the double. I will meet you at the front entrance. We'll be sending you in alphabetically."

Frazier gave Tony a push. "I'll bet you a cold beer I beat you."

Tony rolled his eyes. "You're on, Iron head."

Twenty minutes later, the group was gathered outside building 12. After a couple more minutes, Colonel Pace arrived carrying his trademark clipboard. He pointed to the front door and announced that once they went inside, they were on their own. There were lots of items to notice, but more than a dozen were important and warranted particular attention. And this was not supposed to take all day. The record time for a candidate who had also passed the observation requirements was just under twelve minutes. Pace wished them all good luck and looked down at his clipboard. He called out the name of James Axelrod, a burly guy from Montana. Axelrod stepped forward and was given a sheet of paper, which everyone presumed was a diagram of the interior. "You'll have a minute to look this over," Colonel Pace said. Then he held up his stopwatch and pressed the button with an exaggerated motion of his thumb. Axelrod looked at the paper and smiled. After only a few seconds, he handed it back to Colonel Pace and stepped inside the door.

Frazier's name was fourth on the list, and Tony's was fifth. As Frazier was headed in, Tony called out to him. "Good luck, Ironman." Frazier turned back just long enough to say, "See you on the other side. I'll be looking forward to collecting on our bet." Tony smiled and Frazier was gone.

Then came Tony's turn. He looked at the floor plan and instantly understood why Axelrod had seemed amused. It was a crude crayon sketch, nothing more than a box with four words written in the handwriting of a kindergarten kid. They were "front door" and "back door." He smiled too. *Pretty funny.* But the colonel was holding his stopwatch and looking deadly serious, which prompted Tony to take another look at the paper. He turned it over and noticed what looked like a smudge. He squinted at it closely and saw a tiny scribble. It was too small for him to be entirely sure, but it looked like the word *language* followed by a tiny question mark. He thought to himself, *oh well*, and handed the paper back to the colonel. The door was opened for him, and he moved inside, stepping into a hotel lobby. Tony hadn't been in many, but he had seen enough of them in the movies and on television to recognize the layout. Straight ahead were the elevators. To the right was the front desk. To the left, a couple of couches and some easy chairs were surrounded a rectangular coffee table. A casually dressed man was seated, reading a newspaper and drinking coffee. Beyond him was a hallway.

Tony was impressed by the effort to which the training department had gone. It really looked like a hotel. But he remembered he was supposed to be moving quickly. He instinctively moved left toward the hallway but stopped himself after just a couple of steps. He turned back to look at the front desk. A fastidious-looking gentleman in suit and tie seemed absorbed in whatever it was he was reading. His glasses were perched precariously on the end of his nose. Tony approached him and asked for directions to the restroom. The man barely looked up and gestured toward the hallway. Tony noticed he pointed with his left hand and wore a watch on his right. *Left-handed*, Tony concluded. He wanted to hear the man speak, so he came up with another question. "Have they been cleaned recently?" The man just nodded. No luck. And it was time to move on. Tony thanked him and turned back toward the far hallway. Before he got there, he decided to make another quick stop. He walked to the coffee table and reached for one of the newspapers. Just as he had hoped, the man sitting nearby lowered the paper he was reading to look at Tony. "Do you mind if I look at your newspaper for a moment?" Tony asked. The man only stared. Tony asked again, this time in French. But still the man didn't react. So Tony tried a third time, this time in Spanish. The man smiled and quickly replied, "Si, senor. Por favor." Tony said "gracias" and picked the newspaper up. It was the front-page section of the *Washington Post*—in English. Tony scanned it, noticing the date at the top and the headlines beneath.

Then he put it back on the table, thanked the man again, and made his way to the hallway.

He wanted to keep moving toward the rear exit. Along the way, he entered and surveyed the three conference rooms he found, looking for clues. *Were they set up for anything, and if so, what?* He entered the men's room and searched it for evidence of any kind. He had been taught that there were differences between American bathrooms and those of other countries, and so he scanned the room quickly. Then he left and continued up the hall. He came across a bank of pay telephones and noticed the instructions were written in German. He lifted the receiver on one but got no dial tone. *I guess they didn't go to that much trouble*, he thought, meaning the training department hadn't put in functional telephones.

He walked quickly, stopping to open any doors that weren't locked and taking note of everything he saw inside. He knew it was especially important to discover any secondary passageways. If there were two ways to get from point A to point B, he had been told in class, he needed to know about both of them. The location of staircases was a particular priority. And it was very, very important to take careful note of all exits. Before long he came to the back door. He reached for the handle, then hesitated. He had a nagging feeling that he had missed something important. Without a watch, he couldn't be sure, but it seemed like he had made good time and could spare a few seconds. He doubled back to an alcove where a pair of phones sat on a mantle. He knew the pay telephones weren't live, but he hadn't checked the house phones. He lifted the receiver. A voice on the other end, coming from the man at the front desk who had given him the silent treatment, politely said, "Oui?"

At the pre-breakfast meeting the next morning, Frazier and Tony were both excused from calisthenics. At first, they were too happy to care about which of them had gotten the higher overall score, but after a little while it began to bug them, Frazier more than Tony. He asked Captain Jarvis to settle it. Who had scored higher?

Captain Jarvis promised to check with Colonel Pace and let them know before lunch. Throughout breakfast and later during the day, it stayed on the boys' minds. When they ran into each other on the way to lunch, Frazier began to taunt his buddy. "No way you kept up with me, Tony."

Tony laughed. Ironman would never change. "I don't know, Steve," he said. "I think I did all right."

"Oh yeah," Frazier razzed, "if you feel so good, what say we double the bet?"

"Happy to do it," said Tony. Just then, Captain Jarvis arrived.

"So, Captain," Frazier chirped, "how'd we do?"

"Well, Frazier," the captain began, "I spoke to Colonel Pace. It seems that you beat young Gannon here by almost thirty seconds. The colonel wanted me to tell you your time was good. Damn good."

"Aha," Frazier shouted. "I knew it. Tony, old buddy, you're terrific, but you're not ready to take on the Ironman just yet. I think I'll enjoy one of those cold ones with my lunch, Mr. Runner-Up. And you can buy me the other one tonight. And be sure they're ice-cold, won't you, my second place friend?"

Tony grimaced in exaggerated dismay. But before he could offer his congratulations, the captain interrupted. "Not so fast, Frazier. You didn't let me finish. Your time was better than Gannon's. That's true. But the exercise wasn't all about speed. We told you that. And Colonel Pace said that Mr. Gannon reported more information than you did. I don't know what it was, exactly, but according to the colonel, Gannon won. Something about getting Lefty the Frenchman to talk."

Frazier howled in protest. Tony's smile was stretching his cheeks as he spoke. "You know, a man can sure work up a thirst whipping the Ironman." And with that, they laughed and slapped each other on the back as they entered the dining hall.

# CHAPTER 12

*If your mission is to prevent the spread of Soviet-style communism into the western hemisphere*, Tony observed, *the situation in Chile is bound to give you indigestion.*

In 1970, a socialist physician named Salvador Allende was elected president of Chile. Allende had lost three previous elections, which is perhaps why the efforts of his opponents, and several American corporations with capital interests in Chile, came too late to block him. Allende successfully rallied the support of a dozen or more leftist parties that had never before been more than loosely affiliated to create his Unidad Popular (Popular Unity) party, a coalition of groups whose views ranged from moderate socialism to radical communism. That Allende had been able to unite people of such disparate political philosophies was remarkable and took many interested observers by surprise.

Allende promised to reorganize the economy into socialized, mixed, and private sectors, with dramatic increases in spending on education, health, and housing. The lower economic levels of Chilean society were thrilled. But such programs cost money, and the wealthier citizens knew who would end up paying. To them, Communism was another word for thievery. The philosophical divide was deep, and the population was severely polarized.

Allende's two opponents in the election were Jorge Allessandri, a conservative, and Radomiro Tomic, a moderate Christian Democrat.

Regardless of any political disagreements they had, both men were fervently anticommunist. Allende's platform of socialism for the benefit of all Chileans gave priority consideration to the nation's workers and its lower classes, none of whom had ever felt truly represented by the historically powerful Christian Democrats. Ominously for American corporations and large farm and ranch owners, the peaceful revolution Allende preached also included reforms to the agricultural industries that had started during President Eduardo Frei's administration, and to the very profitable copper industry, controlled by the principal stockholders of the American firms Anaconda and Kennecott.

Washington had successfully influenced the outcome of Allende's previous elections, manipulating labor unions, student groups, truckers, shopkeepers, and even doctors and lawyers. During the 1964 elections the Company secretly underwrote more than half of the expenses of the Christian Democratic Party's campaign against Allende, then a poorly-known leftist. The CIA had no official budget, and therefore no budgetary constraints. If people close to President Nixon decided that money needed to be spent pursuing a genuine national security goal, then funds became available. The Company had financed an extensive anticommunist propaganda campaign using posters, radio, films, pamphlets, and the press, all calculated to convince Chilean voters that Dr. Allende planned to bring communism, Soviet-like militarism and Cuban-like brutality to Chile. The CIA funding had been funneled through circuitous channels so well disguised that even the eventual winner, Eduardo Frei, may have been unaware of its real source.

By the time of the 1970 election, however, Washington had become more sensitive to exposure. The CIA began warning Washington, early on and at the highest levels, that Allessandri and Tomic could split the vote and cancel each other out—which might give the election to the socialist. But since the winner could not be predicted with certainty, there was a risk that support for the loser might anger the winner. It was also hoped that the CIA's role could be smaller and less expensive than in 1964, comprised more of a direct assault on Allende than on support for either of his rivals. Back in America, President Nixon and National Security Advisor (and eventual Secretary of State) Henry Kissinger were dealing with Vietnam and issues of domestic policy, and may have been distracted into missing the urgency of the CIA's Chilean messages.

But the instant Salvador Allende won a plurality of the vote on September 4, 1970, President Nixon and Henry Kissinger, now deeply disturbed, moved Chile's political situation to a front burner, especially in light of Allende's open admiration of Fidel Castro, a man whose very existence caused America to gnash its teeth. Only a few years earlier, the Cuban missile crisis had illustrated the very real danger posed by the communist connection between Cuba—only ninety miles south of America—and the Soviet Union. Allende's foreign policy plans included not only establishing diplomatic relations with Cuba but also moving closer, ideologically, to other communist countries such as China and North Korea.

Although Mr. Tomic and Mr. Alessandri together received more than 60 percent of the popular vote, they split that percentage down the middle, which meant that Allende's 38 percent was the most for any one candidate. "An unfortunate plurality"—as one paper dryly observed. The Chilean Constitution did not provide for a runoff. Instead, the proud Chilean National Congress was left to select the president, choosing between Allende, who finished first, and Alessandri, who finished second. Allende quickly moved to solidify his coalition. He gained the support of the Christian Democratic Party by agreeing to sign a Statute of Constitutional Guarantees, promising to respect individual rights and not to undermine the Chilean Constitution. The Company's reports to Washington predicted that the Chilean congress would ratify Allende as president unless the Chilean military could be persuaded to interfere.

The commander-in-chief of the Chilean military was General René Schneider. He had flatly declined more than one potentially profitable invitation to sabotage or otherwise defeat Mr. Allende's candidacy. General Schneider was a "constitutionalist" and believed in the preservation of the military's apolitical tradition. If his countrymen had elected a leftist government, the army's role was to protect it. The military's sworn duty did not include second-guessing or overruling the voters, but rather upholding the constitution and supporting and defending those entitled to exercise authority under it.

But many military officers had weaker loyalties to Mr. Allende. Most soldiers were conservative philosophically, their personal political leanings decidedly more to the right than to the left. Still, the Schneider Doctrine was holding, and the leadership of the Chilean military remained steadfast in its defense of the process. The Constitution, which had been ratified in 1925, put the decision in the hands of the National Congress of Chile, and General Schneider was content to leave it there.

An increasingly desperate President Nixon authorized the CIA to identify and assist one or more paramilitary groups capable enough and willing to kidnap and neutralize General Schneider. It was believed that without his influence, the army would likely give vent to its anticommunist sentiments. If so, his kidnapping could trigger a violent reaction, disrupting the congressional session and preventing Allende's inauguration. If it went really well, anticommunist factions within the military would take control of the government altogether. Tony read a quote from National Security Advisor Henry Kissinger, which described America's secret, but nonetheless official, policy: "I don't see why we need to stand by and watch a country go communist due to the irresponsibility of its own people. The issues are much too important for the Chilean voters to be left to decide for themselves."

The CIA identified General Roberto Viaux and General Camilo Valenzuela as potential candidates to carry out paramilitary operations against General Schneider. Each was secretly given untraceable equipment, including several machine guns, tear gas grenades and, of course, cash. Their first two attempts failed. Finally, a small group of well-armed men ambushed General Schneider's official car at a street intersection in Santiago. But Schneider refused to surrender. He leaped from his car, firing his gun. The gunmen panicked, and instead of capturing him, they shot him. The general was rushed to a military hospital, but died three days later.

His death provoked a national outrage, and the public and the military rallied behind Salvador Allende. Schneider's second in command, Army Division General Carlos Prats, placed the army on emergency alert. The coup had failed, and Allende was confirmed and inaugurated. A few days after General Schneider was buried with full military honors, President Allende promoted General Prats to commander-in-chief. The unthinkable had come to pass. A Marxist had been duly and democratically elected to govern a country in the western hemisphere.

The moment Allende took office, the effort toward destabilizating his government intensified. The Company had long maintained a working relationship with the owner of the country's largest newspaper, *El Mercurio*. By the time Allende became president, Agustin Edwards, the newspaper's owner, was frantic. For years he had invested heavily in Chilean industry and was dedicated to its modernization. Allende's agenda of aggressive nationalization of private industry represented a complete reversal, and on a personal level, could ruin him financially. But Mr. Edwards had powerful friends. He was, after all, not just the patriarch of the Chilean press. He was also regarded as the country's wealthiest man.

Edwards promptly flew to Washington, where he stayed with Donald Kendall, chairman of PepsiCo and one of President Nixon's closest friends and biggest campaign contributors. Kendall passed Edwards's message directly to Mr. Nixon during a social visit at the

White House, which was followed by meetings with National Security Advisor Henry Kissinger and Attorney General John Mitchell. Not long after, CIA director, Richard Helms, received instructions from the White House to meet with Edwards, or "Doonie" as he was known to friends, to obtain "insight" into the Allende "problem."

Edwards's first request was for outright military action, but the White House, embarrassed by the botched kidnapping of General René Schneider, refused. More appealing to Nixon was a thorough propaganda blitz. Edwards pledged his entire media empire, which included not only *El Mercurio*, but also *Ultimas Noticias*, a second national newspaper, *La Segunda*, Santiago's leading afternoon paper, and a dozen smaller regional journals. A joint campaign waged with the CIA would discredit Allende and terrify the people with tales of communist repression and brutality.

The president directly authorized a $2 million "loan" to Mr. Edwards, and arrangements were made to have the money surreptitiously delivered through a Brazilian intermediary. *El Mercurio* stepped up its publication of anti-Allende propaganda. The newspaper's editorials frequently included impressively detailed allegations of Mr. Allende's complicity with the Soviet Union's communist party, the evil purpose of which was to stifle free expression and crush dissent. Accompanying photos showed Soviet soldiers ripping children from the arms of their mothers, who were to be sent to the infamous Gulags. Routinely, columns cited the Cuban example of how communist rule tended to be totalitarian and self-perpetuating. Bold, inflammatory editorials railed against Allende.

President Allende had approved sharp increases in the minimum wage while simultaneously barring price increases in consumer goods. But that led to a dramatic drop in production. Food shortages became widespread, and inflation soared. Trade unions, initially amongst Dr. Allende's biggest supporters, began turning against his government, and workers had begun to strike.

Demonstrations were becoming increasingly violent. Additionally, the Chilean congress and the middle and upper classes had become critical of the UP and its leaders.

The Allende government was seeking financial support from the Kremlin and from Havana, which made Washington even more uncomfortable. And American corporations reacted strongly to Chile's refusal to pay compensation to Anaconda and Kennecott when the Chilean copper mines were nationalized. Washington authorized American financial institutions to tighten Chile's credit. It saw no reason to support a socialist government's quest for stability, and turned its back on the worsening conditions there, as if to tell those who had voted for the socialist, or failed to prevent his election, "we told you so."

When the Russian and Cuban governments were unable or unwilling to extend themselves, Chile's need for capital, for loans, grants, and other forms of aid, went unfulfilled. Living conditions deteriorated. Right-wing paramilitary groups and left-wing revolutionaries grew bolder. Newspaper editorials described Chile's military as disenchanted and suggested it was reevaluating its loyalties. Allende's administration was in trouble, and he had become a target.

Many in Washington now believed Allende's government had entered a hopeless stalemate: popular enough to do well in elections but not powerful enough to accomplish its idealistic goals. To such people, a coup, the forceful takeover of power by the military, represented the best way to return order and stability to daily life in Chile. The idea was gaining momentum by the day, and its rumblings were being felt across the city, from the boardrooms to the barracks.

Allende's Popular Unity Party may have been popular, at least in the beginning, but it was never, ever united. Violence and disorder continued and increased. The demonstrations and strikes were crippling every aspect of Chilean life. The writing wasn't just on the wall—it was on the floors and ceilings too. Yet President

Allende was not taking strong action in response. His government had passionate critics, and it could not have escaped him that some of his enemies were capable of plotting his downfall. But Allende did not appear to fully appreciate the depth of his predicament. Or else he lacked the ruthlessness required to overcome it. He refused to shut down opposition media and allowed them to continue publishing inflammatory rhetoric. He declined to order dissidents killed or jailed or even beaten. Transition in surrounding South American countries had consistently been violent, and those coming into power usually took enthusiastic revenge on those they had overthrown, often devoting more initial time and energy to purging old enemies than to implementing new policies. Salvador Allende's loyal national police, the carabineros, would undoubtedly have followed that pattern if ordered to do so, but President Allende considered reprisal and repression abhorrent and undemocratic. He listened to his political opponents rather than stifling their voices. He repeatedly spoke of the need to respect freedom of conscience and to uphold political liberties, including those of his opposition. He dreamed of changing Chile's basic capitalist structures without violence or institutional disorder. This was to be the new way, the Chilean Way. He declined to support legislation aimed at outlawing labor unions and student groups whose views were antithetical to his own. And perhaps most fatefully, he did not take over the army, put his most loyal lieutenants in charge, and jail, exile, or kill those whose loyalty was not fully established.

Allende intended to lead according to a democratic, pluralistic, and libertarian plan. Based on the rule of law, political liberty, the security of its people and its institutions and the socialization of the means of production, it was to be the people's democracy. To the leftists, his revolution was doomed because it was insufficient, halfhearted, and impractical. To the conservatives, his revolution was doomed because it was radical, criminal, and impractical. Tony couldn't help but wonder if, after all, both sides were right.

# CHAPTER 13

One of Tony's classes focused on the use of miniature cameras and recording devices. His college work in the electrical circuitry labs made him especially adept at linking electronic components and getting them to work together. At Camp Peary, though, he was also given advanced instruction on multiline telephone systems and state-of-the-art technology—things he had only heard about in his advanced engineering classes at Yale. He particularly enjoyed the complex techniques required to implant tiny relays and registers into the dialing systems of ordinary telephones. When retrieved, a properly installed register could reveal all the telephone numbers dialed on that telephone over a period as long as thirty days. Tony also learned how to implant miniature recorders and even smaller transmitters, how to select the best one for a particular situation and then how to identify suitable places to hide it. Lamps, desk ornaments, picture frames, and furniture all had potential.

Once implanted, the transmitters could relay audible signals, entire conversations, to remote listening posts where they could be monitored, recorded, and studied. Such transmitters, though, were easily detected by antibugging sweeps, routinely conducted in sensitive areas like embassies, presidential offices, and government buildings. Counterintelligence techniques like sweeps were less effective against voice-activated recorders that did not transmit. A record-only device, however, needed to be retrieved by hand and brought back to a safe place. Installations of such devices were often accompanied by an integrated timer connected to the telephone's dial tone generator. In this manner, a technician could plant a recorder and set up the telephone to suddenly lack a dial tone at a predetermined time in the future. This would result in a call for service from the customer. If the operation was set up properly, that call would be relayed to the Company. The resulting service call would be made by a CIA operative, who would then retrieve the full recorder and reset the timer so that it would work perfectly until it failed again later, requiring the technician to "service" it again. Ideally, if everything was done properly and especially when dealing with less sophisticated targets, like those found in third world countries, the entire process could be repeated over and over again.

The CIA had devoted a large amount of resource and effort toward advancing this technology and teaching it to junior officers like Tony, and it was clearly being used extensively around the world. Tony knew that as a rookie officer, he would spend most of his time on the listening end of these devices. But sooner or later he'd get out into the field, and he was intent on learning his tradecraft so that he would be ready when that happened.

The information Tony was receiving was becoming more and more detailed. His tension increased. He was given new clothes and counseled on how to dress, how to order in a restaurant, how to tip, how to hail a taxi. Chileans disliked Argentineans and disrespected Peruvians, which made it acceptable to make jokes about them. There were classes on Chilean music, literature, and art, including an hour-long lecture on the exalted status of Chile's poet laureate Pablo Neruda, who had just been awarded the Nobel Prize for literature. Chileans had their own style, very distinct from other South American peoples, and the more clearly Tony understood it, he was told, the better he could perform in the field and the safer he would be.

Eventually, Colonel Pace himself confirmed that Tony's assignment would be as a surveillance technician for the field station in Santiago, Chile. For an instant, he wished he had learned German or maybe even Russian. An assignment behind the iron curtain was considered varsity. Anything else, including South America, was junior varsity. Nonetheless, the need to prevent Castro from spreading his revolution was very real, and Tony was on a fast track for a field assignment because of his language skill. He really couldn't complain, and Colonel Pace reminded him of that.

Tony wasn't unsure about too many things as his time to leave the country approached. He knew this path was right for him, and he couldn't wait to get started. Nonetheless, as the time for his field assignment grew close, Tony's mind kept stumbling up against one set of issues. What to tell his mom and dad and—the single aspect of the transition that actually hurt to think about—what to tell Carrie.

As to his parents, he expected little difficulty. The Company's experts gave all the new hires counseling on what to tell loved ones and how to deal with the guilt they might feel about lying to them. Tony had been given what amounted to a full script. His reason for leaving the country would be built around his new employment opportunity. He had been offered a challenging technical position with CE, which came with a handsome salary and opportunities for quick advancement. The company was offering even more dynamic advantages to those willing to relocate overseas, and since Tony spoke a fair Spanish, he had been given that choice. A significant premium would be added to his salary along with the likelihood of more rapid promotion.

Tony was encouraged to brag about the numbers being discussed, but he hesitated. Tony knew what his father was paid, after many years of hard, physical labor, and he didn't want to say something that might hurt his feelings. It seemed arrogant for him, as a new graduate, to flaunt his higher salary. "Don't worry," Tony was assured by one orientation officer, "your parents will be proud of you. You went to college, as they had hoped you would, and now you are going to earn some real money, like college men are supposed to. It's a dream come true for them—to see their son succeed. Certainly your mother, but your father even more. That's why he always pushed for you to get your education so you wouldn't have to break your back like he did."

But Carrie was not likely to be supportive of this whole "going to South America" thing. Tony was sure of that. She wasn't going to understand Tony's willingness to leave her, indefinitely, to go to some third world country. Why not take the Westinghouse job, where they could be close to their families, where they might be able to get married, settle down, and maybe start a family of their own? And, if not that, weren't there good jobs in New York or Boston or even Philadelphia? Tony knew that Carrie's dreams took her to that place in her mind where families sat down to supper at six o'clock every evening and talked about the day's events, dealt with the minor problems of life, shared the joys and were just, well, happy. But that was no longer Tony's dream.

To Tony, Carrie had been all the things he wasn't. Straightforward, forthright, and sweet. Never secretive or sneaky. She was honest and decent, sensitive and caring. Always wanting to do the right thing, never manipulative, like him. She was open-minded, kind and patient, not moody or temperamental. She looked for the good in people, unlike Tony, who could be harsh and judgmental. She didn't care how rich a person was or how good-looking.

The upcoming departure for foreign shores represented a crossroads. Tony could feel the process pushing him and then pulling him. He didn't want to lose her and knew it would hurt. But at the same time, he didn't want to be tied to anyone right now. He rationalized that it would be best for Carrie to move on, herself. She was a pretty girl, and smart, and she had too much going for her to be happy sitting home waiting for him to return. Chances were he would be gone for a year, maybe more. Unable to predict for sure that he would ever want to return, much less how he would feel if and when he did. She deserved a better deal than that.

He had invested so much in their relationship and winced at the thought of giving her up or hurting her. Which is why he had always been so careful to keep his adventures secret. Having to keep his mischief from his sweetheart in order to protect her heart had forced him to develop techniques that might now enable him to "work in the shadows." By the time the CIA entered his world, Tony Gannon already had a long, personal investment in "undercover work." On that scale, at least, he could cover his tracks with the best of them. Tony supposed that in time he might mellow, and that his need to wander might subside. But he wasn't at all sure that he could ever be completely monogamous. So was he really in love? Hell if he knew.

Little by little, Tony could feel himself drifting away from Carrie in his mind, until finally, his mind was made up.

On April 21, 1973, Tony was summoned to the office of the director of training. It was time. He had devoted himself to the program and had absorbed every bit of training and instruction. He had been tested and tested again, physically, emotionally, and psychologically, and he had passed. His security clearances were in place. He had prepared his parents, and in an emotional session with Carrie, he had taken his leave of her. She cried; so did he. But now he needed to move ahead.

# CHAPTER 14

On May 5, 1973, Tony Gannon flew to Chile. The Trans World Airlines jet left New York at eight am and didn't arrive at Ezeiza Airport in Buenos Aires until eight that night. There, an exhausted Tony boarded an Aerolineas Argentinas propeller plane to cross the Andes to Santiago. The flight was too rough for sleep. Stewardesses lurched down the aisle, casual and unimpressed, even as the drinks on their trays sloshed and spilled. He hadn't flown often and was not a good flyer. Tony Gannon, secret-agent, retrieved the barf bag from the seat back in front of him and tried not to hurl.

At the airport in Santiago, a tall slender gentleman seemed to recognize him, asking, "How was the weather in Montreal?"

"Sunshine and rain," Tony responded.

Tony had been given the name Andre A. Stephens. The fellow smiled and held out his hand. "You must be Andre. I'm Paul R. Beard." Undercover officers were instructed to religiously use their cover names, including middle initial, in all reports and at all times. Cover had to be maintained, no matter how relaxed one felt or how safe. By strict adherence to that approach, it was hoped that the officer would not slip up under duress. All trainees were tested: for instance, occasionally addressed by their real names during drills or exercises, and in particular if they were tired or if they were focused on a complicated mental task or even if they had just finished drinking a couple of beers. They were expected to point out their correct name or ignore the reference altogether. Trainees were always being judged, and they could not advance unless and until they mastered the basics. In the field, their lives, and the lives of their fellow officers, might depend on it.

"Yes, I'm Andre," Tony said happily. He put his bags down and shook Beard's hand.

"How was your trip?" Beard asked.

"I didn't think we were going to make it over the mountains."

"Yeah, I know what you mean," Beard said. "I've felt like that myself a couple of times. Every once in a while the Andes swallows up one of those old DC-9s." Beard chuckled. "Not often enough to be too concerned though. Here, let me help you with that." He reached for Tony's suitcases and led Tony out of the airport.

Tony was glad for the assistance. He was so tired the bags felt like they weighed a ton apiece. But even in his exhaustion, he was excited that his new life as Andre A. Stephens had begun. Before he left he had written the name down on paper and stared at it, trying to burn it into his subconscious. He wanted his brain to regard itself as the brain of Andre A. Stephens. To examine the name from every angle, like a schoolgirl who fantasizes marrying her boyfriend and scribbles her new name, her first and his last, all over her notebook. Now finally in Chile, Tony knew he would be Andre A. Stephens, even in his dreams.

Tony's apartment was located on Montana Boulevard, in a middle-class neighborhood less than two kilometers from downtown Santiago. The apartment had a small kitchen with a square table and four chairs, a refrigerator, a stove, and a tiny oven. A compact couch and easy chair made up the living room. The bedroom held only a bed, a clock radio, a telephone, and a black-and-white television. Tony had been instructed to watch the government-sponsored programs and those of other political institutions, including channels produced by the University of Chile and the Catholic Church. He was also tasked with monitoring Radio Magallanos, the main pro-government radio station. In short: plenty of speech making and political commentary.

The Company leased apartments around the city, under the guise of civilian contractors like Chase Manhattan Bank or 3M Manufacturing. Some were close enough to strategic targets, like the presidential palace, to enable audio receivers to pick up signals broadcast in real time from planted transmitters. Tony's studio had become available when the previous tenant had been forced out of the country during one of Allende's purges of a particular American company.

Tony had learned that American efforts to foment popular opposition to Allende had strained the socialist state's economy, but the results of subsequent congressional elections were, from Washington's perspective, disappointing. In April 1971, Unidad Popular candidates won just under 50 percent of the total vote, representing a gain of more than ten percentage points since the presidential elections seven months earlier. In July, a by-election was held in Valparaiso to replace a deputy who had died. Again, the Unidad Popular candidate received almost 50 percent of the vote. Evidently, the socialist model for a "People's Democracy" had gained support among the idealistic Chilean public.

In November 1971, President Allende had invited Fidel Castro for a visit. It was supposed to have lasted ten days, but it stretched out for more than three weeks. Castro toured the country from north to south, often escorted cheek to jowl by Allende himself. Their message of socialist unity was impossible to ignore. Washington's determination increased.

Continental Electric had become a perfect cover for penetrating Chilean society. One of the American corporations most affected by Allende's nationalization efforts was International Telephone and Telegraph (IT&T), the owner of more than two-thirds of the Chilean Telephone Company, Chiltelco, an interest valued at more than $150 million. In June 1970, the IT&T board of directors had privately discussed Chiltelco's vulnerability to nationalization should Allende become president. One of IT&T's directors, John McCone, had served as director of the CIA from 1961 through 1965, and was still a consultant to the agency. Cone was able to talk directly with the current director, Richard Helms, and the picture that emerged was indeed disturbing. IT&T decided to take sides against Allende by opening its pocketbook, offering more than a million dollars to fund agency efforts to stop Allende's election.

The CIA's western hemisphere chief, Bill Broe, declined the money but introduced McCone to *El Mercurio's* Doonie Edwards, and to Mr. Allessandri, Allende's political rival. IT&T quietly contributed more than a quarter of a million dollars to the Alessandri campaign and more than $100,000 to the newspaper. After Allende's election victory in 1970, IT&T renewed its offer to contribute to efforts to block Allende's confirmation by the Chilean Congress. When that failed, IT&T executives worked to coordinate a plan with other U.S. companies to delay credit and slow deliveries of goods and spare parts to Chile. The U.S. government was to play its part by withdrawing technical assistance. The goal was to crush Chile's economy and doom Allende to failure.

Columnist Jack Anderson learned of IT&T's connection to Washington's anti-Allende efforts and publicized it in his syndicated column in early 1972. Allende likely knew that he had an enemy within his country's own telephone company even before that. But reading Anderson's fully and accurately detailed columns was humiliating. His patient forbearance of antagonistic corporate American interests in Chile and their opposition to his leadership had been pushed beyond tolerance. He issued an angry edict, sending several high-level IT&T officials home and forbidding the Ministry of State to extend any more visas to its employees. Chiltelco would need to look elsewhere for new technicians and engineers. Continental Electric, a highly regarded provider of technical support, was a natural replacement. With admirable foresight, it already had a lot of young fellows trained and ready to travel. Including one named Anthony Gannon.

Tony worked in a small well-equipped office that Continental Electric subleased from the American embassy. The embassy and its subtenants occupied the top three floors of a nine-story grayish office building in downtown Santiago, across Agustinas Street from the Hotel Carrera and diagonally across Constitution Square from La Moneda, the presidential palace. The structure had the nondescript architectural style of many conservative institutions, although the lobby had recently been modernized at the expense of the building's major tenants.

The Santiago station chief was Gilberto D'Onofrio, a CIA veteran with twenty-five years under his belt. Tony's direct supervisor was Mike Henderson, another veteran case officer. Tony was a tech, and a rookie at that, with no military experience. He sensed that Mr. D'Onofrio and Mr. Henderson were disappointed with his resume, kind of like racecar drivers who were hoping for a Corvette but wound up getting a Volkswagen. But the station had lost several officers in the IT&T purge and needed whatever replacements the Company could send. At least Tony was a Spanish speaker.

At Tony's orientation, D'Onofrio and Henderson gave what was meant to serve as a pep talk. "You will listen, and you will report. Audio surveillance is important work. We need to know who has access to Allende, who's in his inner circle. You're going to help identify who's who, so their relative value to us can be determined," Mr. D'Onofrio explained.

"Then the process of learning their pressure points begins," Henderson added. "If any of Allende's close associates has a weakness, our goal is to find it. Just before you arrived here, one general complained about an associate's gambling problem. Can you see where that might be useful?" he asked.

"Sooner or later he'll need cash that he can't get legitimately," Tony answered quickly. He was thinking of his Uncle Johnny who liked to bet on football games. And baseball. And the horses. He was always falling behind to his bookies and had come crying, more than once, seeking "loans" from Tony's dad. Dignity goes out the window when a gambler gets in over his head.

"Another guy might have a sick mother or a sick child that needs the kind of advanced medical care not available here in Chile," D'Onofrio continued. "We have the ability to provide such a person with a quiet flight to a modern hospital in Houston or New Orleans or Miami, where medical miracles can be found. America can give hope to people in that kind of situation. But we need to know about it so we can make a timely and discrete offer."

Henderson picked up where D'Onofrio had left off. "There was a colonel who liked young boys. By some unfortunate accident, he had been caught on film. He, of course, could hardly allow his shameful weakness to be revealed. So blackmail, to use the nasty word for it, was a very effective tool. But the moviemakers wanted more money than he had. We were able to help make a deal with his blackmailers. He got the tapes, and nothing was ever disclosed. You can imagine the man's gratitude. It was a delicate process, of course, because we had to make sure the poor fellow didn't find out that we kept copies of the films, or that we were responsible for the blackmailing in the first place. We also needed to make sure the colonel didn't panic. Deep despair can prove counterproductive. He needed to be scared enough to shit himself but not enough to shoot himself." Henderson and D'Onofrio were both smiling. "We don't want anyone reading about our operations in a suicide note. Besides, assets are only effective if they're alive. So they have to be handled tactfully. Our officer was very reassuring. He told him, 'All is not lost, dear colonel. No one need ever know.' I don't mind telling you that the colonel has been helpful ever since."

D'Onofrio's spoke again. "We don't brag. We are out here in the trenches, and we do what needs to be done. It's always for a good cause. Don't you agree?"

Tony was full of loyalty. "Yes, sir," he said, ready to salute.

Henderson finished up. "We're not above providing the young boys or the young girls or the drugs or the cash or whatever it takes. And targets have to be carefully selected. The Russians are here too, and they're pretty sly. Don't want to blow cover by approaching a plant. So we rely on building surveillance to reveal the faces of people going in and out and tell us how long they stayed; but only by listening can we figure out who the decision makers are and how they think. Your time is going to be spent with headphones on, listening, making notes, and reporting. Your sources will include transmissions from bugs we've placed all around the city."

What D'Onofrio and Henderson told him was true. After a few weeks, Tony's days took on a familiar routine. At 8:30 AM, he reported to the CE offices in the embassy building, retrieved the stack of documents and tapes that had been left for him, grabbed a cup of strong coffee, and went to his desk where the headphones waited. He sat in the hard wooden chair for hours, sometimes all night long, listening to the muffled voices, or sifting through the media for clues about the issues and activities of the important players in an increasingly polarized political atmosphere. Sometimes, before he put the next tape into the playback machine, he read through the notes and reports of others who were doing similar work elsewhere around the country. The focus of these information-gathering efforts was to identify the players and help the analysts determine who was loyal to the government, who opposed it, and who was on the fence. Loyalists could be targeted for discrediting and, in the event Allende fell, could then be dealt with. Those that were antagonistic to Allende could be approached. South America was a culture replete with disgruntled politicos. Identifying the enemy of one's enemies was very valuable to those working against the current regime.

Mike Henderson and Gil D'Onofrio had a relaxed coolness about them. They had been in Chile for years, and knew who would be willing to help and who wouldn't, and about who needed to be watched carefully and who could be trusted. Changes were coming, and D'Onofrio and Henderson knew who might want those changes. And who might be in position to help make them. And who would resist. Tony devoured their reports.

From time to time, he was given complete transcripts of intercepted communications. This did not happen often, because only the most important conversations warranted the time and cost needed to transcribe them. He wished he knew the local people as well as D'Onofrio and Henderson did, but that would take time. In the meanwhile, he was getting to know his way around and meeting people. As he listened to their conversations and read the reports and transcripts, the secrets of strangers were revealed. It was like having a subscription to a daily gossip column. Gradually, he felt like he knew the characters in his stealthy soap opera better than their own friends and relatives did.

# CHAPTER 15

One afternoon, the intercom on Tony's desk buzzed. "Hey, Andre. This is Mike. Would you mind coming into my office for a minute?"

Tony quickly made his way there. Before he could knock, Henderson called out, "Come on in. I've got someone wants to see you."

Tony opened the door and almost yelled. It was Steve Frazier. Ironman. He was so happy he felt his eyes moisten. He didn't realize just how lonesome he had been until he saw his old friend. The two men hugged and slapped each other on the back.

"They told me you were floundering, so I agreed to come down here and back your sorry ass up."

"Ironman," Tony exclaimed. "Damn, I'm glad to see you."

"Actually," Henderson said, "Allende sent another one of our mechanics home, and we've been having trouble keeping our vehicles running right. Besides, we could always use another good driver."

"You know I'm just the man for that job," Frazier said. A little too exuberant for a new guy, maybe, but his confidence was just as much a part of him as ever.

Frazier was assigned to work as a mechanic at the embassy motor pool. He struggled with Spanish and so was limited in the kinds of assignments he could be given. But he had an aptitude for mechanical things, especially cars. Since he was a boy, he had been a garage rat, and back in New Haven had spent his spare time working on a 1964 Mustang. He could service motorcycles and half-ton trucks and just about everything in between. Replacing gaskets and hoses or rebuilding transmissions, Steve Frazier was at home.

On slow days at the garage, he was given driving assignments, which he looked forward to. His training had included advanced techniques in the operation of all kinds of vehicles, both old and new. He was taught high-speed driving and evasive maneuvers, including driving while being shot at, operating with one or more flat tires, limited visibility operations—all manner of emergencies. And the man flat-out loved to drive. Heck, Frazier could reverse down an alley while ducking under the dashboard better than most people could manage puttering down a country road on a sunny day.

It was part of Tony's job to go out when he wasn't working. Henderson and D'Onofrio had given him a list, which they updated frequently, of places where he might cross paths with people of interest. Tony and Ironman embraced the aspect of their assignment for which they were ideally suited: hanging out. Acting like twenty-two-year old men normally act after work. They searched the list for the best restaurants and nightspots. Heck, it wouldn't violate any rules if, while they were developing contacts in the community, they happened to meet some good-looking women.

All case officers learned that the key to the development of local assets, native agents, was getting to know people with information and discovering their motivations or their weaknesses. Most frequently, at least in the Third World, with its shortages of goods and rampant inflation, the pressure point would be financial. Security officers and local police could always use extra cash, to take better care of their families or get themselves into or out of trouble. Alcohol, drugs, gambling, women or other obsessions could cause problems for a man. And just about anyone in Chile could use money beyond what they received in their paychecks. But that wasn't all. In order to serve as a truly valuable agent, a foreign citizen needed to lack full political or personal loyalty to his employers or his government. Ideological differences, disloyalty, and the need for cash. That was the formula. Tony had been instructed to remain alert to the hoped-for combination of an "axe to grind" and access to information. Such people were out there, and every political development and every vote in parliament had the potential to create new winners and losers. But these things were never obvious. That's why there were funds in the station budget for young officers like Tony and Ironman to get out around town.

"Just put yourself in position to meet folks," Henderson told each of them. "Make yourself a part of the social scene and hang out where people are having fun and getting loose. Spend a little money. Not conspicuously. Just enough to show you're doing all right. Listen to anyone willing to talk to you. Once people recognize you, they'll trust you. Share a few drinks, and maybe one of them will tell you something useful."

D'Onofrio had discouraged Tony and Frazier from spending too much time together at night. Case officers were usually loners. They weren't supposed to get too chummy in the field. The life of an officer in clandestine operations was supposed to be solitary, because if one officer's cover was compromised, it could expose anyone closely associated with him. Officers were also prevented from knowing too much about other operations that they were not involved in, a principle called "compartmentation." But Tony and Frazier weren't overly impressed and ignored the rule whenever they could. As far as they were concerned, they had perfect roles to play—just a couple of North Americans working in Chile who were both a little homesick. And they had the kind of boyish confidence that made it difficult to anticipate that either of them would ever lose his cover. Beyond that, they had been relying on each other for years and couldn't imagine anyone they'd rather look to for support if trouble did come their way. So they spent some evenings together, Frazier looking for women and Tony not exactly looking away. As long as nobody at headquarters got overly upset about it, they intended to continue.

Frazier hadn't been in Santiago for even a month before he wrangled an invitation to a big party at the home of Tucho Colon, the owner of Le Boit Noir, one of the city's most popular nightclubs. Colon was a well-connected businessman who had been building a nightlife dynasty for years. His home was on a beautiful street in the foothills of the Cordillera, an exclusive neighborhood of hidden mansions several kilometers outside of the city. Even the lush trees overhanging the roadway were elegant, a stark contrast to the crowded barrios surrounding downtown Santiago.

Colon was on a first name basis with most of the important "movers and shakers" in town, which was remarkable when you considered he was gay. Chilean society was heavily influenced by the Catholic Church and very conservative on social issues, so Colon's sexual orientation was a closely guarded secret, one that he necessarily took great pains to disguise. It helped that he had the ability, because of the great number of women he employed, to surround himself with beautiful and affectionate females. And, in truth, Tucho enjoyed the company of women, so the charade wasn't difficult for him to sustain. But Tucho's affinity for young men with sharp features had been well documented in the CIA's files. And, as was also documented, well exploited.

Tucho's circle of friends included several members of the Chilean parliament and two very influential ministers. So what if he had some disgusting habits and was, in blunt terms, a pervert? His need for illicit excitement and secrecy made him a particularly easy target. More than once the company set him up to embarrass himself and then rescued him, and his reputation, before the situation got out of hand. Tucho Colon was slow to learn his lessons or too weak to control himself. As the list of his transgressions mounted, he became more and more beholden. And he was in position to express his gratitude by passing along the kind of information that only a member of Chile's innermost political circle could obtain.

The names of a Russian agent and a Cuban agent, both of whom had been sent to Chile to engage in counterespionage operations, had certainly been helpful. Once the Santiago station had learned their identities, care had been taken to ensure the foreign agents were denied access to any ongoing American clandestine operations. Then they were purposely fed false information, which they passed up their chain of command all the way back to Havana and the Kremlin. And perhaps most delicious of all, eventually violent and disruptive actions were attributed by the press to the unwitting enemy agents. How simple it was to reveal in the morning papers the names and Russian or Cuban affiliations of the "thugs and hoodlums" that had been sent into the streets of Santiago by Salvador Allende to tyrannize and terrify the good people of Chile. D'Onofrio wrote in one account that his officers had proven themselves better framers than the clerks at the local art gallery. It had taken finesse and a lot of careful planning, but it had only been possible because of information provided by a grateful Tucho Colon.

On this particular night, Colon was celebrating the opening of a new club, his fourth. Tony and Frazier took a taxicab, but the driver wasn't able to get them within three blocks before they were bogged down in the traffic mess caused by Colon's guests. They paid the cabbie and walked the last blocks. The house was at the end of a tree-lined boulevard, with a wide grassy median separating the lanes of traffic. Music could be heard for blocks, and people with drinks wandered outside as Tony and Steve hopped up the three steps leading to the porch that surrounded the mansion. A couple sat in an oversize lounge chair on the porch, kissing. The front doors were massive wooden structures, the floor was genuine Italian marble, and the walls were finished with panels of real walnut. Well-dressed guests sipped champagne from glittering crystal flutes. Tony and Steve exchanged cheerful greetings with a few as they headed for the bar.

"Remind me how you swung this invite, Murphy?" Tony asked.

"Maria Elena, that secretary at Central Bank, the friendly one who always offers me a *pastelito* when I go there, she knows Colon's cousin or something. She told me to come and that I could bring a friend. And you were the closest thing to a friend I could manage."

But Tony was no longer listening. His attention had been seized, completely, by a tan, slender woman who was standing in the doorway to the dining room. She was wearing a dark brown leather skirt with a suede jacket that had buckskin tassels hanging from the midriff down to the waist. Her hair was shoulder length and brown with streaks of blond. She was pretty, all right, but more than that, her faced conveyed a strong sensuality. She had the exotic, sexy look of a woman who thoroughly enjoyed all of her senses. Bedroom eyes, you could call them, that blinked slowly—with long, full eyelashes. Long legs and slender hips gathered into a narrow waist. Tony couldn't really tell how she was shaped under the vest, but there was more than a hint of curve pushing out against the suede that covered her chest.

Tony figured her to be in her late '20s or early '30s, which meant she was older than him. She was talking to a heavyset, pleasant-looking woman who was eating hors d'oeuvres from a round dish. But she wasn't focused on her chubby friend, who was chewing vigorously and talking at the same time. Instead, she lazily scanned the room until her eyes met Tony's. A smile started to form, but she caught herself and demurely returned her attention to her friend. But Tony had seen it. He kept his eyes on her, hoping he hadn't been mistaken. He looked at the people near her. Was there a husband or a boyfriend among them? He didn't see one. A few seconds later, she glanced at him again and flashed another smile. He felt electricity crackle from her eyes to his. She turned away, but it was too late. Tony knew that they had connected, and he felt his heart race.

"Hey, Andre!" Frazier interrupted. "Here's your drink, buddy." Tony needed a moment before he was able to reach for the rum and Coke. He actually had trouble catching his breath. But the drink tasted good. He swallowed and then turned slowly toward the doorway where she was standing. But she was no longer there.

"Frank," Tony said quietly to Frazier, "I just saw the most spectacular woman."

"Where?" Frazier asked, whipping his head back and forth. Subtlety had never been Ironman's forte.

"I don't know. She was standing by the doorway just a second ago."

"Let's find her. That is, unless you've got something better to do."

Tony and Frazier meandered through Tucho Colon's magnificent home. There were many lovely women at the party, and Frazier was taking mental notes. But Tony's heart was still beating too fast. He tried to remind himself to relax. She was just a girl.

Several large rooms were filled with people, but she was nowhere to be seen. Ironman struck up conversations with several women, as was his style. He had always taken a volume approach to meeting girls. Back at Yale, it was not unusual for him to show up with three or four or more. He would invite them back to the house to meet his roommates for a nightcap. The ladies were always at ease. Safety in numbers, or so they thought, and an opportunity to meet Yalies. The "volume theory" of seduction became Frazier's trademark. He was relentless and had little in the way of standards. He would talk to all the girls in the group, laughing and joking and making them feel welcome. He took his time, getting to know each one. He didn't care who was prettiest. Attitude—that's what he was looking for. He wanted to find the most responsive lady. If the prettiest one wasn't receptive, he'd cheerfully turn his attention to one of her less attractive friends. They're even more grateful, he observed. His goal, after all, was sex. He didn't plan on falling in love. They were challenges to be conquered. He wanted to sweet-talk, make out, get naked, have his way with their bodies, and add another notch to his belt. If they had fun going along with his program, and many did, he would see them again. If not, well, there were lots of fish in the sea. And if it were up to Frazier, he would hook each and every one.

He was always friendly and outgoing anyway, and when he had female company at home, he was an enthusiastic host. He kept his bar well stocked and knew how to prepare almost any drink. He could serve them each their favorite until a simple nightcap turned into two or three or more. Ultimately, someone's defenses would wilt and handsome Steve, the Ironman, would move in. He would invite her to stay after her friends left and promised to take her right home when she was ready. The method worked well throughout his years at Yale, and he saw no reason to change it now. Tony just shook his head. It might not have been his way, but you couldn't argue with success. At school, Frazier had gotten more women into the sack than some entire fraternities.

But tonight Tony hardly noticed the ladies that were being drawn into conversation by his friend. Where was his mystery woman? Had she left? After another half an hour of searching with Tony, Frazier had had enough. He had become engaged in conversation with a group of four or five women, and he was measuring them all up. Tony was on a different mission. He wandered away in his mind and then he just wandered away.

Bars had been set up throughout the cavernous house, and it seemed to Tony a good idea to head toward the one closest to the dining room. A few feet from the doorway, a bartender was pouring a glass of red wine. Tony waited until he was finished and then stepped up.

"*Que quiere, senor?*" the bartender asked cheerfully.

"*Rum y coke*," Tony responded. The bartender went right to work and soon handed Tony his cocktail. As Tony began to pivot back toward the interior of the room, he almost knocked shoulders with a short, stout woman who was rumbling into position at the bar. Tony immediately recognized the mystery girl's chubby friend. *Thank you, Lord*, he whispered to himself.

"I'm sorry," said Miss Chubby.

"No, no," Tony said, cordially. "Entirely my fault." As he spoke, he glanced casually beyond her to see if mystery woman was nearby. But she wasn't. Still, Tony knew Miss Chubby could be his link to her, and he wasn't about to let the opportunity get away.

"I am so clumsy," Tony said. "I almost knocked you over."

"Not at all," Miss Chubby replied. "I was in too much of a hurry."

Tony gave her the most cheerful look he had in his repertoire. She was overweight, but her face was pretty, with curly hair and big brown eyes. Of course, Tony didn't care about that. His focus was her friend.

"This place is really beautiful, isn't it?" Tony asked in his best Spanish.

"Yes, Mr. Colon's house is a palace," she replied.

"May I introduce myself? My name is Andre Stephens."

"Hello, Mr. Stephens," Miss Chubby responded. "I am Maria. Maria Cueto." She held out her hand, and Tony drew it to his lips. He kissed it as regally as he could. Maria giggled.

"Please call me Andre, won't you?" Tony insisted. He was still getting used to Chilean formality.

"Of course, Andre. And you may call me Maria," she responded.

"Thank you, Maria," Tony said. "So how do you know Mr. Colon?"

"Oh, I really don't know him," Maria answered. "My girlfriend, Cristina, does. Actually, she doesn't really know him either. She knows a friend of his. That's how we were invited tonight."

Tony hoped Cristina was his mystery woman. But it wasn't time yet to inquire. He needed to be patient, but it wasn't easy. "Really?" he said. "That's how I got invited, too. My friend knows a lady that works at the bank who is Mr. Colon's cousin or something. I think. Anyway, she invited my friend, and he invited me."

"Well, I guess we have something in common then, don't we?" Maria asked. She raised her glass and offered, "to friends!"

Tony raised his glass and repeated her toast. "To friends!" Tony saw Frazier approaching from across the big room with a frown on his face. "Speaking of friends," he announced, "here comes mine."

Maria turned toward Frazier. "*Aye Dios mio,*" she said. "That's your friend? I noticed him before. He's really cute! And so tall."

Tony made a pouty face, as if he felt slighted by her comment. Back home his expression might have said, "What am *I*, chopped liver?"

Maria smiled and apologized. "You're really cute too, Andre."

"No," Tony answered, perhaps a bit too quickly. "Don't worry. I am happy to introduce you."

Just then Frazier arrived. He smiled at Maria and pulled Tony's sleeve. "Man," he whispered, "this place is full of lesbians. I thought I had something going with a girl back there, but it turns out she likes women as much as I do."

Tony was hoping that Maria hadn't heard him. He introduced Frazier, who took Maria's hand. But when he did, she pulled him toward her and leaned close enough to offer her cheek European style. Frazier didn't miss a beat. He kissed her on one cheek and then the other. Her flirtatious nature was coming through loudly and clearly. And while, yes, she was just a little heavy, she did have a very pretty face. All in all, just right for Ironman, and he didn't hide his interest.

Meanwhile, Tony could bide his time. Sooner or later, he figured, Maria would be rejoining her friend. Assuming she was his mystery woman, he was already in place to be introduced. He just needed to wait and let it happen. For now, he could relax and enjoy watching Frazier do his thing.

A little while and a couple of drinks later, though, Maria announced it was time for her to leave.

Frazier said, "I'll be glad to take you home." Tony shook his head. How was Ironman gonna do that? They'd come by cab, remember? But it didn't matter. Maria wasn't going for it. She liked this tall, dark, and handsome man. And she was hoping to see him again. But a girl mustn't make it too easy. Men appreciate a woman more if they have to work a bit. Now her telephone number was a different story. That she would give him. All he had to do was ask.

"Thank you for that kind offer. But I came with my friend, and I would never abandon her. She's probably already outside waiting. I really have to go."

Tony began to panic. Frazier repeated his offer, "Are you sure I can't take you home?"

"Yes, I am quite sure," she said. "I have to go home with Cristina. Perhaps we can see each other another time," she continued, "For now, you will please escort me outside, yes?"

"Of course," Frazier answered, in his most courtly manner. The three of them walked toward the front door. It was then that Tony saw her. His mystery woman. She was seated in the backseat of a shiny black sedan. The window was open. Maria was holding Frazier's hand as she moved quickly toward the car. "Look, Cristina. I have a new friend. This is Frank Murphy. Isn't he good looking?"

Cristina responded to Maria but looked directly at Tony. Their eyes were exchanging sparks again. "Yes, Maria. He is very handsome." She was smiling like the Mona Lisa. *Cristina*, Tony said to himself. He was convinced she was directing her words at him. His heart jumped so hard, it threatened to leap from his chest.

Maria kept on, giggling. "He wants to see me again. Should I let him?"

"How naughty you are, Maria," Cristina scolded playfully. Tony had already fallen in lust with her voice.

Maria turned back to Frazier, no doubt to give him her telephone number, and they spoke quietly before she began to get into the front seat. Tony took the opportunity to approach Cristina. "I have been wanting to talk to you since I first saw you. I was trying to find you inside. How can I contact you?" He spoke in a hush, wanting only her to hear.

"Sadly," she whispered, "that is not possible." With that, the car pulled away.

# CHAPTER 16

Cristina de la Vega was indeed a beautiful woman. She was five feet six inches tall, which gave her stature above the average Chilean. Her legs were long and slender with the firm muscular contours of an athlete's. Her eyes were a very distinctive green, which also set her apart from other Chilean women, most of whom had brown eyes. Cristina had very long eyelashes, which added a powerful sensuality to the simple act of blinking. She was thin through the waist with gently rounded hips and a full bosom. Her skin was dark tan and as smooth as cocoa butter. She kept her hair cut to her shoulders. It was full and wavy—the color of caramel with streaks of gold. She had full lips and teeth that were a little crooked but absolutely white. Altogether, Cristina had the kind of look that men noticed and women envied.

But there was a lot more to Cristina de la Vega than her appearance. She had grown up in the Bermudez neighborhood of Santiago and had excelled in school, both academically and athletically. She was a talented soccer player and quite adept at tennis. After high school, she went to the University of North Carolina at Chapel Hill, where she became fluent in English while earning a bachelor's degree in comparative literature. The combination of accents in her speech, Latina mixed with southern belle, added to her allure. Every boy on campus noticed her, and if she spoke to one for even a few minutes, he would inevitably ask her out. She dated a few of the attractive ones, but the dates were always the same: a cheap meal somewhere, a couple of beers, maybe a movie, and then back to the dorm. So she accepted invitations from two professors, but she was still disappointed.

Cristina had a very strong libido, and men were necessary for her physical satisfaction. There were occasions when she was attracted to a man and went to bed with him. It was the height of the sexual revolution in America, and everyone was supposed to be having fun; but none of her affairs had depth. Any thrills were fleeting. Afterward, she felt hollow and alone, and a little guilty. She seldom went out with the same man twice.

By the time she graduated and left the States, she had not given herself in a meaningful way to any man. Her lust had sometimes been indulged, but any satisfaction was short-lived. Overpowered by her beauty, in awe of her flawless, smooth skin, her long legs and full, rounded breasts, all her lovers treated her like a goddess. But she wanted to be treated like a whore. Their lovemaking was workmanlike, as if they were applying techniques learned from a how-to book. They approached tentatively, desperate to please her but uncertain about how, alert for her signal to slow down or back off entirely. That was not the stuff of which her deepest fantasies were made. She wanted someone who couldn't back off. A lover consumed by a need he was unable to restrain, who did not ask permission, whose passion would overtake his soul and then hers, sweeping them both away to explosive ecstasy. The dreams that aroused her, that had her squirming and sweaty, short of breath and soaking wet, were about being taken. Not raped, and not hurt, just overwhelmed by a man who wanted her too much to back off. A strong man, reckless with desire and confident in his prowess.

Eventually, she went on fewer dates, preferring to spend her time alone, cooking for herself, reading, and listening to music on her record player. She was never sure why it was that way. Perhaps it was something she saw in her parents' marriage.

Raul de la Vega had been a handsome man and a skilled carpenter. At one time he ranked among the most elite tradesmen in all of Chile, and had participated in the construction of many of Santiago's finest homes and offices, even becoming acquainted with President Allende during the remodeling of the presidential palace. But he preferred drinking and womanizing to staying at home. Ana de la Vega wanted a traditional marriage, with a dutiful and doting husband who would slow down and put on weight and make everything comfortable. But she had married the wrong man for that. Raul de la Vega was a drunk and a philanderer and eventually, he broke Ana's heart. She made Raul leave their home. They divorced shortly after Cristina returned from America. Ana de la Vega sold the house she had grown up in and went to live with relatives in Montevideo, the capital of Uruguay. She tried to explain what had happened and why the marriage had ended, but Cristina already knew. She had seen it coming.

With no wife to tether him, Raul's life spiraled out of control. At work, his artistry suffered dramatically. It wasn't too long before the good contracts stopped coming, and he was forced to get by on small jobs that paid poorly. Cristina watched her father first squander his gift for woodworking and then his health. She wistfully remembered those days, not too long before, when she had marveled at the polished surfaces of the wood paneling her father had built, the smooth, quiet workings of the hinges and the richness of the sound the doors made when they closed. During La Moneda's remodeling, one night after everyone had gone home, her father had taken her to the Toesca assembly room, the Cabinet Room, the Independence Lounge, and the upstairs dining room and auxiliary kitchen, through the false walls and trapdoors and crawl spaces that weren't shown on any plans. His affair with the bottle had taken all that away.

But Cristina loved him deeply, in the unique way that little girls love their fathers, and despite her disappointment in him, she recognized that she shared some of his adventurous ways. Having observed firsthand the sadness and failure visited upon a talented but irresolute man, one would have expected her to recognize and reject the company of men with such flaws. She should have learned from her mother's broken heart, but in the curious way that marks human nature, Cristina de la Vega found herself most attracted to men who were daring, if not reckless.

# CHAPTER 17

Even before the black sedan had pulled fully out of sight, Ironman was ready. "Let's go back inside for another drink."

"Okay," said Tony, "if you must. But there's no one else I want to meet."

"Speak for yourself," Ironman replied. Meeting Maria had only whetted his appetite. And there was an open bar inside. Several, actually. He wasn't even close to quitting. "I've got it in my head to offer the cure to one of those good-looking lesbians I saw inside."

Tony shook his head. "Still the king of volume sales, I see."

The party was less crowded now, but still fully active. Tony was content to sip his rum and coke, but Frazier was working hard on whatever lady happened to squeeze in next to him. He wasn't having any luck. One after another collected her drink from the bartender and moved off.

"I told you they're all lesbos. I can't even get one to smile at me."

Tony hadn't been paying attention. "What have you been saying to them?"

Frazier paused. "Well, I think I've got it right but you know, maybe not. Damn complicated, their language."

"Just tell me what you've been saying," Tony repeated.

"I've been asking, *Puedo comprarle una vecina?* Just like you told me. But I can't get a bite."

"You dummy, that's not even close," Tony laughed. "You've been offering to buy them a neighbor. Drink is *bebida*, not *vecina*."

"Jeez," Ironman said. "I wish people would just speak English, make it easier."

"Come on," Tony said. "Let's call it a night."

"I guess," Ironman said. But he was reluctant. They were still pouring free liquor inside a beautiful mansion with good-looking women to be tracked. One of them had to be getting lonely; he just needed to find her. Besides, closing time was when he usually got his best results. He ordered another drink. "This will be my last," he assured Tony, whose scowl was plain. "Just give me one more shot." He turned his gaze halfway across the room to a disheveled brunette leaning against a high table. He drained the last of his drink and reached for the new one the bartender was placing before him.

That has to be his sixth, Tony observed, amazed that his friend wasn't completely trashed. A slur in his words might be detectable by someone who knew him well, but other than that, nothing.

"There she is," Ironman said. "If I don't get somewhere with her by the time I finish my drink, we'll go. I won't be happy about it, you understand. But I'll go, if that's what you want. Just don't go calling that taxi quite yet. I've got a good feeling about this one."

"Fair enough," Tony replied. The woman was clearly older than Ironman. But she was fairly attractive and the faraway look in her eyes suggested she'd had a few too many. *Oh well*, Tony thought. *No supermodel, but definitely a perfect Ironman target. Hopefully she'll shoot him down fast.*

Ironman's path to her table wasn't exactly a straight line, but it got him there. And once he arrived, all six foot three of him, he had no trouble getting the brunette's full attention. Ironman may not have had full possession of his faculties, and wouldn't have been too smooth in Spanish even if he did, but he was still ruggedly handsome and full of healthy male hormones.

Tony's curiosity was piqued. The blaring stereo prevented him from making out much of their conversation, but if a smile was what Frazier was after, he succeeded right off the bat. In fact, by the looks of it, the lady was delighted by whatever Frazier was telling her. Tony's hopes for a quick ending were fading.

That is until a well-dressed, clearly unhappy man joined the duo. He was huge, bulging across the chest and serious. *Time to go, Ironman*, Tony thought. But his buddy wasn't sharing that thought. He was still focused, laser-like, on his prey, her boyfriend's size and negative body language notwithstanding. And the drunken lady wasn't discouraging him. Not a bit. At first, her boyfriend tried to look bored, nodding patiently as Ironman rambled on. But his face gradually transformed into a glower, directed first at his girlfriend and then at Frazier. Still, Frazier wasn't going to be deterred. Then Tony saw the man set his shoulders and narrow his eyes. Several possibilities flashed through Tony's mind, most of them ugly. He headed toward the trio. Now the man was telling Ironman to move on, that his lady friend wasn't interested in a rude foreigner. But that lady wasn't sure about that, or at least she wasn't signaling her agreement, which was all the encouragement Ironman needed. The boyfriend might as well have been invisible. Ironman reached across the table to take his new friend's hand. The boyfriend pulled her hand away, then pushed Ironman in the chest. Ironman looked surprised, but whether due to the woman or the booze, he still wasn't accepting the idea that it might be time to leave.

Tony took Frazier's left bicep. "Come on, Frank," he said, "the taxi's here. Time to go." Then he addressed the agitated boyfriend. The last thing they needed was to get into a fight at Tucho Colon's party. "Please excuse my friend," Tony said. "He's had too much to drink. He meant no disrespect."

Before the boyfriend could respond, Ironman turned his head toward Tony and smiled. "Hey, buddy," he stammered. Have you met . . . ." he began, but then stopped. "Hey, senora," he said turning back to the brunette, who was still smiling at him. "What'd you say your name was?"

Immediately the boyfriend was stepping toward Ironman. But Tony was quick. He pulled his friend with his left hand and pivoted to the right, just in time to intercept the charging man. "Hang on, sir. Please. We are leaving. It is better that you let us go."

"Better for who?" said the boyfriend, hotly.

"Better for everyone," Tony answered. He had to look up to lock onto the bigger man's eyes, but the deliberate tempo and tone of his words said, *don't test me.* Boyfriend stared back. Tony had him thinking.

Which is when Frazier bellowed, "I need to take a piss. Necesito tomar una meiada."

The boyfriend exhaled heavily, his expression softened and he shook his head. "Take him home," he said. "He's not smart enough to be mad at. And when he's sober, you better teach him Spanish, too."

Tony smiled and agreed. Later, he would explain to Ironman that several Spanish verbs meant "to take," but the one he had used, *tomar*, was associated with drinking. *Tomar una bebida*—to take a drink. No wonder the boyfriend had been amused. The literal translation of Frazier's announcement established that he couldn't speak the language. Or else he was much thirstier than most people ever get.

# CHAPTER 18

Confined to his desk, bored with listening to headphones and writing notes about what was said, Tony begged Henderson to let him do something else, even if it was just for a couple of hours. "Come on, Mike," he pleaded, "Can't you take me with you on something, even something small?" So Henderson took him on a "service call." He introduced Tony to the guard at the building and to the receptionist. They showed their Chiltelco identification cards, picked up an old IT&T telephone and intercom, and replaced them with new units made by CE. They left two other telephones in place, resetting the auto fail mechanisms that had been installed a few weeks earlier. Tony enjoyed it and prevailed on Henderson to take him again. The next time, Henderson let him disassemble the units, remove the old recording devices, and replace them with new ones.

Eventually, Henderson felt comfortable enough to send Tony out on his own, to the offices of Jorge Alessandri's pulp and paper company, *La Compania Manufacturera de Papeles y Cartones*. La Papelera, as it was called, was located in the same downtown building as the United States Embassy. Still, cover needed to be maintained; any undercover officer might himself be under surveillance. Tony left the embassy, rode the elevator down to the lobby, left the building, and drove around the block a few times until he was satisfied he wasn't being followed. Then he parked, reentered the same building he had left earlier, and took the elevator up to the offices of La Papelera. There, he deftly disassembled two telephones, replaced the full voice recorders with new ones, and reset the failure relays. On his way out he fairly skipped with self-satisfaction.

Tony received a Continental Electric paycheck every two weeks. Actually, he received a receipt showing that his salary had been deposited directly into his US bank account. Whatever cash he needed to carry out his duties in Chile was given to him by Mr. Henderson. He couldn't believe how much he was earning for sitting around with his headphones on. It seemed to him that any minimum-wage clerk could do his job, so long as they spoke the language. To his knowledge, he hadn't produced a single piece of valuable information, nor had he written any meaningful reports. Only recently had his assignments included some work in the field, servicing a telephone or two in a government office. Other than that, all he did was go to bars to meet people and talk with them.

From what Tony could see, the CIA was spending a fortune in Chile, and he was confident he didn't know the half of it. The CIA's finances were secret, and it received its money by way of disguised allocations included in the massive budgets of other government agencies. Only a few people at the very top knew how much it actually was, and such information was never revealed to field officers like Tony. But it was a plain fact that building networks of reliable sources and then supporting their efforts around the world was expensive. Very expensive.

The Santiago station was home to several officers. Salaries and expenses just to maintain cover, like rent, food, living and spending money like regular people, had to cost a ton. And the station used top-notch technology. Not to mention the big crates and boxes Tony noticed whenever he passed through the embassy garage. The ones that appeared suddenly and then disappeared. Whatever expensive equipment those crates contained was being passed along to Chilean agents.

And how much more was spent developing assets in local communities? Cash that went directly into the pockets of Chilean nationals? How better to quickly develop the "loyalty" of a local worker or politician or union leader than to straight out buy it? Say a construction foreman with a wife and three kids happened to be supervising the erection of a big hacienda in the Santa Carolina suburb. And say the home was being built for a particular government official. If the foreman was more concerned with his own standard of living than he was with political considerations, he might be willing to provide access to telephones and electrical systems in exchange for a pile of money, especially if that pile exceeded what he could earn for an entire year. That foreman might then turn a blind eye toward a couple of new workers, in clean uniforms, who showed up at the job site for a day, with pockets full of eavesdropping devices. And guys like Tony would end up listening to conversations recorded by bugs that had found their way into telephones right on that official's desk.

When an opportunity like that arose, the station needed cash. The men in charge, guys like D'Onofrio and Henderson, handed out the peso equivalent of thousands of U.S. dollars to people from whom they could not get receipts. And spies like Gil and Mike knew how to hide things—in a false panel in a suitcase, a book or a camera, a phony can of shaving cream or the heel of a shoe. But these men had been carefully selected for their integrity. They were not common crooks looking to skim money from a Vegas casino. They were proud officers of the American Central Intelligence Agency, putting the money to good and proper use.

Tony came around to accepting that his high salary made sense. The CIA was in Chile to manage a serious risk to America's security, and intelligence gathering was essential to its success. This was not an exercise. This operation mattered, and Tony's contributions would be important. He could feel it.

# CHAPTER 19

Carlos Gonzalez de Pinero smiled. He was a short man, not quite five and a half feet tall, with straight jet-black hair. He was relatively plain looking, but when he smiled, his face transformed him. In the two years since Salvador Allende had come to power, Carlos had a lot to smile about. His beloved Chile was the most beautiful country in the world. He was born there and had never stepped foot outside its borders. He couldn't imagine any place better. He happily accepted Allende's rhetoric and the idealism of the Unidad Popular because he just knew that people could live together in peace and harmony. He saw the good in everything and refused to dwell on the bad. His happiness each day began with the love he felt for his pretty wife, Diana, and blossomed out to every aspect of his life. He paid little attention to politics and did not allow himself to be disturbed by the hardships taking hold in Santiago and across Chile. He reflected on the unpleasant events reported in the news, and then let them go. Surely they were temporary. He preferred to keep his thoughts on more pleasant subjects. To Carlos Gonzalez, the universe consisted of his home with Diana and their flourishing floral business. Someone else would have to worry about other matters.

Carlos Gonzalez's younger brother, General Agustin Gonzalez, was as different as a brother could be. He had joined the Chilean military at the age of eighteen and never came close to taking a wife.

He was married to the army. A head taller than his older brother, he was also broader across the shoulders. There was no laughter in his eyes, which were set close together and gave him the piercing look of a bird of prey. He loved discipline and, from the start, trained harder than anyone else. He became expert in all forms of martial arts and a marksman with all pistol and rifle models. He loved military history and the tactics of war. He rose quickly through the ranks and by the time he was twenty-eight, he was promoted to colonel and given command of more than two thousand soldiers. Few people outside Allende's inner circle, and not all inside it, liked General Gonzalez. But almost all feared him.

To Agustin Gonzalez, a soldier's loyalty did not belong to any particular political party or ideology. It belonged to Chile and its constitution. If a cocker spaniel had been lawfully elected to the office of president, it would be entitled to the full protection and support of Chile's military. Colonel Gonzalez himself was a conservative and would never vote for Salvador Allende or any other socialist. But he had no qualms serving the leftist president. In fact, he was proud to do so.

The instrument of executive authority within the Ministry of Interior was the corps of carabineros, Chile's national police. A full regiment of well-trained soldiers and officers selected not only for their skill and experience, but also for their discipline and loyalty to the president. The best among them were selected to join the president's *Grupo de Amigos Personales*, literally his Group of Personal Friends. GAP officers served as palace guard and personal police force. When General Schneider, a former instructor of Agustin Gonzales, rose to the position of commander-in-chief of the army, he recommended that President Allende give Colonel Gonzalez a major leadership position. And later, after Schneider was killed in the botched kidnapping shortly before Allende's inauguration, the president looked to those who shared Schneider's loyalty to the constitution. As soon as he was sworn in, Allende elevated Colonel

Gonzalez to the rank of general and gave him command of the carabineros.

Carlos had been married to Diana, a slip of a woman, for four years, which had been wonderful for them both. She was pretty, certainly, but she dressed plainly and had the reserved personality of a serious, thoughtful woman. She smiled less frequently than Carlos and always had a little tired look to her, reflecting the fatigue that comes from hard work mixed with a bit of fear. Unlike her husband, Diana could not fully ignore the discontent rumbling in the streets of Santiago. She could not set aside the sadness and guilt she felt knowing that she was doing well while so many of her countrymen struggled. Still, Carlos's happy spirit was contagious, and she quietly reflected his contentment whenever they were together, which was almost all the time.

Diana Gonzalez had learned to play the piano as a girl and would play in the evenings for Carlos. Their love affair had started their last year at the university where she studied art and music while Carlos majored in finance. They had been inseparable ever since. Carlos Gonzalez was a good student, at the top of his class. He faithfully attended his classes and studied hard in the evenings, unlike boys from affluent families whose positions in life were assured. She admired his work ethic and his cheerful nature. He was polite, a gentleman, and he escorted Diana to church every Sunday. He made her feel comfortable and secure and loved.

As soon as they graduated, they married and started a flower business, which they operated out of the living room of a modest house they rented together. Diana had an eye for beauty, as well as a green thumb. She selected the flowers to buy, and Carlos negotiated the price. She was content to leave the "number crunching" to her husband. They went about the city taking orders for their floral arrangements, and one or both of them would make the deliveries. As partners, they made a very good team. They also made a good team in the bedroom. In the tradition of their families, they had waited until their wedding night to become lovers. And now, four years later, even that aspect of their marriage was a success. Carlos was a respectful and considerate lover, but his feelings for Diana were strong and his passion evident. Whenever he took her in his arms, she felt herself melting inside. They continued going to church together, where they said prayers of gratitude, so happy were they that they had found each other.

Carlos and Diana Gonzalez worked well together and steadily built their flower business into a profitable enterprise. Of course it didn't hurt that Carlos's younger brother was the powerful General Agustin Gonzalez. General Gonzalez was rapidly becoming one of Salvador Allende's most influential military supporters, as well as commander of Chile's national police. With a word from him, wonderful things could happen quite quickly. And, it need not be added, with another kind of word, terrible things could happen just as fast. If General Gonzalez suggested to any member of the government, any local businessman, or, for that matter, anyone in position to purchase anything, that they should consider patronizing his brother Carlos's business, it was hardly considered optional. As loyal and respectful as the general was to his president, he could be impatient and vicious with his enemies. He was a military man, not a businessman, but the influence of the military on Chile's business community was increasing in proportion to the unrest in its streets. Where the viability of a civilian institution was threatened by a lack of security, the correct deployment of soldiers could provide stability. General Gonzalez had the authority to provide considerable protection from boycotts, violence, or other threats. He could deliver the resources needed to keep a shop open and operational or a trucking company or a factory or a medical clinic or a bank or a lawyer's office. It wasn't just for his brother's floral business. Protection by military forces was an essential element of any business plan and was rapidly becoming a part of most commerce in Santiago.

But Carlos Gonzalez was oblivious to such things. He had no interest in the workings of government and no need to fear the partisan sniping going on around the city. All that mattered was Diana and, of course, flowers. After church each Sunday, they would ride through the Chilean countryside, meeting with the growers of the prettiest carnations and roses. They would smile as they toured a farm, genuinely uplifted by the heavenly colors bursting from the ground in robust blossoms. When they found a farmer whose fields were fertile and well tended and were producing beauty on the stem, they could offer cash on the spot. They sold a lot of flowers, and therefore they could buy a lot. Sometimes they would purchase the farmer's entire crop. They could send trucks to collect the harvest. Few other florists could compete.

A business relationship with Carlos and Diana was a profitable one for a grower, and the countryside was full of farmers who recognized and benefited from it. Sure, human nature being what it was, there were occasional "disagreements" about what had been promised, or when it was to be delivered. But if a farmer worked hard and the misunderstanding was honest, Carlos and Diana were generous and supportive. Such situations were resolved promptly and usually contributed to an improved and continuing relationship.

However, on those rare occasions when a farmer tried to take advantage of Carlos's gentle nature or fell behind because he spent too much time drinking or gambling and not enough tending to his fields, Carlos was not above mentioning his brother's name. He preferred to handle his business without such intimidation, and he was not proud of exploiting his brother's tough-guy reputation, but it was undeniably effective. All people in Chile knew General Agustin Gonzalez, and those with any sense respected his authority. In a socialist state, the land belonged to everyone and was to be used for the benefit of all the people. Those lucky enough to control a ranch or farm were wise to avoid arrogance. A farmer who offended a government official, especially one with a military command, could find himself planted in his own fields, and the people's farm thereafter tended by a new guardian. It was a privilege to be allowed to serve as a conservator of any piece of ground, one that should not be taken for granted. Understandably, it didn't take long for word to get around. Cheat Carlos and Diana Gonzalez and you won't get very far or last very long. And so disputes were routinely resolved quickly and favorably for them. And Carlos and Diana's business continued to grow and flourish.

The first time Tony saw him, Carlos Gonzalez was delivering a lush bouquet of fresh flowers to the palace. Carlos was arranging it in an aqua-colored ceramic vase on the desk of one of President Allende's secretaries, Maria Rosa Alcorta. Every Thursday, Carlos or Diana would carefully place fresh arrangements on tables and desks in various government offices, where their color and beauty would brighten the room until the following Thursday, when they would again be replaced. Carlos did not see Tony working quietly in the corner of an adjoining room, but it was part of Tony's job to notice everyone. He watched the Flower Man admire the vase for a moment before leaving the room. He was smiling as he left.

The Chilean Telephone Company, Chiltelco, had contracted with Continental Electric Company to upgrade several telephone and intercom systems in the presidential palace, the Supreme Court, and other buildings in the capital. The Company had chosen CE as cover in Santiago because Chiltelco had access to just about every important office in the city. Tony's engineering background provided him a lot of theoretical knowledge about electrical circuitry, and he had been given specific instruction at Camp Peary on hooking up telephones, intercoms, and other office equipment. But that didn't exactly make him a real repairman. Tony faked whatever expertise he lacked. Most of the time, all he needed to do was bring in new equipment and replace the old. He wanted to do a good job and project reliability because obvious incompetence could make people suspicious, but the inefficiency of putting in new units instead of fixing old ones wouldn't raise any eyebrows, so long as the equipment worked properly when he left. So while he carried a variety of manuals and books, and an impressive array of tools, for the most part he just came in, replaced whatever needed replacing, made sure the bugs were working, filled out his paperwork, and left. The company would generate an invoice for his service call, and the Chilean department or ministry would send a check. The arrangement was profitable for both CE and Chiltelco, but Tony thought it was funny—the Chilean government was actually paying to be spied on.

It was during another "service" call, while Tony was fiddling with some wires and a compact soldering tool, that he saw Carlos Gonzalez again. Carlos was of slender build, but his loose-fitting clothes made him appear stocky. He was an inch or two shorter than Tony, with a shock of unruly black hair and sparkling black eyes. His mouth was turned up at the corners, just waiting for a reason to smile, but underneath his eyes, Tony could see some darker patches with wrinkles at the corners, suggesting a contemplative side. As he entered the room, he was whistling. Then he softly sang a few words, clearly absorbed in his work. When he noticed Tony, he smiled and said cheerfully, "Buenos dias. I am Carlos Gonzalez. They call me the Flower Man. It is a pleasure to meet you." He bowed slightly.

Tony felt uneasy. He was afraid that a mistake with his Spanish could make the man suspicious. And there was no disguising his accent. "Buenos dias," he responded cautiously. "My name is Andre Stephens. I work for the phone company."

But Carlos Gonzalez was not a suspicious person and had no reason to play detective. He was nothing more and nothing less than he seemed—a conscientious man doing work he enjoyed. Nonetheless, Tony had first picked up Spanish when he worked in a Puerto Rican bodega. There was a big difference between that and the Spanish spoken in Chile. Carlos didn't recognize the accent but knew that Tony wasn't a native. "Where are you from?" he asked.

Tony responded as he was trained. "I'm Canadian," he explained, "French Canadian, actually. French was my first language. I also speak English, of course. Spanish is only my third language, and as you probably already noticed, I am not very good at it. I am still learning."

"You speak very well," Carlos answered. "And you have a good pronunciation. Not like a gringo."

"Thank you," Tony replied. "Thank you very much."

"Perhaps you can teach me a little English," said Carlos, pinching his thumb and index finger together. "My wife and I have spoken of visiting North America. We heard that Canada is very pretty. Maybe with your help, I can learn enough to get around there."

Tony smiled again. He had been taught to trust no one and not let his guard down. But this little Flower Man was disarming.

# CHAPTER 20

One morning, Tony's telephone rang before his alarm. He reached for it without opening his eyes.

"Andre?" It was Henderson.

"Yes."

"Meet me at the loading dock in the back of the American embassy. Don't wear a uniform. And be prepared for a little heavy lifting," Henderson directed. "Thirty minutes. Don't be late."

Tony scrambled and made it in twenty-nine. Henderson was already waiting, standing alongside the open tailgate of a truck. A dozen burlap sacks lay on the loading dock behind him. Tony squinted in the dim light of the early dawn. He saw the words *arroz blanco* printed on the sides. White rice.

"Are we delivering care packages now?" Tony asked.

"Special groceries. Courtesy of the U.S. government," Henderson responded. "Now stop askin' questions and help me lift 'em into the back of this truck. Time's a wastin'."

Tony went to grab one of the sacks, but Henderson stopped him. "Those go in last. First we load these." He was pointing at two wooden crates stacked one on top of the other at the side of the dock. Danger—Explosives! was stenciled on the side. Tony looked at Henderson. "That's right," Henderson said. "So don't drop this shit, okay?" Tony felt strange, like he was dreaming. Uncomfortable but more excited than afraid. "No problem, boss," he said, and he meant it.

"When I count to three, we lift together. And then we slide it, gently, into the truck. You ready?"

Tony nodded. Henderson counted to three. Together they lifted the crate, swung it around, and walked it to the back of the truck. It felt like it weighed a ton. "Gently, now," Henderson cautioned. Tony didn't need to be reminded. They placed it gingerly on the tailgate and slid it into the truck bed, stencil side hidden. Then they turned back to the other crate. Tony recognized NASA's logo printed in blue on it, above the word "Fragile." He couldn't help but look at Henderson in surprise.

"Electronics," Henderson said. "Spare transmitter parts that some friends need to keep a wildcat radio station on the air. Our little way of helping them get their message out."

After the truck was loaded, Henderson went inside the embassy. "Wait here," he told Tony. "I need to make a phone call before we go."

A couple of minutes passed before Henderson emerged. During that time, Tony tried to stay composed. It was off with the headphones and out into the field. His anxiety level was high, and what Henderson said next didn't do much to decrease it. As soon as he climbed up into the driver's seat and started the engine, Henderson asked, "Will you be able to take over if anything happens to me?" He jerked the gearshift into position and let out the clutch.

Tony said, "What?"

"Can you drive this old six speed?" Henderson asked.

"Standard shift? I think so," Tony said. He smiled.

"What's so funny?" Henderson asked. "It's a serious question."

"Last time somebody asked if I knew how to drive stick was the summer I applied for a job with the Good Humor Ice Cream Company. They had these white freezer trucks, and they drove around the neighborhoods and played carnival music on loudspeakers and sold ice cream to kids. The guy told me he only had one truck left, and it was standard transmission. If I could drive it, he'd give me the job. I didn't know shit about shifting. All the cars I had ever driven were automatic. But I wanted the job. So I told him, "No problem." I was thinking, how hard could it be? Didn't realize 'til later that I was starting it in second gear instead of first. I can still remember that old guy with his arms folded, shaking his head as I lurched through the parking lot. Stalled out twice before I got to the street. But I learned."

"Interesting," Henderson said. "But we ain't selling ice cream. There are people out there who would object to this delivery. Armed people. We should be all right, but you never know. Things can always get hairy."

Tony remembered the mixture of fear and excitement he felt the first time his football coach sent him into a varsity game. "I won't let you down," he had said then. It seemed to satisfy the coach, so he said it again. Henderson nodded just like the coach had. They drove off and before long were well out of the city, heading south on the coast highway.

After a while Tony asked, "How long is this trip?"

"We should be there in less than two hours," Henderson replied. "Assuming no trouble." He paused. "I hate this kind of assignment. Glorified delivery boys, is what we are. Everybody in Santiago has an agenda or a grudge. And most of 'em have weapons. We never used to do this kind of shit. But the carabineros have turned up the heat. Can't have the locals we'd ordinarily use come around the embassy, 'cause if they were recognized picking up anything, it could blow us all out of the water. So I'm stuck making this run with a damned rookie." He glanced over. "No offense or anything."

"None taken," Tony replied, but he felt his jaw clench. He was determined to hold up his end of this deal.

The Flower Man's Daughter

They rode along, doing about sixty kilometers an hour, not talking much. Tony looked out the window at the ocean. He wondered what Carrie Barber was doing. He hoped she was happy, but he also hoped she missed him. He pictured her sitting at her desk scribbling in a notebook. He felt the love and guilt in his chest like bad heartburn. He had left her, hurt her, so he could do this—drive a secret shipment of weapons and electronics down a seaside road in a foreign country. He hoped it was worth it.

Henderson's "uh-oh," interrupted Tony's reverie. A line of cars had stopped ahead of them.

"What's that?" Tony asked, his throat tightening.

"That, my young friend, is a roadblock," Henderson answered. "I was afraid this might happen."

"It's bad?" Tony asked

"Sure as shit ain't good," Henderson said. "But how bad depends on who they are."

"What do you mean?" asked Tony.

"Well, it could be the MIRistas, radical leftists. They'll want to know where this shipment is headed. If they don't like our answers, our goose is cooked. Then again, it could be Patria y Libertad. That'd make it easy. Or it could be some other group. We'll know soon enough."

A flagman, a young carabinero, stood in the middle of the opposite lane. Tony recognized the uniform at the same time as Henderson spoke. "Allende's men. That's good. I'm better prepared." The carabinero signaled for Henderson to pull in behind the line of stopped cars. He couldn't have been more than eighteen, and looked just as nervous as Tony felt. By the time the boy approached Henderson's open window, Henderson had his paperwork out.

"We're bringing rice to the orphanage at Sister Teresa's convent in Las Palomas," Henderson said smoothly. "Under authority of the president himself." The carabinero examined the papers Henderson handed him. Tony caught a glimpse of a letter written on elegant stationary. At the bottom, Tony saw an official seal. The carabineo looked impressed. "We're in a hurry," Henderson said. "The sister has a lot of hungry children to feed."

The officer crossed himself. "Of course, senor, please pass. And *vaya con dios*. May God bless you."

Henderson put the truck back in gear and pulled out. Tony exhaled slowly in relief. But as they accelerated past the waiting cars and approached the front of the line, two carabineros leaped in front of them, pointing their rifles directly at Henderson's head. A third took a firing stance and aimed at Tony. Henderson screeched the truck to a halt. Still clutching his papers, he threw his hands in the air. Tony did the same, the sound of his own heartbeat pounding in his ears.

"Where the hell do you think you're going?" asked the one in charge.

"Las Palomas," Henderson said calmly, his hands still in the air. "To deliver food for the orphans. Your comrade back there told us it was okay to pass." Henderson turned his head and pointed back over his shoulder with his chin.

"I don't care where you're going. Nobody passes without inspection. I am Captain Mendez." He gestured to the roadside with his rifle. "Give me your papers and pull your truck over there." Henderson did as he was told. The other two officers had not lowered their weapons. Staring into the black hole at the end of the rifle barrel, Tony was as scared as he had ever been.

Captain Mendez took a minute to read Henderson's documents. Then, expressionlessly, he gave Henderson another order. "You, come with us. Show us what you've got back there." Henderson slowly exited the truck and walked with the soldier to the back. He opened the doors. Tony wasn't sure how to act, so he tried his best to look bored. He smiled at the rifle barrel, stretched his arms back behind his head, and yawned for all he was worth. The soldier noticed and seemed relieved. At least he relaxed his stance a bit.

But he didn't lower his rifle, and he wasn't smiling. Tony hoped they had arranged the sacks of rice properly. He wondered what would happen if the true nature of their cargo was discovered. He said a silent prayer and held his breath.

After a few minutes that seemed like hours, Henderson came up on Tony's side and spoke quietly and calmly. "These fellows want us to give 'em two sacks of rice. I guess they're hungry, but at least they don't mind sharing with the orphans. Otherwise, they'd take 'em all. Then we'd be in real trouble. Now come down, nice and slow, and help me lift 'em out of the truck."

Tony and Henderson hefted two rice sacks and lugged them to a nearby military truck. As soon as that was done, Henderson went and shook hands with Captain Mendez. He was smiling. *The man has nerve*, Tony thought. Then Henderson climbed back into the truck, which was still running, put it in gear, and moved on down the road. He was whistling a Chilean song like he hadn't a care in the world.

Once they were fully out of the soldiers' earshot, Henderson stopped whistling but said nothing. Tony had plenty of questions but waited. Only when they had gone a few more kilometers did Henderson finally speak. "I bet nothing like this ever happened when you were selling ice cream, huh, kid? Consider this your graduation. Welcome to the world of special ops. Maybe not as glamorous as you had imagined. But it gets better. Or maybe you'd rather be sitting in the office, listening to those headphones?" Tony, drenched in sweat and his mouth so dry he could barely swallow, wasn't sure.

They soon turned off the beach highway. "Where are we actually going, Mike?" Tony asked.

"What, you don't want to go see Sister Teresa at the convent? You want the orphans to starve."

"Come on, Mike. Doesn't having a rifle pointed at my head make me eligible for the truth?"

"All right, all right," Henderson answered. "We're headed to Cactin." Tony recognized the name of a rural town about one hundred kilometers out of Santiago, the headquarters of Patria y Libertad. Patria y Libertad had been waging a guerilla war, complete with bombings and assassinations, for more than a year, and were considered "arrest or shoot on sight" by the Chilean national police. The right-wing group was rapidly gaining strength, at least partly because of support from the CIA. The Fatherland and Liberty Nationalist Front was strongly anticommunist; like a lot of conservative groups, they didn't hate Allende so much as what he stood for. But what set them apart was their willingness to resort to violence. Patria y Libertad had started out as a ragtag paramilitary group formed by disgruntled soldiers, but their ranks grew with the influx of farmers and ranchers whose property had been nationalized away from them. Talk of a socialist utopia was wasted on such men. Take someone's farm without compensation and give it to strangers and you were likely to make him awfully grumpy. Add to that the Catholic Church's distaste for communism and many across a wide spectrum of Chilean society had become grumpy together. Those willing to do something about it joined Patria y Libertad. Patria y Libertad wasn't just capable of violence—it was enthusiastic about it. Its members lacked the patience to try to change course democratically, which made them a natural ally for the Company—a fact that had not gone unnoticed by the Santiago field station. A significant amount of cash and equipment was devoted to the cultivation of this effective asset in the destabilization campaign. Chile had lost a lot in Allende's push toward agrarian reform, and many Chileans were happy to be "cultivated."

About an hour later, they arrived at Cactin. It wasn't much of a town. A dusty, unpaved main street bordered on both sides by simply-constructed storefronts and bars. Henderson drove slowly through the downtown section and soon came to a stop near a chain link fence. A rough-hewn man was holding a machine gun. The sign on the building behind him read Auto and Truck repairs, and two old gasoline pumps stood in the building's shadow. Another couple of men, also holding automatic weapons, emerged from the building. Tony was relieved to see they weren't pointing them at anyone.

"Patria y Libertad?" Tony whispered to Henderson, who nodded.

"Don't worry. They're expecting us."

A husky man in a dark military uniform stepped up. The insignia on his arm was a swastika-like spider. Tony had seen a graffiti version painted on walls in town. The man was smiling, but his bad teeth and scraggly beard gave him an unmistakably sinister appearance. "Gentlemen," he said with a sweeping bow, "welcome to the convent at Las Palomas. I'm Sister Teresa. What have you brought for my children today?"

"Sister Teresa" told one of the other men to open the gate and directed Henderson down the gravel driveway which ran along the service station to another gate at a fenced area in the back. A soldier with an AK-47 strapped across his shoulder slung the gate open.

Tony was surprised at what he saw: an enormous field, with maybe a hundred trucks of all sizes parked in rows. Drivers were sitting on makeshift chairs at makeshift tables, playing cards or dominos. All of them were drinking, or so it seemed by the number of beer bottles. The drivers watched Henderson and Tony roll past. Henderson pulled in front of a large barn located in the middle of the field. Tony and Henderson got down from the truck and started toward the back. As they opened the truck doors, the surrounding group of men snapped to attention and saluted. A tall dark haired-man in military garb was approaching. Tony had seen pictures of him. Colonel Gustavo Gutierrez. Gutierrez greeted Henderson warmly, and Henderson introduced him to Tony. Tony was a little awestruck, like he was meeting a celebrity, someone famous, or, more accurately, infamous. The colonel thanked them both for making the trip and asked whether it had been difficult. Henderson laughed and told of the roadblock on the coast highway.

"They are getting desperate, aren't they?" said Gutierrez.

"I guess so," said Henderson. "Some of the carabineros were so young they should have been carrying schoolbooks instead of automatic weapons." Both men chuckled. "My young friend here was sure he was going to get shot. Next time he'll have to bring them some ice cream." Tony smiled but kept quiet. He wasn't going to try to say anything clever.

Colonel Gutierrez directed his men to unload, and they swarmed the truck bed. The two crates came out last and were carried off in separate directions. The colonel invited Henderson and Tony to take lunch with him. Tony was glad that Henderson declined. "We've got to get back. Please excuse us. Next time, for sure."

"Yes, my friend," the colonel said. "Maybe soon we'll dine together at La Moneda." He handed Tony and Henderson each a shot glass of dark rum that an attendant had brought over. "But we must make a toast before you go." He raised his glass. "To La Moneda. May it soon be rid of the socialist fool!"

During the ride home, Henderson asked Tony what he thought of Colonel Gutierrez.

"Interesting man," Tony replied. "Have you known him long?"

"Not really," Henderson said. "I've met him a couple of times. His family used to have money, not exactly high society, but definitely upper middle class. Then Allende got elected and started nationalizing. A lot of their land was taken and redistributed. It didn't sit well with Gustavo. He brought his passion and his military training to Patria y Libertad and helped to radicalize it, and he moved the operations to Cactin. I didn't realize he was so popular with the truckers. I guess in this country you take your support where you find it."

Tony had heard of places like that, hideouts for striking truckers who feared seizure of their vehicles by the Chilean army. The truckers' strike was really hurting the country. Farmers and manufacturers couldn't get their goods to market, and the retailers couldn't get delivery of items to sell in their shops. The shortages and resulting inflation were choking the economy and ratcheting up the people's discontent. Those on the left, like the MIRistas, impatient for a complete nationalization of the transportation industry, felt Allende wasn't moving forcefully enough against the striking truckers. They wanted the vehicles seized and replacement drivers put to work restoring the stream of commerce. To those on the right, like Patria y Libertad, socialism was nothing more than collective theft, and any efforts to seize trucks were illegal and needed to be resisted at all costs. The right-wingers were fighting to protect private ownership rights while the leftists were fighting to nationalize them. The country was caught in the middle.

"I hope you don't mind me asking," Tony said. "But I can't help wondering why we're giving Gutierrez dynamite?"

"Listen, Stephens," Henderson answered. "There are a few things you should know. Frankly, I would have thought you'd know them already. The Company has a task here in Chile. But the people keep voting for this communist or socialist or Marxist or whatever Allende is, and his unity party. So we are increasing our efforts. Developing new assets and new strategies. We've had success finding country boys willing to move from their small towns into Santiago, where they get union jobs. The unions make the government look bad when they strike. Sooner or later, people who don't have bread and milk for the table stop supporting the incumbents. And that's a good thing. People who work for a living, who own something, who don't want to lose it, they need law and order. Our goal has always been to help the citizenry discover the error of their ways. You listening, Andre?"

"Yes, sir, Mr. Henderson," Tony answered quickly.

"Okay. So the next target on our list is the media, mostly the newspapers, but also radio and television. We want the people to know how bad they have it, and how bad the people have it in other socialist states like Russia and Cuba. One good story about how hard life is behind the iron curtain, or how Castro imprisons anyone who doesn't salute with a smile, or how the price of butter and eggs keeps going up for those lucky enough to get them at all, can have an effect, and a series of such stories over time can change public opinion. We don't have official pollsters here in Santiago, but there is a pulse, and we take pride in our ability to feel it. That's why guys like you eavesdrop all day.

"You'll never hear it said in public, but the word is destabilization. The wealthy never embraced Allende, and they're already fed up. When the middle class and especially the working people lose confidence in him and where he's taking their country, they'll get fed up too. And then good things will happen. Counterrevolution. We're working our tails off helping the seeds of that counterrevolution take hold and grow.

"Beyond that, of course, is the normal spy stuff. Knowing what Allende is planning so we can get in his way. That's not as easy, but just as important. The development of agents within the Allende government willing to pass along information is dangerous but worthwhile. In order to develop a relationship with one, even a low-level official, an aide, or a deputy, for example, requires our officer to reveal himself. And don't forget that Allende gets help from the Russians and their Eastern bloc buddies. There's always the chance the official we're working with will sell information back to Allende, and if that happened, the whole station here in Santiago, every single officer, would be at risk." Henderson paused long enough to scratch the inside of his ear with his pinky. Then he continued.

"Or false information fed to us could send us in the wrong direction. Hell, it could expose an operation that took months to assemble. Allende may not be vicious, but some of his people are. Look up General Agustin Gonzalez in your manual. Allende's security people know we're running intelligence operations here. We know the Soviets are giving them the technical tools they need to conduct surveillance, including the finest East German electronics. Our embassy in Santiago is constantly being watched, just like we watch the Soviet embassy. But we've gotten lucky in one respect. The Soviets haven't really stepped up to help Allende in Chile on the scale they are doing for Castro in Cuba. Maybe the Kremlin is reluctant to support a second revolutionary economy in the western hemisphere. So Mr. Allende has to maintain a relationship with America and its corporations. Kind of hedging his bets."

"I've heard that," said Tony.

"Good," said Henderson. "So you know Allende's more radical supporters are frustrated because he tolerates American interests. They want him to be more like Castro, cut off relations and close the American embassy. Thus far at least, he hasn't gone for it. He wants his revolution to be different."

"Yeah," said Tony. "He calls it the Chilean way."

"Right," said Henderson. "So our embassy is still here. And our corporations are still here. And hidden within them, we're here, too."

"But dynamite?" Tony interjected. "Can't we just increase support to opposition parties and their candidates?"

"We've tried that. Hasn't worked so far and we can't keep waiting. Too much damage is being done. So we're turning up the heat. As valuable as individual agents are, or media rhetoric, they cannot match, for sheer power, what Patria y Libertad brings to the table. Propaganda is important, no doubt. Strikes and food shortages are helpful. But violence represents a quantum leap. The impact is immediate and undeniable. It hits people's consciousness hard, and gets to 'em on an emotional level. Scared people crave security and stability. They'll give up their ideals and a lot of freedom for it. Patria y Libertad can do more with one bomb than we can with a hundred newspaper stories."

Henderson paused, letting his words sink in. And he could tell that Tony was absorbing them, so he continued.

"Besides, Colonel Gutierrez didn't need our encouragement to hate Allende's government. He used to be a captain in the Chilean army. His family built their fortune over generations. They grew grapes, primarily, and after every crop was sold, they put away money. Eventually they had enough to buy the neighbor's tract. And the neighbor next to him. Land was cheap back then, and the Gutierrez's family holdings grew and grew the old-fashioned way, by working the ground and saving money. By the time Chile's politics began moving to the left, the Gutierrez family owned more than a thousand acres of prime, fertile farmland. Hard work, sure, but they were set forever, or so they thought. Then came Salvador Allende. His concept of socialism is a lot like Robin Hood's. You know, take from the rich and give to the poor. Agrarian reform may sound nice in theory, but in practice it meant landowners, like Gutierrez's daddy, got their wealth "redistributed." Wealth that had taken no small amount of blood, sweat and tears to accumulate was confiscated and given to owners selected by officials in Allende's administration. When the Gutierrez family protested, they were threatened and told to be grateful for the little compensation they got.

"Kennecott and Anaconda, the American corporations that owned half of the entire copper industry, got kicked out without so much as a fare-thee-well. Not a dime. They're still fighting about it, but Allende's position has been that they made obscene profits for a long time and had already been paid, many times over, for their investment. It was only right for the government to stop the exploitation by nationalizing the mines and returning the profit streams to their rightful owners, the people of Chile."

"I don't know, Mike." Tony said. "I can see where Gutierrez has a legitimate beef. And maybe you could make a case for violence on his part. But why are we supplying the weapons?"

"Just think of it as eliminating the middle man, kid," Henderson said. "We'd be giving him money for whatever he wanted anyway, and he'd probably get his supplies from American dealers after all. Shit, we're also giving a ton of dough to the MIRistas, the hoodlums on the left. They're blowing up things because Allende isn't revolutionary enough. We're egging 'em both on. Like that Tim Hardin song, *Old Time Smugglin' Man*, we're giving guns to the Arabs and dynamite to the Jews. In the end, the roof will fall in on Mr. Allende and Chilean socialism."

Tony reflected on Henderson's comments for the rest of the ride home, which was uneventful. Tony knew that insurgents have a distinct advantage. The saying was, disruption is easier than construction. Or in the version offered by one of Tony's farm-raised instructors, it takes a team of pretty fair carpenters to build a good barn, but it only takes one stubborn jackass to kick a hole in it.

About a week later, El Mercurio reported that the railroad bridge in Rio Claro, an important link in Chile's transportation system, already reeling from the ongoing truckers' strike, had been dynamited and severely damaged. No casualties were reported, but the bridge would take months to repair. Reported elsewhere in the same edition was an unrelated story announcing that Radio Libertad, the voice of Patria y Libertad, had recommended broadcasting from an unknown location.

# CHAPTER 21

One afternoon while Tony was working on an intercom system at one of the receptionist's desks at the palace, someone entered the room and took all the air out of it. At least that's what it felt like to Tony, who had trouble catching his breath. It was Cristina. She was wearing a well-tailored dark gray business suit that looked expensive. As she stepped past the desk, Tony watched her walk. Her black high heels made her calf muscles ripple subtly. Her legs were a perfect color brown, and she was not wearing hose. She had some folders in her arms, which she held against her chest as she headed past Tony toward one of the inner offices.

It took him a second to be able to activate his voice, and even then, "hello" was all he could muster. Cristina turned toward him and stopped. "Oh, hello," she said with just a hint of a smile. It wasn't enough to establish that she recognized him, but enough to give Tony hope that she did.

"You're Cristina, aren't you?"

"Yes, yes, I am," she answered, looking a little curious about how he knew her name.

"You . . . you were with Maria Cueto at Mr. Colon's party, weren't you? I heard her say your name when she introduced my buddy Frank to you."

"Really?" was Cristina's only comment.

"Yes," Tony replied. "Perhaps it sounds curious, but you made quite an impression on me, even though we only spoke for a second. I'm Andre Stephens." Tony got up and moved quickly from behind the desk to extend his hand. Cristina offered her hand back, and Tony took it. Her fingers were long and slender and her skin silky smooth. He was sure she could hear his thumping heart.

"Of course, I remember you," Cristina said. Her tone was unmistakably flirtatious. "I even asked Maria about you." Tony restrained himself from shouting in exhilaration. "Really?"

"Yes, as a matter of fact. She was excited about your friend, and when we were talking about him, your name came up. She told me you were nice." Tony's spirits sank a bit to think the mention of his name had only been incidental, but it was better than no mention at all. Something to build on, at least.

"I am very happy to see you," Tony said, trying not to overanalyze. "I'm glad you were wrong."

"I don't understand," Cristina said.

"When I told you that I would like to talk to you, you told me it was impossible."

"Yes, I did, didn't I?" Cristina said. "And since you are talking to me now, I was wrong, wasn't I?"

"I really was hoping to see you again. Today is my lucky day," Tony gushed. "So what brings you here to La Moneda?"

"I am at the palace often," she said. "I work for General Lorenzo Fox in the finance ministry. In fact, he'll be here for a cabinet meeting in about ten minutes." She looked at her watch. "Which means I need to get going. I have to organize some reports and things for him."

"But I would really enjoy talking," Tony said. "Do you have to leave right now?"

"General Fox is a very impatient man. What will I tell him if he doesn't have what he needs for his meeting? That I preferred chatting with a charming young man instead of doing my job?"

Tony felt himself blush at the compliment.

"And by the way," Cristina continued, "what are you doing here?"

Tony looked down at the Chiltelco emblem on his shirt. "I fix the telephones."

"I see," Cristina said. "I hope you do a better job than whoever did it before. The phones here are notoriously bad."

"Yes, ma'am," Tony said, snapping off a clumsy salute and smiling for all he was worth.

Cristina smiled back, and Tony could swear someone had turned on a bank of bright lights. "Anyway, Mr. Telephone, I really must go. It was very nice to see you again." She held out her hand.

Tony felt desperate. "Can I invite you to coffee? After your meeting. There's a great café just a block away."

"I would like that," Cristina said before adding, "but it's not a good idea."

Tony thought the regret he saw in her expression was genuine, so he pressed. "Some other time, then?"

"I'm afraid not," she answered. "It was nice to see you again, but let's leave it at that." She turned and walked away. Tony stood but said nothing. He was sure their paths would cross again.

"I ran into Cristina," Tony told Frazier as they cracked open a couple of beers at Tony's little apartment.

"Who?"

"Cristina de la Vega. You know—the one I went nuts over at Tucho Colon's party," Tony answered.

"Oh yeah. I remember," Frazier said. "Maria Cueto's friend. I thought you told me she shot you down."

"Yes, she did," Tony said. "And she did it again. Told me no thanks."

"Too bad," Frazier said. "So where'd you see her?"

"I was at the presidential palace, and she came walking right in like she owned the place."

"Really?" said Frazier, whose interest in scoring was followed only by his interest in hearing about his friend scoring. "How'd she look?"

"Hot," Tony replied. "Very hot. Which was impressive considering she was wearing a business suit. But it fit her perfectly. And she was wearing high heels. Man, she's got great legs and what a shape. She looked even better than she did at the party, if that's possible."

"Nice," said Frazier. Tony could hear the leer in his voice.

"But I have a feeling there's more to her than that," Tony continued. "I didn't get to talk to her for very long, but I could just tell. She's smart."

"So she's got brains," Frazier replied. "Nobody's perfect."

Tony shook his head. Unlike his buddy, he found intelligence in women attractive. "I like that combination. And if I'm not way off, there's a pretty good-sized adventurous streak there too. I could see it in her eyes. A frisky babe with smarts. You gotta love it. I'm telling you, Steve, this one's special."

"Uh-oh," Frazier replied. "Now don't go falling in love."

"Don't worry," Tony said. "There's not much chance of that."

"So what was she doing at La Moneda?"

"She works for some general. Name of Fox. You heard of him?" Tony asked.

"Sure have," said Frazier. "General Lorenzo Fox. His picture's in the book. He's big in the Ministry of Finance. Supposedly more of a banker than a soldier. Too capitalist to make a good communist, but he's tight with Allende, anyway. She works for him, does she?"

"That's what she told me," said Tony. "Said she was on her way to a meeting with him."

"Impressive," said Frazier. "Could be good for a variety of reasons. Are you going to see her again?" he asked.

"I don't know. I asked her to have coffee. But like I said, she turned me down. Again. Maybe she's devoted to a boyfriend or something. I don't know. But the way she looked at me, Steve . . . I still have hope."

"I knew this city had some good-looking women, but I was still surprised by the amount of talent that turned out for that fiesta."

"No kidding," said Tony. "I guess by now you've had a chance to consummate your friendship with that little cute one, Maria."

"Not exactly," said Frazier. "I called the day after the party, and we made a plan to meet for lunch, but she stood me up. I tried calling a couple of times after that but was never able to reach her. I don't know what her problem is, but I gave up. Too many fish in the sea and all that."

Tony frowned. "That's too bad. She seemed like fun."

"Yeah," said Frazier. "I don't understand it myself. I thought Maria and I had something going there, but I guess not.

# CHAPTER 22

"So," D'Onofrio said, "how'd you enjoy your trip down to Cactin with Henderson? There are some characters out there, aren't there?"

"You could say that," Tony said. He wasn't sure where D'Onofrio was taking the conversation, so he kept his response short.

"Mike told me you stayed cool. Nice work. But I bet you're happy to be back at your desk."

"I don't know," Tony answered. "There were a couple of moments when I felt that way. But overall, I'd say I enjoyed myself."

"Good. Because I have another little job for you, if you're up for it."

"Of course I'm up for it," Tony answered.

"Don't get overanxious, son," D'Onofrio said. "You're just beginning. And this time you'll be on your own. To be honest, I wouldn't send you, but Raymond got sent home. Allende's still spanking IT&T. It's Allende's country, at least for the time being, which means he can do what he wants. So now I need to take a chance on you."

Tony wanted to tell him, I won't let you down, but held back. He had used the phrase too much already and didn't want it to become his cliché.

"You have a good disguise kit?" D'Onofrio asked.

"Yes, sir," Tony said. Excitement was fluttering in his gut.

The preoperational briefing was short. Tony was to join a demonstration being organized by the Movimiento de Izquierda Revolucionaria—the Movement of the Revolutionary Left or MIR—and to march among the demonstrators. It was hoped that there would be violence. And if it didn't get that way all by itself, Tony would be prepared, at the right time, to incite the demonstrators and push the government's security forces to react. The media was already set to blame any violence on Allende, with extensive reporting of the event, followed by another series of editorials all of which were calculated to reinforce the basic theme that every socialist leader inevitably ends up stifling opposing views with force. Photos of a few bloody faces would highlight the coverage of the episode, another example of a Marxist government crushing freedom of expression as it moved to solidify its totalitarian control.

Tony was given two stink bomb canisters and shown photographs of the leaders of MIR, including one American, Ira Baumel. Baumel had come to Chile to teach at the Catholic University of Santiago after Nixon and Agnew trounced McGovern and Shriver in the 1972 presidential election. Baumel had been active in the McGovern for President organization, and his work had earned him a spot on President Nixon's list of enemies. McGovern, a World War II combat veteran, was a vocal critic of the war in Vietnam and a staunch proponent of withdrawal. His campaign platform included deep, across-the-board cuts in defense spending. Understandably, neither the military nor the intelligence community had any love for him or for those who supported him. They were only too pleased to add young Mr. Baumel to their own list of persona non grata.

The CIA took Nixon's grudge as license to target Baumel upon his arrival and to investigate and monitor his activities. Baumel wasted little time giving them good cause to do so. He immediately joined the radical Marxist wing of Chile's student movement, whose favorite outlets for the expression of their revolutionary views were occupation of campus buildings and marches in the streets. Students, professors and administrators from both the Catholic University and the University of Chile attended their assemblies. Student-led demonstrations had spread to campuses in Valparaiso and Concepcion. The demonstrations were intended to be peaceful and orderly but frequently ended in clashes between demonstrators and police, who employed tear gas and Billy clubs. Despite considerable effort by President Allende and his UP, young Marxists like Baumel were able to maintain leadership positions in the most active student organizations. They had even been able to seize control of the university's TV station, which they then operated illegally for months.

In July 1973, Jaime del Valle, dean of the law school at the Catholic University, published a study suggesting that more than two hundred thousand fraudulent UP votes had been cast in the March congressional elections. President Allende was livid. So radical campus intellectuals, like Baumel, were natural enemies, and using the media to portray him and his colleagues as the target of police violence was not difficult.

Tony would have to wear a disguise—a reddish moustache and long brown wig. It was important that Andre A. Stephens, CE technician, not be identified as politically active, much less antagonistic to the government. It was quite likely that within days of the demonstration he would be back at La Moneda, or some other government building, servicing the telephones, and it would not do for someone there to match him to a newspaper photo taken at an antigovernment event.

The next day, Tony went to Bulnes Square, an open area across Alameda O'Higgins Boulevard from Liberty Square. On the opposite side of the plaza he could see the windows of the Foreign Ministry wing of La Moneda. A throng of sign-carrying students were waiting to begin marching northward across Alameda and along Morande Street past the state bank, the government radio corporation, the garage and offices of the Ministry of Public Works, and the offices of the Santiago provincial governor. Then they would cross Moneda Street, past the Social Security Building and Central Bank, and left into Constitution Square. Police and soldiers had already taken formation along the route, holding black batons and rifles. Tony could see the bravado and fear, even through their helmets and face guards.

When the crowd started moving, Tony quickly strode toward the middle, blending in like any other longhaired youth, periodically raising his fist and shouting along with the slogans coming from the bullhorns at the front the bellowing mob. There must have been a thousand or more protestors. An older man passed by, handing out signs. Tony took one that urged a swift end to capitalism. "Afuera las corporaciones!" "Corporations get out!"

A podium had been erected at Constitution Square, just across Teatinos Street from the Ministry of Finance and Economy. A young man was already railing through a bullhorn. Tony recognized him as one of the leaders of the Socialist Youth movement. After about fifteen minutes, the young man reciting anti-corporate rhetoric seemed to tire and was replaced by another shouter. The speeches sounded as amateurish and juvenile as the ones Tony had heard from college kids protesting the war back in New Haven. For more than an hour speakers took their turns at the podium. They seemed satisfied to express the same themes over and over again, with no perceptible increase in intensity. Nothing about it suggested the crowd would lose control of itself. The tension and anxiety Tony had seen in the soldiers' faces to begin with was gradually being replaced by boredom.

Eventually, though, Ira Baumel stepped up to the lectern and took the bullhorn. Tony recognized him immediately. It was time. Tony slowly and nonchalantly reached into his pocket.

"Hey, friend, you want to come with us?"

Tony stood still. The voice had come from someone close. He kept his hand in his pocket but loosened his grip on the metal canister. He waited.

"Brother, did you hear me? I asked whether you want to come with us." The voice sounded harsh and impatient, and Tony no longer doubted that it was meant for him. He had to make up his mind quickly. Do I speak English? He wasn't Tony Gannon or Andre Stephens. He was some guy in a disguise. With an exploding stink bomb in his hand. He turned.

A group of students stood together, all in jeans and tie-dyed tee shirts and all about twenty years old. The scraggly one in the middle had been the speaker. "Hermano," he said, "I'm trying to invite you to our after-demonstration party. Back in the dorms. We're getting ready to leave, and my friend here thinks you're cute." He gestured toward the girl next to him. Tony looked them over. Definitely not cops or soldiers. That's a relief, he thought. And it got better. The girl was pretty, with long dark hair and big brown eyes. Tony did a quick calculation. Four girls and only three boys. Which is where I come in, he concluded. I'm all for balancing out the male-female ratio.

"Maybe he doesn't speak English," Brown Eyes said. Tony realized he hadn't yet spoken. But he still couldn't make up his mind what language to use. "Do you speak English?" she said. "Habla Ingles?"

Tony's hand was still in his pocket. Still on the canister. He wanted to jump in and get to know these people, especially the girl. But he had a job to do. He pulled his hand out and held up his thumb and forefinger, borrowing the gesture from the Flower Man. "A leetle beet," he said.

"Oh, he's so cute," the girl squealed. "Ven con nosotros a la fiesta," she said. "Come with us to the party."

Tony pursed his lips and shook his head back and forth. "No puedo," he said.

"You're missing out, pal," the shaggy fellow said. "She makes a helluva Pisco Sour. Uses egg whites and sugar. It'll be a good time, I guarantee it."

Tony kept shaking his head. "No puedo," he repeated. And what else could he say? Maybe I can join you after I toss these stink bombs through the window over there and start a riot? He looked again at Miss Brown Eyes. Man, he thought, I must be crazy. Then he turned his back.

"Your loss, brother," he heard Shaggy say as the group walked away, and Tony couldn't have agreed with him more.

The next day's newspaper headlines decried the latest example of the government's shameful campaign to stifle peaceful dissent. According to reports, the riotous events began when Ira Baumel, the outspoken leader of a radical student group, began calling for an escalation of antigovernment activity. Enraged soldiers, it was reported, began attacking defenseless students. Photographs showed two officers clubbing the cowering Baumel. Blood was splattered across his forehead. The articles repeatedly emphasized that the demonstration had been peaceful until the soldiers began their unprovoked attacks.

Nowhere in the reports was it mentioned that the police had been completely restrained until someone threw a couple of smoking stink bombs through the front window of the Ministry of Interior. When the police moved to push the crowd back and secure the building, out-of-control students rushed them from all directions. What resulted was pandemonium, hardly an orchestrated effort to suppress or stifle anything. But the newspaper descriptions clearly gave the opposite impression—that Chileans were no more protected from tyranny than people in Havana or Moscow or East Berlin. Tony rubbed his temples. He had done his job. He just hoped Miss Brown Eyes and her friends hadn't been hurt.

# CHAPTER 23

A few afternoons after the demonstration, Tony was back at work, servicing the intercom system at the very same Interior Ministry offices that had been the site of the socialist student demonstration. The broken window had already been replaced, but a tinge of odor—like rotten eggs—remained in the air.

After the first couple of times Tony was in the palace, he became more comfortable wandering around, though he kept an eye out for places to hide, just in case. He looked for alternate ways to gain access to offices that were supposed to be off-limits to the civilian help, especially foreign contractors like himself. He had discovered ways that made it possible for him to sneak into rooms located close to the inner sanctums where meetings took place. A maze of dark closets was connected by narrow crawl spaces and trapdoors. Most of the floors in the palace were tiled, and Tony believed he would be able to hear someone approaching. More than once, he strayed from a room where he was working on a telephone or intercom to enter another room several doors down, always scouting for places to plant recording devices, under a couch or chair or under a conference table, so that anyone who spoke at a meeting there could be overheard. He was emboldened by the belief that his uniform shirt, with the Chiltelco logo on the chest, and an innocent smile, were all he would need to allay the suspicions of anyone he might encounter. He was just a telephone technician, whose presence was perfectly appropriate.

Tony had replaced a half dozen monitoring devices in various meeting rooms and hoped to be listening one day to a conversation that he himself had helped to bug. So far that hadn't happened. Nonetheless, he figured his work had been satisfactory because nobody had complained or told him otherwise. And Mr. D'Onofrio was still giving him assignments away from his desk and headphones.

The ministry offices were housed in the western wing of the Palacio de La Moneda, sharing the building with the presidential offices and the Foreign Ministry. On the north face, the windows looked out onto Constitution Square, where Tony had launched his attack. To the west, the windows faced across Teatinos Street to the comptroller's office. Several museums were located on the same street, including the Museum of Pre-Columbian Chilean Art, the Museum of Colonial Art, and the Ralli Museum, which featured contemporary art from around the world. Farther south, past Bulnes Square was the Chilean Academy of Painting where many native painters were schooled. Chile had a rich tradition of fine art, along with government-sponsored orchestras and ballet troupes.

But these days, the Chilean economy was in disarray, and tax revenues were at an all-time low. The ministry's budget had been cut and then cut again. Still, Chile yearned for world-class status, which required modernization of its transportation system and other utilities, and improving its network of highways and rail lines. The international airport was especially important to the image Chile conveyed to its neighbors and the world. And of course, President Allende was also interested in upgrading and modernizing the power supply grid, communication systems, water and sewer systems, and the collection and processing of trash. His goal was to provide a strong foundation for all commerce so that businesses and industries, including banking and tourism, could flourish. This was essential to the economic prosperity of the country and to the degree of prestige it could achieve internationally.

Tony was at the building to install a new power supply module for the intercom system. Of course, his agenda included taking several hours to do what could be accomplished in less than one, thus prolonging the opportunity to observe the comings and goings of people within the offices. Before going on the assignment, he once again reviewed the station's collection of photographs of people believed to be Cuban or Russian agents.

Tony was working and taking his time when Carlos Gonzalez entered the office carrying a flat cardboard box with bunches of brightly colored carnations. There looked to be a few dozen, each a different shade. Pink, white, brilliant red, yellow. As usual, Carlos was smiling. He had the kind of face muscles that formed a smile just by relaxing. He cheerfully greeted Tony, whom he recognized immediately. "How are you, my Canadian friend?" he called out in heavily accented English.

"Ah, Carlos," Tony answered. "So nice to see you."

Carlos smiled even more broadly. "Today I make Diana's delivery for her. She promised that if I carried these here, she would cook my favorite dinner, arroz con pollo. How you say in English, chicken and rice?" Carlos rubbed his stomach. His eyes were closed and his head was tilted back, savoring the air as though he was already bathing in the aromas of his wife's kitchen.

For a moment, Tony also imagined the sweet smell of onions cooking and chicken simmering with garlic and paprika and ripe bananas being fried. Tony loved arroz con pollo and platanos maduros. He had found a couple of restaurants that served wonderful plates full and ate there whenever he could. He thought how much better the meal would be, cooked at home by Diana—who added love to her husband's favorite recipes. His mouth began to water. Tony hadn't had a home-cooked dinner during his time in Chile, which was stretching into its third month.

As if reading Tony's mind, Carlos invited him to dinner. "It's just going to be Diana and me, and I know she'll prepare enough to feed all of Valparaiso. And there'll be homemade dulce de leche for dessert." The effervescence in Carlos's voice made it clear his invitation was genuine. "You tell us about Canada, and we will teach you about Chilean food and drink. We have been saving a bottle of the best cabernet sauvignon from the Bouchon winery here in the Colchagua Valley. It is aged in French barrels for more than a year. If you come, it will give us an excuse to open it. Diana will be delighted. Please say you will."

Tony was touched by the warmth of this affable Chilean man who was inviting Tony into his home, and he was hard-pressed to think of a reason not to go. He had no special plans for the evening, just the usual routine—exercising on the mat on the living room floor, then dinner at a nearby restaurant. Some nights he was able to link up with Frazier, but for the most part, he was alone. He would order a steak or chicken and rice and sit by himself, reading a newspaper. Afterward, when he got home, he would read some more, listen to the radio, and think. Tony missed his life in America, and he missed his sweet mother and his tough-guy father. He missed Carrie. As much as he hated to admit it, he was getting homesick. A nice dinner at Carlos and Diana's sounded good—very good. Then he realized he had a problem. He had walked to work. "I would enjoy that," Tony told Carlos, "but I don't have my car today."

"Andre," Carlos replied. "It would be my pleasure to carry you to my house and take you home after." And so Tony accepted the invitation.

Carlos and Diana lived in a quiet upper-class suburb of Santiago called Las Condes. Carlos took a couple of turns and was quickly out of the city. The road narrowed, twisting and turning. Carlos kept up a steady stream of chatter. It was obvious he was a thoughtful man who had given deep consideration to many of life's more esoteric issues. He spoke of books he had read and ideas he had absorbed and embraced. The car radio was tuned to a music station, and Carlos frequently interrupted his discussion to sing along. He knew every word to a song by Victor Jara, a popular singer and songwriter. He proudly pointed out that Victor and his wife Joan, herself a well-known dancer and choreographer from England, were neighbors.

Tony listened intently. It was not his plan to exploit Carlos and Diana or pump them for information. But he had been trained to listen whenever Chileans spoke, and he was content to let Carlos pick the subjects. Perhaps Carlos would get around, on his own, to a discussion of people connected to Allende, and if that happened, Tony would take it all in. But he did not relish the idea of misleading a nice man like Carlos, who was taking him home to dinner, or of steering him toward such topics. Tony reminded himself of the lessons he had been taught at Camp Peary—the benefits obtainable from the cold manipulation of people and the need to suppress any emotional attachments. This was fundamental to spying, and the good ones had no problem with it. But as much as Tony understood the principle, his nature hadn't allowed him to get there. Yet. He was hoping that nothing controversial would come up. At least nothing that might reflect badly on Carlos.

When they arrived at the Gonzalez home, Diana was playing a melancholy love song on the piano. As soon as Carlos heard it, he held up a fist as though it were a microphone and began to sing into it. *"Estoy en un rincon de la cantina. Me estan sirviendo ya, mi tequila. Y como siempre, mis pensamientos andan a ti."*

Diana laughed as she played. "My husband thinks he's Victor Jara, you know."

Carlos smiled sheepishly and bent to kiss his wife's cheek. As he did, Tony surveyed the room. The table Diana had set was truly beautiful. The starched linen tablecloth was gleaming white. In the center were two impressive arrangements of roses and lilies. The polished silverware was set in perfect alignment beside the china plates. The crystal glasses reflected the light from the chandelier. Tony was impressed.

Diana arose from the piano and greeted Tony. Then she tied an apron around her waist and got right to work. She served each course with care, explaining where she had gotten the recipe. Soup. Salad. Appetizer. Entree. Homemade dulce de leche for desert. Each dish was more delicious and certainly more lovingly presented than at any fine restaurant. In between courses, Carlos retrieved the next bottle of wine. "This cabernet sauvignon is from the Los Lingues estate in the Colchagua Valley," he boasted, displaying the bottle to Tony with the elegant flourish of a sommelier. He made an elaborate ceremony of screwing the cork and pulling it as Diana stood behind him, rolling her eyes and shaking her head. Yet she was smiling and obviously sharing his joy. He enjoys it so much, her body language said, how can we not enjoy it with him?

And the conversation was stimulating. Tony hadn't expected Diana to participate as actively as Carlos, but she was just as intelligent and every bit as articulate as her husband. This couple may have made their living selling flowers, but they were well educated and thoughtful. Eventually the discussion got around to the "messy political situation" in Chile. They acknowledged that their country was becoming increasingly polarized and unstable. Strikes and demonstrations were growing more disruptive and more violent every week. Carlos and Diana spoke about Allende's decision to appoint some of Chile's generals to cabinet positions. They were both uncertain of the wisdom of the move, although they conceded that such drastic measures might help to restore order.

As an example, they pointed to the dramatic influence of General Carlos Prats, who had recently been appointed minister of the interior. His heroism in confronting the Tanquetazo at the steps of La Moneda was admired by all. Carlos and Diana credited him with single-handedly reversing what they believed might otherwise have been a violent, even disastrous, confrontation. Tony knew exactly what Carlos meant by "the Tanquetazo," and he was also familiar with the role that General Prats had played in quelling it. The reports he had read described Prats as a key figure in Allende's effort to keep his government afloat. Several military leaders had been invited to join the government as a way of restoring order. General Prats shared the late General René Schneider's philosophy about the limited role the military should play in civilian affairs, and he was therefore reluctant to accept the appointment. But he recognized that the army's loyalty to Allende's office could serve as a lynchpin in the effort to prevent its collapse, and that without the army, the viability of the Allende government was in immediate jeopardy. So he, and several other military figures, accepted their appointments.

The Tanquetazo had occurred just a few weeks earlier. An increasingly vocal element within the middle ranks of the Chilean armed forces had lost respect for Allende's administration and had begun to openly question its ability to govern. On June 29, 1973, reports came in to the CIA's Santiago station that an antigovernment conspiracy within the army's Second Armored Battalion had been discovered at the Santiago garrison. When Lieutenant Colonel Roberto Souper learned that he was about to be relieved of his command for his part in the conspiracy, he led a column of some sixteen armored vehicles, including several tanks, into the center of Santiago. Accompanied by about eighty soldiers, he surrounded the presidential palace and the Ministry of Defense. Shots were fired, and some casualties were reported. But for the most part, there was a pronounced lack of resistance. The city seemed on the brink of an unopposed revolution. The rank-and-file membership of the Unidad Popular, the workers and farmers, stayed away, thus depriving President Allende of any support in the streets. He hurriedly summoned the loyal General Prats, who rushed downtown to confront the mutinous soldiers.

The general walked directly in front of the lead tank. His stature among military men was already considerable, and the courage he displayed was impressive. He was able to persuade the soldiers to give up their rebellion without another shot. Most of the participants were allowed to escape, and those that surrendered were treated leniently. But the episode—dubbed by the press as the Tanquetazo—served to remove all doubt about two things, both of which were duly noted at the Santiago station and elsewhere. First, the potential for a military coup was indisputable. And second, Allende's supporters in the working classes were not likely to marshal themselves into any significant counterrevolutionary force.

After dinner and the last of the wine, Carlos asked Tony if he was ready for his ride home. Tony thanked Diana and told her again how much he had enjoyed himself. "It was a delicious dinner."

"Ah, the food was just ordinary," she protested. "It was the company and the conversation that made it special." She embraced Tony. "I am so glad that Carlos invited you."

But Tony would not give in. "The company was indeed wonderful. But the food was truly exceptional. Your cooking must be the finest in all of Chile." Tony tried to imitate one of Carlos's grand gestures by sweeping his arm across the sky. He was feeling the wine more than a little, but he really had enjoyed himself. Being with Carlos and Diana was like visiting old friends. They had made him feel so welcome, so comfortable. He started to say how much his girlfriend would enjoy meeting them and even thought about pulling Carrie's photo from his wallet. But he caught himself. Carrie was not his girlfriend. Not anymore. He didn't even know why he still kept her picture with him, and he didn't want to explain and risk ruining the cheerfulness of the moment. So he let it go. "Thank you so much for having me to your home."

"It was our pleasure," Diana said. "I hope we can do it again soon."

"I would like that very much," Tony replied. "I will not forget your gracious hospitality."

# CHAPTER 24

Soon after he had spoken to Frazier about them, Tony requested permission to review the dossiers on General Lorenzo Fox and his aide, Cristina de la Vega. Of course he was most interested in the lady, but he thought it best to request the files on both. No sense revealing that he was motivated more by lust than by duty. "I met Ms. de la Vega at Tucho Colon's party," Tony told D'Onofrio. "Saw her again the other day at La Moneda. I might run into her again, and I thought it would be helpful to know something about her and her boss." Tony left out the rest of the story and kept a very straight face.

D'Onofrio told him that he didn't remember seeing much on the girl, as he called her, but there was plenty on General Fox. D'Onofrio said he would make the documents available, but they were to be read in his office and then placed into the burn bag, the big cardboard sack that went directly to the incinerator at the end of every business day. Sensitive documents had a very short half-life in the field and had to be disposed of with care. Wastebaskets just wouldn't do.

The pile of material on General Lorenzo Fox didn't include much on Cristina. Only that she had been working for the general for nearly two years. Native of Chile but educated in the States. A member of the UP but not politically active. Lived alone. Never married. No children. Father deceased. Mother living in Uruguay. Tony was able to read it all in just a few minutes. Then turned his attention to the material on Fox, which consisted of several reports from a company officer, code name Rubio, the Spanish word for blonde, including several transcripts of conversations between the general and Rubio, and one actual tape.

It was immediately apparent why Mr. D'Onofrio had described the Fox dossier as "sensitive." Fox had been recruited as an agent for the CIA a year earlier. General Fox became a widower when his wife was killed in a car accident. They had no children. He received a bachelor's degree in finance from Northeastern University in Boston. He believed in market economic theory. Supply and demand. Understandably, he had strong reservations about Allende's socialist form of government, and was considered "reachable."

The general was an avid gun collector. By "coincidence," Rubio showed up at an antique gun show and expressed admiration for the same pieces as General Fox. Later, Rubio ran into Fox at gun shops and antique auctions. Soldiers, even high-ranking ones, weren't paid much in Chile; and the General didn't have the money to match his taste. But Rubio did. And it wasn't long before their shared interest grew into something of a friendship. And so Rubio was able to reveal to his friend that he was wealthy and could afford to be generous. Did the general admire the German-built Walther PPK model S pistol? Did he prefer shiny nickel plating to the factory original flat black? The exact version of the weapon James Bond used in the popular movies? Well, Rubio had two of them, as it turned out, and would enjoy nothing more than to share one with an aficionado like the esteemed general. A fellow collector who would truly appreciate it. And if the general was uncomfortable accepting it as a gift, then they could consider it a long-term loan. He could always just give it back. Fox wanted it very badly. Badly enough to take it, even if it meant compromising his ethics.

And later, Rubio explained quite innocently that he knew some people, North Americans and wealthy Chilean anticommunists, who resented the path that Chile was following under Allende. Some good and honest businessmen who were intent on defeating him at the voting polls, if possible, and if not, perhaps by other means. He wasn't specific, and the general didn't ask him to be. But the point was made. Rubio's friends were serious men, with serious plans, and the wherewithal to carry them out. They would surely succeed. And, dear friend, these people are paying very well, right now, for information. Why shouldn't you get some of that money, General Fox? You know that Allende is an idealistic fool, and that ultimately his government will fail. Why shouldn't you profit from these circumstances, just like others are doing? The general should not doubt that Allende's "experiment in socialism" was doomed. It was a question of when it would end, not if. Rubio was persistent and skillful. Reading the transcripts, Tony was impressed by his cunning approach, like a wolf stalking a sheep, intent on separating him from the herd.

Then Tony put the tape into his machine. Rubio's voice was distorted to protect his identity, but the general's speech was clear and easily understood. He liked and respected Salvador Allende and was reluctant to betray him. And he felt a strong loyalty to Chile's constitution. Like so many others, he had been inspired by the Unidad Popular's goal of balancing individual rights with its socialist ideals. He admired the president for including the political opposition, not suppressing or excluding it. Citizens with widely disparate views were part of his coalition. The Chilean Way had offered hope. Like Allende, General Fox wanted to believe that the people's patriotism was stronger than their partisanship.

But Fox's idealism was eventually supplanted by his pragmatism. Necessary efforts to fortify the government against political attack lacked presidential enthusiasm, which permitted the dissenters to strengthen. Allende's virtue seemed also to be his biggest weakness.

Fox knew that political naiveté rarely goes unpunished, and Allende would likely enjoy no lasting exemption.

Though his words were garbled on the tape, Rubio's arguments were eloquent. "In his aspirations for a more civilized government, Allende has sown the seeds of his own destruction," Rubio insisted. "It is fatal to be so tolerant." Rubio pounded away and found an increasingly receptive ear. Soldiers have a low tolerance for chaos and disorder. It's in their nature, which Rubio was doing his best to manipulate and exploit. "You have every right to protect yourself," Rubio implored.

So the general began describing conversations he had with other officers in the national police. He recounted things that were said at finance-department meetings. At Rubio's direction, Fox identified the people and what they sounded like and what they said so they could be matched to the voices recorded on tapped telephones. The information provided by the general enabled the Company's analysts to see differences between things some officials said when the president was present and what they said when he wasn't. The greater the differences, the shallower the loyalty.

The Company was well pleased by the flow of good information being produced by Operation Henhouse Fox, and Rubio's budget was increased commensurately. General Fox enjoyed the lavish gifts and was soon fully on board. He had thrown his lot in with the Americans and could count on their support if and when things went awry. "My friends are specialists at making arrangements," Rubio bragged. "They can get a man out of a bad situation. Even out of the country." Fox was reassured.

# CHAPTER 25

Tony stayed alert for opportunities to return to La Moneda. Mr. D'Onofrio thought he had developed an admirable enthusiasm for his work and sent him there whenever possible. Of course, the truth was that Tony was hoping to run into Cristina. He hadn't given up. Her unavailability, accompanied by her willingness to flirt, made her all the more attractive. He was playing with fire, lusting after an assistant to a high-ranking official in Allende's government. But the risk was part of the excitement, and Tony Gannon was up to the challenge.

A few weeks after his first "lucky day" at the palace, he was walking across the Plaza de la Constitution when he saw her. The plaza was a square block of open space in the business, cultural, and educational center of the city, surrounded by the Supreme Court, the central bank, the Hotel Carrera, the Social Security Building, and the Ministry of Finance and Economy. The corner farthest from the palace, at the intersection of Agustinas and Teatinos streets, was the U.S. embassy. A large fountain had been erected in Constitution Square, with a statue of Bernardo O'Higgins, the national hero who led the Chilean struggle for independence from Spain in the early 1800s. All around him were crisscrossing walkways, lined with flagpoles displaying Chile's flag. Across from the grandest walkway stood the presidential palace, La Moneda—the most important symbol of Chile's democratic government.

Tony was at least one hundred feet behind Cristina and couldn't see her face when he first spotted her. But she had an unmistakable grace that was at once athletic and sensual. He had no doubt it was her. She was wearing a dark skirt suit with black leather pumps. The jacket had padded shoulders and was snug around her waist. The white sleeves of her shirt extended an inch or more beyond the cuffs. The skirt was a little looser than the jacket but still didn't hide the curve of her hips. She looked very conservative but at the same time very feminine. She carried a briefcase, an umbrella, and several books. Tony saw his opportunity. He jogged toward her, and as soon as he got close enough to be heard, he shouted, "Let me help you!"

Cristina turned her head and looked back over her shoulder at Tony but didn't stop. Which was a mistake. She tripped over a crack in the sidewalk and plunged forward. Her briefcase, umbrella, and books went flying.

Tony helped her up. "Are you all right?" he asked.

"Yes, yes," she answered as she got to her feet.

Tony began gathering the books. "Are you sure?" he asked. "It looked like a nasty fall."

"I am fine," she replied, "except for the embarrassment. You must think me a clumsy fool."

"Not at all," Tony insisted. "I am sorry for surprising you. It's my fault."

"Oh, how gallant you are," Cristina said with a wry smile. As she reached to retrieve the books Tony had gathered, she noticed the muscles rippling in his forearms. There was more to this young man than the sparkle in his eyes.

"Please, let me carry these for you," Tony responded. "I am on my way to the palace anyway."

"Well, that's very gracious," Cristina said. "I suppose I could use a little help. My boss needs these books for his meeting, and they are very heavy."

Their eyes met, and like every time before, Tony felt the electricity.

Cristina felt it too. She knew she should brush him off, because any indiscretion could cost her dearly. General Fox was a possessive and jealous man. But it was getting more difficult to ignore this boy. He was very good-looking in a rough way, and she liked that. He was eager and bold, especially for a young foreigner, and Cristina liked that too. Her body was responding, whether it was a good idea or not. There was no denying the delicious tension she was feeling. And what was the harm in a passing flirtation? She would put a stop to it before it developed into anything serious.

When they got inside, Cristina thanked Tony again. She gestured toward a table in the foyer. As he put the books down, he looked at their titles. Fiscal Policy in a Socialist State. Modern Economic Strategies. Principles of International Banking.

"Forgive me for saying so, but these don't seem like stimulating reading," Tony said.

"Maybe not," Cristina responded, "but I don't think General Fox reads them for pleasure. The president relies on the general for guidance on very technical subjects. Besides," she continued, "when did technicians become experts on stimulation?"

Tony smiled. "Touché," he said. He was well aware of the reputation engineering types had. They were nerds. Geeks. He remembered the joke, how can you tell an engineer that's taken assertiveness training? He's the one who looks down at the other person's shoes when he is talking, instead of his own. Tony bristled at being associated with that image, but he was supposed to be a nerd. That was part of his cover.

He should excuse himself and get back to work. But she was so sexy, so alluring, so irresistible. He couldn't help himself. He had to go for it. There was no guarantee he'd ever see her again, much less have the chance to talk to her alone. This might be his only opportunity to get something started, and he would surely kick himself later if he didn't at least try. He owed it to himself. So he plunged ahead. "I guess there's always a risk of being misjudged," he said. "You stumbled out there, so I could think you are clumsy and without grace. And I work on telephones, so you could think I am boring and self-restrained. And, Cristina, isn't it possible we'd both be wrong?"

"I suppose," she said thoughtfully.

"Really," Tony confirmed. "Maybe I am just a fool. I am sure there have been many before me. Fellows who saw your beauty and couldn't resist you enough to behave properly."

Her lips curled as she looked at him, and her eyebrows arched. "You're a very brave man, Mr. Stephens,"

"Why do you say that?" Tony asked.

"You have only met me a couple of times, but from the start your eyes spoke like they knew me. And now you are wondering if I am stimulated by these books. And you tell me I am beautiful and irresistible and all these things. How do you know I won't tell my jealous boyfriend and get you in trouble?"

"Do you?" he asked.

"Do I what?" she responded.

"Do you have a jealous boyfriend?"

"As a matter of fact, I do. A very jealous and powerful one, too. And I don't think he would like finding out that I was talking to a . . ." she paused. Tony looked at her and waited for her to finish her sentence. He anticipated a snobby put-down. A reference to his working-class status. But her next words were, "a stimulating young man." Tony felt his face flush.

"Really?" he said slowly. He was taking his time, savoring it. "Well, thank you for saying so."

She was waiting to see what he would do. He moved toward her, slowly but deliberately. She put her hands up, like a traffic cop. "Don't," she said firmly. "Let's go take that coffee we spoke of last time. I know where there's an espresso machine. I will make us a cup. But we will only have five minutes."

"I would travel two hours to spend five minutes with you," he told her, and they both knew it was true.

"If you will carry my books down the hall and upstairs for me, I will show you."

Tony picked up the thick and heavy volumes, but they felt like feathers. His heart had changed gears, and his motor was racing. She smiled, looking like a mischievous schoolgirl, and started off down the hall. Tony was grateful there were no other people around. He had no doubt they could see he was out of place and up to no good. In more ways than one. But the hall was empty, and, regardless, there was no turning back.

He followed Cristina up a wooden staircase at the back of the Morande Street side of the palace. When they came out of the stairwell, she led him down the second floor hallway, past some offices and the Independence Lounge, and through a set of double doors at the entrance to the auxiliary kitchen. The room was large with high ceilings, which had drop lighting above plastic panels. Pots and pans and other cooking utensils hung from a bronze harness over the island in the middle. There were two refrigerators and a freezer on one side. Along one wall were the stove and ovens beside large pantries that stretched to the ceiling. Some of their doors were open, revealing sacks of sugar, flour, and beans. Tony noticed an aluminum stepladder—no doubt needed by the cooks to access the higher cabinets.

"Welcome to the auxiliary kitchen," Cristina said cheerfully. "It was added to La Moneda a few years ago. My father built it and the lounge next door. He was very proud of these rooms."

Tony glanced around, more interested in locating the exits and doorways than in admiring the workmanship. But he could tell Cristina wanted him to acknowledge her father's artistry, and so he did. "It's a great kitchen. The cabinets are beautiful. Your father is quite a craftsman."

"Yes, yes, he was," she answered. "This was his last important project. He died two months after it was finished."

"I'm sorry," Tony said.

"Thank you," Cristina answered. "But enough about sad things. Let us enjoy our coffee."

Tony watched Cristina scoop coffee beans into the grinder and activate the machine. The aroma wafted throughout the room. Then she measured the ground coffee into a silver espresso fixture and deftly swept a knife across the top to remove the excess. She placed the fixture up under the espresso brewer and secured it with a half turn. Black liquid began to drip into the metal cup she had placed below. She retrieved a carton of milk from the refrigerator and poured some into two china cups, which she held up to the steamer nozzle. She added several small spoons of sugar to the coffee, and poured the steaming dark brew into the cups. The coffee and steamed milk combined to create a dark tan color. When she turned to put Tony's cup and saucer down in front of him, he was smiling from ear to ear. "I can see this is not the first time you've done this," he said.

"It's easy. Everyone in Chile knows how to make café con leche. Next to pisco, it is our national beverage. We drink too much of both, I'm afraid."

Tony smiled again and then lifted his cup to his lips. He wanted to look sophisticated, so he was careful not to slurp. "Ahhh," he said. "Its wonderful. Really, really delicious."

"Thank you," Cristina said. "I hope you like it sweet. That's how I make it. We have an expression, 'Sweet enough to please a girl raised on a sugar cane plantation.'"

Tony had not stopped smiling. The situation was thrilling to the point of intoxication. He was on a secret adventure with a beautiful woman who was serving him coffee. "I knew it would be sweet," he said. "After all, look who made it."

Cristina's sat across from Tony and raised her cup. "To sweetness," she said.

For a moment, Tony wanted to sweep the cups off the table and reach across to engulf Cristina in his arms. But he held back. "To sweetness," he toasted. Then he lowered his cup and looked into her eyes. "I am so glad I saw you today."

Cristina smiled demurely. She wasn't sure what to make of this fellow. She wanted to be smart, to resist the temptation, to avoid the risk he represented, but he was making it so easy not to.

"So tell me," he went on. "How's your friend, Maria Cueto?"

Cristina stiffened. "She's fine. Why do you ask?"

"Well, actually, I was hoping she would be getting together with my friend, Frank Murphy. You know, the guy she met at Mr. Colon's party. She seemed to like him. To be honest, I was hoping their friendship would allow me to get in touch with you."

"Really," Cristina replied. But it was not a question. She was guarded and waiting.

"Murphy told me he called her the day after the party, and they planned to meet for lunch, but she didn't show up. He tried to call her a couple of times afterward but was never able to reach her. I'm curious. Is she okay?"

Cristina's expression remained serious, even somber. "She had a big problem. Nothing to do with your friend. You can tell him that, if it will make him feel better."

"What kind of problem?" Tony said. "If you don't mind me asking." He could see Cristina think about it for a second. "It wasn't her fault, you know, but she is embarrassed. I'm not sure she would like me talking about it."

"I understand," Tony said. "I hope she's all right, though."

"Well, the truth is that she went out with a macho idiot who got drunk and attacked her. He beat her and forced himself on her. She didn't leave her house for quite a while. The last thing she wanted to do was make a date with another man she didn't really know. Like your friend Mr. Murphy."

"That's awful," Tony said somberly. "I can't imagine how a man could do such a thing, but I've heard it happens."

"Yes," Cristina said. "You never know about people. But she is getting better. I spoke to her yesterday, and she sounded good. She's strong. It will take time, but she'll recover."

"I hope so," Tony said. "She seemed like such a happy person."

"Oh yes. You're right about that. Maria is a wonderful girl. I call her Miss Personality. Always making everyone laugh. I could tell you some stories about that one. She's a great friend. And I work for her uncle, you know. General Fox is her mother's brother.

"Really?" Tony said. "Well, I'm glad she is feeling better. Tell her not to lose her faith in men. We're not all animals."

Cristina smiled. The cloud was lifting. Of course she had no reason to trust Tony. He was as much a stranger to her as the attacker had been to Maria. But Cristina's instincts about people had always been good, and she had confidence in her ability to judge character. And this man, sitting across the table from her, did not scare her. She felt a lot of things when she looked at him, but fear was not one of them.

They engaged in pleasant conversation for several more minutes. Then Cristina finished her coffee and told Tony she had to go. "The general will be looking for me." She stood up and brought the cups to the sink. Tony got up from his chair and watched her rinse them. He was looking for a cue. But Cristina wasn't giving him one. He walked with her to the back staircase. "I am very grateful for the coffee and for this time with you, Cristina," he said, staring as deeply as he could into her eyes.

"Me too," she answered. "You are a very interesting man. But now I have to go."

"Of course," Tony answered. "You go ahead. I will wait here a few minutes, and then I will go back the way we came."

"Thank you," Cristina said, and then she paused. It was the signal Tony was waiting for. He took her in his arms and pulled her to him, steadily but gently. She didn't pull away. He moved his face closer to hers, careful to give her the chance to stop him. But she didn't. He kissed her, softly at first. Still going slowly enough not to scare her, to allow her to protest. But she wasn't scared. And she didn't protest. She kissed him back, and their kiss quickly intensified. Tony felt his eyes starting to close, but he kept them open to see what hers were doing. Only when he saw hers close did he close his own. His head was spinning. He ran his tongue over her lips and felt her tongue come out to respond. It made him giddy. After a few seconds, he withdrew his lips from hers and whispered softly, "Whew."

She said nothing.

"You better go now," Tony said. "But before you leave, will you do me two favorcitos, two little favors?"

She smiled. "Perhaps. Tell me what they are."

"First, promise me I can see you again soon," Tony said.

"Yes," she replied too quickly to catch herself. "Although we'll be taking a big chance."

"You won't regret it," Tony said.

"I will if anyone finds out," Cristina said. "You must promise me that you will tell no one. Otherwise, it could become a disaster. For both of us."

"I promise," Tony said, his eyes serious.

"Okay, I am probably making a mistake. But we'll soon see. Can you meet me here a week from Thursday at five thirty in the evening?"

"Yes, yes," Tony said. "I will be here waiting."

"Now what was the second favor?" she asked.

"Let me hold you one more time before you go." Tony didn't wait for her to answer. He drew her close, firmly. He kissed her cheek and moved his face along it until his nose was snuggled against her neck. Then he drew in a deep breath, inhaling her fragrance. After a moment, he pulled back, but only enough to position his lips against hers. They kissed again. Deeply. Every nerve fiber in his body flashed and tingled. The electric current flowed between them as their mouths melded. He was fully aroused and pressed his hips forward, mashing himself against her. She felt him and pressed herself against him in return. Then she pulled away, turned, and disappeared out the doors. Tony sighed and shivered as his senses whirled in a cyclone of excitement.

# CHAPTER 26

The next day D'Onofrio approached him about an even more delicate assignment.

"You did a good job at the demonstration, Andre," D'Onofrio told him.

"Thank you, sir," Tony said.

"In fact, you've stood up to everything that's been thrown at you. Maybe you've been lucky, but that's good too. And you're been in La Moneda more than anyone else, so they're used to seeing you there."

"Yes, sir," Tony said.

"Allende's been working out of a small private office in the palace," D'Onofrio continued. "On the second floor. We had a device in there a while back, but a Soviet security adviser found it in a sweep. They couldn't pin it on us because we'd used an East German device. Allende had his suspicions, but nothing concrete, and our ambassador, Nathaniel Davis, insisted it wasn't us. He asked Allende how he could be sure the Russians didn't put it there so they could "discover" it just to impress him. Or maybe they were spying on him themselves. Made Allende think. You don't always get help from ambassadors like that, but Davis is a good one. I don't know if Allende bought it completely, but whatever the case, he's been making calls from that upstairs office and we'd like to

have a listen. And we got a break. Chiltelco has a new work order
to upgrade the intercom systems in the Red Room and the Cabinet
Room, which happen to be on the second floor, just around the
corner and down the hall from the president's upstairs office. This
time we'll use a brand-new voice-activated recorder with minimal
power requirements. It'll run off the phone's internal power source.
No signal emissions and no batteries. Chances are it won't be found,
even if they do another sweep."

"Great, chief. I'm ready," Tony said. "Will I be on my own?"

"Pretty much. We wanted to send someone to the palace with
you, but we're short. You'll have to penetrate the target yourself.
Now these rooms are upstairs, on the second floor. You haven't been
up there."

"No, sir," Tony heard the sound of his own voice. *Why did I
just lie?* he asked himself. But he knew why. He was keeping the
promise he had made to Christina. Romantic and stupid. He regretted
it instantly, but it was too late. He couldn't fix it now, so he'd have
to let it go.

"Security upstairs is tighter than on the first floor. At least one
carabinero on foot patrol in the hallways. Luckily we have reason
to believe they've gotten lackadaisical, a little lazy. But he'll be up
there somewhere, and we can't predict with certainty where he'll be
when you go in. You'll have to be quiet and you'll have to be alert
and you'll have to be quick. And if you get caught, well . . ." He
hesitated. "Son, you just can't let that happen."

Tony braced for just a second and took stock. He didn't feel
scared and he certainly didn't want his chief to be. He wanted to
say something to reassure D'Onofrio, but he didn't want to sound
frivolous. So he sat still and waited.

Then D'Onofrio continued. There was a new resolve in his voice.
"Andre, I have confidence in you. And I need that phone tapped.
So we'll just have to prepare carefully and make sure it goes down
like we plan."

"Yes, sir," Tony replied. "Piece of cake." He was trying to look and sound like a veteran.

"We have a pretty accurate diagram of the second floor—a detailed schematic of the layout."

"I've seen the floor plan," Tony said, "and I think I can get into the president's office easily enough. Early in the morning, before everyone comes to work. Most of the offices are empty until at least eight thirty. I can be done and back downstairs well before that. It'll be quiet and so will I. Don't worry, sir. We'll get it done."

"Good," D'Onofrio said. He sounded calm, matter-of-fact, even upbeat, but the deep furrows knitted across his brow belied the confidence in his voice. He was about to go out on a limb with a rookie, and he was worried.

On Monday, Tony began to prepare. He checked the official agendas. On Wednesday the president was scheduled to lead a delegation to Valparaiso to attend the funeral of Arturo Araya Peters. Captain Araya, Allende's naval aide, had been gunned down while standing on the balcony of his house, an automatic weapon in his hand. The socialist newspaper Ultima Hora reported that a member of the Cuban embassy had been in the street below, and the two men were arguing over a woman. Some accounts suggested that the woman was Allende's daughter, who was married to Luis Fernandez Ona of the Cuban diplomatic corps, but was believed to be having an affair with her father's loyal captain Araya. Other accounts blamed the assassination on Patria y Libertad, whose criminal hit squads were targeting military officers loyal to Allende. A third theory appeared in the communist newspaper El Siglo, suggesting that the American CIA and the U.S. embassy had instigated the attack as part of an ongoing campaign to incite the government against the Cubans. Allende reacted by sending several more American contractors home. But the truth wasn't known, and as with so much in Santiago, people believed what they wanted to believe. What mattered to Tony was that Allende would not be at the palace on Wednesday. Many of the members of his government would also be with him on the coast. The timing was right.

Next, Tony studied the upstairs floor plan. The auxiliary kitchen and dining room, where Cristina had made him coffee, was on the east side of the building, its windows facing out onto Morande Street. Moving north along the hallway, the next room was the Independence Lounge. Then came the offices of Allende's executive secretary, Osvaldo Puccio, followed by the stairwell to the first-floor exit to Morande Street. Beyond that were security rooms of the president's bodyguards, the Grupo de Amigos Personales or Group of Personal Friends. At the northeast corner of the building was a large office used by Allende's private secretaries. It included a small bedroom and two bathrooms, one of which connected to Allende's office. It became Tony's target. A quick left turn before the bathroom and the entrance to the president's office would be on his right. Tony could exit the Cabinet Room, move quickly down the hall in front of the Sala Toesca, past the back stairs Cristina had shown him, turn left up the hallway past the GAP security room and reach his destination in seconds. That is, assuming he didn't encounter any security guards. On the way out, he could exit the president's office through the bathroom, go through the small bedroom, and then be back out into the hallway. No sweat, he told himself. No sweat at all.

Wednesday morning came quickly, but Tony felt thoroughly prepared and ready to go. He stuffed the recording device into the deepest pouch on his tool belt, between the screwdrivers and hammer. He put on his telephone company uniform and made sure the Chiltelco badge was securely fastened to the chest pocket. He arrived at the palace with his work orders and a box marked Electronics and entered through the front doors.

"Early for you, isn't it?" the security guard asked.

Tony nodded. "A lot to do today," he said, holding out his stack of work orders. "Replacing the intercom system in the Red Room and the Cabinet Room."

The guard looked at the papers and opened the box Tony was carrying. He withdrew one of the CE intercom modules, examined it briefly, and pushed the talk lever. "Ms. Contreras, come in here and take a letter," he said, imitating the president directing his secretary. Tony smiled and shrugged. The guard smiled back. "Up the main stairs. Turn left and then right. The Red Room will be the first set of doors on your right. The Cabinet Room is the next room down."

Tony thanked the guard and moved on. He was soon in the Red Room. He unhooked the old intercom monitor and ran the input leads into the new one. Then he moved to the Cabinet Room, where the process was repeated. It hadn't even taken ten minutes to complete his official tasks. Now it was show time. He put the old units in the box and walked out into the hallway. It was empty and very quiet. The floor was carpeted in this part of the building. He could step quietly, but he would also have difficulty hearing anyone else approach. *It is what it is,* he told himself. His heart was beating quickly, but he kept himself calm. He took a deep breath, exhaled, swallowed hard, and began his trip down the hall.

He couldn't help but think about his date with Cristina. She had told him to meet her in the auxiliary kitchen. Right down the hall. A smile started to work its way into the corners of his mouth, but he stopped it. Keep your mind on what you're doing, he chided himself, or you won't be meeting her next week or ever. He shook his head at himself disapprovingly. You have a long way to go before you can call yourself a professional.

Tony made it to the doors to the president's office without seeing or hearing anyone. And his luck continued when he found the doors unlocked. He entered the room and scanned it quickly. The door to the bathroom was open. There was another door inside, which Tony opened slightly, exposing a small bedroom. Tony could see that the room was empty, so he stepped into it and located the exit out to the hallway. It was basic technique to identify all exits in case a quick escape might be required. Tony then returned to the president's desk and began working on the telephone. He was focused enough to ignore his pounding heart. He removed the bottom plate and then retrieved the bug from the tool belt around his waist. He wedged the voice-activated transmitter into the telephone casing and clipped its leads to the wires coming from the receiver and going to the speaker. It would be powered by the current that the telephone itself supplied, which made it harder to detect than if it drew its power from a battery. Whenever the telephone would be used, either making or receiving a call, the device would transmit the conversation to a recorder on a desk in the CIA offices in the U.S. embassy, located just across Constitution Square.

Tony finished his work and gave the bottom of the phone a rapid once over. He tugged on the wires gently until he was satisfied he had done his job correctly, and that the bug would do its job too. He reinserted the plate back into the bottom of the telephone, returned it to where it had been on the desk, hooked his tools back into his belt, and moved toward the bathroom door. Before he knew it, he was through the bathroom, out the bedroom door and back in the hallway.

He decided to move west down the hallway toward the main stairs, instead of going back the way he came. It was a quicker route and would avoid taking him past the security room. But it did take him directly past the Military Aides Office, which is where he ran into trouble.

"Stop right there," came the carabinero's words. Tony knew they were directed at him. He turned to face the soldier, his heart already in his throat.

"Who are you? What are you doing here?" the soldier demanded. His hand moved toward his holstered sidearm.

Tony kept his cool. He had planned for this. He smiled and answered in French. "Excusez moi. Je cherche la salon du bain."

"Speak Spanish," the carabinero shot back, his voice rising angrily. "Who are you, and what are you doing here?"

Tony pointed to his Chiltelco badge. "I am here to fix the intercom," he explained, this time in Spanish. "I was looking for the bathroom."

The carabinero eyed him and the box he was carrying. "What's in the box?"

"These are the old intercoms," Tony answered. "Here, see for yourself," Tony opened the box and offered it to the carabinero.

The carabinero took a look and then looked again at Tony, who was still smiling. But he was not satisfied.

"Do you always take a tool belt and a box of equipment with you to the bathroom?"

"Oh, that," Tony laughed. "I am so used to it, I don't even feel it anymore. And these modules are valuable. I'd get in a lot of trouble if I lost one. I have to keep an eye on everything or the boss will give me hell." Tony tried to chuckle, in that you-know-how-it-is kind of way, but the sound got caught in his throat. He was starting to sweat.

"I think you better come with me. The sergeant will want to know about this."

# CHAPTER 27

Carlos Gonzalez had just finished putting a bouquet of fresh flowers on a secretary's desk when he came upon the curious scene. First he thought he heard French being spoken. Then he saw Corporal Francisco Garcia clamping a tight grip on Andre Stephens's arm. Carlos wasn't sure what was going on, but judging from the distress in Andre's eyes, he needed some help.

"Oh, Andre, I am so glad to see you," Carlos said. "I could use your help. Are you busy right now?"

Tony did not respond other than to look down at the carabinero's hand gripping his biceps. Carlos looked at the carabinero too. "I need to mount some flowerpots in the windows overlooking the winter garden. Andre has the right tools, you know. He could be a big help." Carlos was smiling, but the carabinero wasn't. "I'm sorry. Is there a problem?"

The carabinero relaxed his grip a bit. "You know him, Carlos?" Tony was thrilled that the carabinero knew Carlos by name.

"Yes, I do. Andre fixes the telephones," Carlos said. "What did he do to upset you?"

"Nothing, nothing," answered the carabinero. "I was just surprised to see him up here. He said he was looking for a bathroom and I wasn't sure . . . . But if you know him, I guess it's all right."

"I can assure you, Francisco, it's quite all right. Your prisoner has been a guest at my home. Now may I take custody of him? I would like to put him to work."

Tony looked at Carlos and then at the policeman, who let go of his arm. "I'm sorry for putting you to such trouble," he said.

"No," Garcia said. "It is I who should apologize. You took me by surprise. I hope you will forgive me."

"Of course," said Tony, "don't worry about it." The two men shook hands. Then Carlos led Tony down a hall which served as a gallery of ornately framed portraits and other paintings. The hallway surrounded the patio and winter gardens, which were in the center courtyard on the ground floor. When they got to the bank of windows on the other side of the gallery, out of anyone's hearing, Tony said, "Thank you, Carlos. I'm not sure why, but he was really upset. At least until you got there."

"I've known Corporal Garcia since he was a boy," Carlos said. "He's a good man. I'm sure he was just being careful."

"I suppose," Tony said. "Anyway, thanks."

"I'm glad I could help. And I really could use you. I have these flowerpots and some mounting brackets. I think they would look good in the windows, don't you?"

By then, Tony's heart was no longer galloping and he could breathe. Another close call, but he had installed the phone bug and was out of danger. Better lucky than good, he told himself, but he knew he owed a lot to the Flower Man. He would have agreed to do anything Carlos wanted. Helping him hang flowerpots would be a pleasure, and Tony happily said so. After they had gotten the first one up, Carlos asked Tony what he had been doing on the second floor. His tone included no detectable hint of suspicion.

"Just looking for a bathroom. I guess I got lost and wandered down the wrong hall or something. That Garcia fellow scared me so badly, I started speaking French, my first language. And that seemed to upset him even more."

"Yes, I heard you," Carlos said. "It's a beautiful language, French. Very charming, under different circumstances. But let that be a lesson to you. From now on, use the bathrooms on the first floor. It's not a good idea to get too near to the president's office. The carabineros are under a lot of stress. They are not sure what will happen next in this city or who they can trust. I am afraid that, like Corporal Garcia, we have all become a little nervous. Certainly the carabineros can't be counted on right now to appreciate the charm of a foreign language."

Tony looked at Carlos. The man may have been small and humble, but when he spoke, he was impressive. "So I noticed," said Tony, and the two men laughed before hanging another plant.

# CHAPTER 28

Tony sat at his table, struggling. He had completed some difficult tasks since arriving in Chile, but this one was giving him a different kind of trouble. He needed to respond to a letter he had just received and his response could not be truthful. The letter, written by his father, lay on the table in front of him: a single sheet of paper, filled on both sides by his dad's choppy handwriting, and an article clipped from Tony's hometown newspaper. The headline read, "Richland Set to Hire 200 More Engineers."

Tony had heard of the company. Richland Research was a medium-sized engineering and manufacturing operation located in Allentown committed to futuristic projects like solar energy and hydrogen-powered cars. Recent developments in the Middle East had given it a huge boost. The Organization of Petroleum Exporting Countries (OPEC) had been formed at a Baghdad conference in 1960; seven of its twelve members were Arab countries. Syria and Egypt were incensed by America's support for Israel, which occupied land it had captured during a stunning victory in the 1967 Six Day War. When OPEC began threatening to limit, if not entirely cut off, the flow of crude oil to the United States and its allies, Washington began preparing for an embargo. Nixon created the President's Energy Council, whose director began issuing warnings, supported by Interior Secretary Rogers Morton, to consume less gasoline or face rationing. But Americans were addicted to oil, to power their automobiles, run their appliances and heat their homes. Washington awarded several large grants and contracts to companies that were already engaged in the effort to identify and develop alternative sources of energy. What many had privately regarded as Richland's folly now seemed positively visionary. And so, when the Energy Council went looking for worthy projects to fund, Richland found itself on the top of the list. A huge research and design grant allowed it to expand its physical plant by some 100, 000 square feet, and, more importantly to Tony's mom and dad, to hire an entire cadre of new engineers.

"Tony," his dad's letter implored, "your mother misses you terribly." Frank Gannon didn't mention his own feelings but Tony knew they were in there. Men like him had feelings. They just didn't talk about them. "With your background, you'd be a shoe-in. Probably get yourself a raise. You could be home in time for your mother's birthday in August. The whole family is going to Sabatino's, your favorite. It's going to be a good time, son. But it would be even better if your mother had you there, too."

The letter stung. Tony knew he was missing milestones at home. It was a price he had agreed to pay. But he hadn't anticipated how much he'd miss it. And what could he say to his father now? "I am not really an engineer, Dad, so I won't be taking that job at Richland. I am a spy for the CIA and by the way, sorry for lying to you and mom all this time."

Just then, there was a knock at his door. Tony glanced at his watch. Ten PM. He didn't get many visitors and the late hour instantly made him uneasy. "*Quien es?*" he said, loud enough to be heard through the door.

"Its me, Andre. Murphy."

"Frank?"

"Yes, its me."

Tony could hear the urgency in Ironman's voice. He rose quickly. "One second."

"Hurry, please."

"Okay, okay. I'm coming. Tony put the letter and clipping back in the envelope, then slid them under some other papers on his table. The subject was too private to share, even with Ironman.

Frazier's face was pinched in distress. *Uh oh,* Tony thought. He couldn't remember the last time he had seen his friend looking so distraught. Perspiration had gathered across Frazier's brow, and a few rivulets meandered down his cheeks. Tufts of hair stuck out at odd angles. He looked like he had just gotten out of bed and run a mile.

"What's wrong, big guy?"

"I think I may have stepped in it this time," he said. "I need your help."

"Tell me about it."

"I don't have much time. Can I explain on the way?"

"On the way to where?"

"Ah shit, Tony. I can't believe what I just did. I'm such a dumbass. Please, come with me. And we need to take your car. I don't have one right now. I came on foot."

"All right, Frank," Tony said as he reached for his car keys. "But you need to calm down. Whatever it is, we'll handle it. We always do."

Two minutes later, Tony was driving while Ironman finished his tale of woe.

"Remember that brunette I met at the end of Tucho Colon's party? Just before we left."

"The one you gave that lesson in mangled Spanish to."

"Yeh, yeh," Frazier said sheepishly. "That one. Well, her name's Celia. Celia Barone. She's really hot. But the guy that was with her at Colon's place—that was her husband. Alessandro Barone. You might recognize the name."

"Barone . . . Barone. Isn't he the Italian ambassador's bodyguard? The one who shot at a guy in the street a couple of months ago?" Tony suddenly remembered the look in the large man's eyes when Ironman wouldn't back off at Colon's house.

"Yes, yes that's him. Apparently some teenager patted his wife's butt and the man went crazy. You can imagine how he'd react if he knew what I just did with her."

"What exactly did you just do with her?"

"Well, earlier tonight, I ran into her, to Celia, outside the grocery store near my apartment . . . ."

*Oh, no*, Tony thought. "It was all I could do to keep her husband from going after you at the party. I'm glad I didn't know what kind of guy he was at the time and how close we were to real trouble."

Ironman rubbed his fingers across his eyes until they met in a pinch at the bridge of his nose. "She saw me carrying my groceries. Offered me a ride. I know I should have said no, but man, she was making it easy."

"Resisting women was never one of your strong suits."

"This is not funny, Tony. I mean, Andre. One thing led to another and I kissed her, right there in the car. Next I knew, we were at her place, going at it like rabbits on her couch."

"So what's the problem?" Tony asked. "So far it sounds like your favorite sport, couch diving. Meet girl. Screw girl. Isn't that Routine A for Ironman?"

"Sure, that's how it started, all right. The woman's an absolute nympho. She gave me a helluva ride, and, I didn't exactly let her down, either. We had a damn good time. No question. But afterwards, she got jittery. Told me to get dressed and go."

"I still don't see your problem." Tony said. "Sounds like it was time for you to head out anyway. Oh, I get it, you wanted her to set a place for you at her dinner table? So you could relive the table top threesome you had with her and her husband at Colon's party?"

"This really isn't funny. Yes, I was ready to get out of there. I was feeling great. But about half way home I noticed my wallet was missing. I turned around and ran back. But by the time I got there, her husband was home. I didn't know what to do. So I came here."

"Oh, shit! You think she took it?"

"No, no. It probably just fell out when we were rolling around on the couch, maybe when she was pulling my pants off. I can't be sure. But I know I had it with me when I went in and I didn't have it when I came out. If her husband saw it, my goose is cooked."

"Don't tell me you left something in it that could blow your cover?"

"No, but the guy's crazy. Maybe he'll come after me like he went after that teenager in the street. Or maybe he'll complain to his boss, who's got mucho clout. If that happens, I could get kicked out of Santiago. Either way, it wouldn't go over well with the boss."

"That would not be good," Tony conceded. "In fact, none of this is good. With a wife like that, he might be in the habit of searching his sofa cushions whenever he comes home. You gotta take it easy and keep your fingers crossed. Hope he doesn't see it before he leaves for work tomorrow. Then you go back and retrieve it. Knowing you, you'll probably get an encore from his missus in the bargain."

"I wish. But I can't do that. I'm supposed to be at the airport in Valparaiso at 8 in the morning to pick up a couple of Naval intelligence hot shots from D.C. I can't be late and I can't be at two places at the same time. After I pick 'em up, I'm supposed to drive them around all day, wherever they need to go. I can't risk leaving my wallet at Celia's house all that time."

"You want me to pick up the Navy guys for you?"

"No, no. That we'd have to explain to D'Onofrio and somehow I don't think he'd understand."

"No, I see your point. So what *is* your plan?"

"Tomorrow morning, you go there and get my wallet back."

"I had wondered what all that stateside training was for. Now I know. Tradecraft is not really for spying. It's for getting a buddy's ass out of a jam. Or should I say, another jam?"

Frazier shook his head and tried to smile. "You can do it, Tony. I know you can."

The next morning, Tony got out early. If his little mission went well, and Mr. Bodyguard didn't take too long to leave the house, he could get Ironman's wallet and still be at his office on time. If not, he'd call. The schedule was flexible. Some days he stayed late. Some mornings he came in early. If he arrived late this morning, it wouldn't be the first time. Sometimes Henderson hadn't even asked why. But, if he did, Tony would just have to come up with something.

Tony drove to the street the Barones lived on and found their house. Then he drove around the block a couple of times to get a picture of the surrounding neighborhood. *This shouldn't be too complicated,* he thought. Certainly, he'd been in tenser situations, with a lot more at stake, but he still wanted to prepare thoroughly and be as careful as possible. At 7:30 am he parked half a block away: close enough to see Mr. Barone leaving, but far enough away to avoid suspicion. Right next to his car was a telephone booth. If Barone hadn't emerged by 8, Tony planned to call the Italian embassy to see when the ambassador was due in, which would give him a good clue as to when the ambassador's bodyguard would be reporting.

Tony kept his eyes fixed on the mirror. *Shouldn't be long now.*

Then it happened. Barone had emerged from his house in a suit and tie. He looked even bigger than Tony remembered, and meaner too, or maybe it was just the frown on his face. *As soon as he's out of sight,* Tony thought, *I'll ring the bell, introduce myself to his wife, explain why I came, get the wallet and be on my way.*

But right behind Mr. Barone was Mrs. Barone. Also, frowning. Also dressed up. The unhappy couple was going somewhere together. *Now what?*

Tony had a risky decision to make. The answer came quickly. Frazier would be in jeopardy until it was done and Frazier was his friend. He got out of his car and headed down the street. To get to the Barones' front door, he'd have to pass an unlocked wrought iron gate and a small, sparsely landscaped courtyard. That's a break, he thought. Only one lock to pick and it's set back from the street. Harder for anyone to see me working. Tony knelt to tie his shoe so he could survey the scene. It was clear. He swung the gate open and stepped quickly to the front door. He knocked twice. If someone was inside, he wanted to know. After a couple of seconds, he knocked again. Still no response. Tony reached into his pocket and pulled out a cloth pouch tied around the middle. He untied the pouch and unrolled it. Inside was a ring of metal probes and tiny hooks. If anyone was watching him, well, that was a chance he had to take. As he worked he listened, but he heard nothing. Exactly two minutes and fifteen seconds later, Tony was standing inside Mrs. Barone's living room.

He closed the door behind him but couldn't lock it without the key. There were two couches in the room. Tony decided to search the bigger one first. It was the one Ironman probably would have used. He examined the cushions and felt along their edges. Nothing. Then he pulled them up and looked underneath. Still nothing. *Its not here. Must be the other one.* He sprung across the room to the second couch and was halfway through his search of it when the front door swung open.

Celia Barone entered and looked right at Tony. She had been dabbing a tissue against her eyes, which were red and wet. "Who are you? How did you get in?"

Tony looked at her and then behind her. She was alone. "I'm Andre Stephens. I'm here for my friend Frank. You remember. I was with him when you met. He left his wallet last night and asked me to come for it. No one was home but your door was unlocked," he lied, "so I let myself in."

Mrs. Barone pressed the tissue to her nose and appeared to be thinking it over.

"Are you crying? I'm sorry. I didn't mean to scare you."

"Yes. I mean no," she sniffled. "It's not you. My husband is so mean. He was supposed to take me with him but we argued. We always argue. So I came home."

"I'm glad you did, because I didn't see the wallet. Can you help me find it?"

She was no longer crying. In fact, her mood seemed to be improving quite dramatically. "As a matter of fact, I already found his wallet." She stepped toward a desk in the corner of the room and pulled out the top drawer. "We're both lucky I found it, not my husband." She held the wallet up. "Is this what you came for?"

'That's it," Tony said. "Thank goodness you found it." He moved to get it, but she stopped him.

"Now wait a second. Can't we talk for a moment? Here, let me fix us a drink." She put the wallet on top of the desk and took Tony by the arm. "My husband keeps a full bar." She squeezed Tony's biceps as she escorted him to the other side of the room.

"No, no thank you, Senora. I think I should just take it and go."

"You know I was happy Frank left it here. A friend like him is hard to find. I knew he'd have to come back for it and I was glad. My husband is never home. I get lonely."

"I understand," Tony said.

"Tell Frank he needs to come again."

"I will, of course." Tony answered.

"Good," she said. "He's lucky to have a friend like you. Let me make you that drink."

Tony smiled. He hadn't expected this. *There are always surprises,* he thought. *And some are better than others.*

"You're a very good-looking boy. What did you say your name was?"

"Andre."

"Ah yes, Andre. Are you different, too? Are you a good man, like Frank?"

Tony held his tongue and watched her fill a shot glass with Pisco, then raise it to her lips. "Want a taste?" She held the glass out and Tony took it. He sipped and handed it back.

"My husband told me I am old and fat. He no longer makes love to me. But I think people need to make love to be happy. I know I do. What about you?"

Tony looked her over. Celia Barone was in her 40's and attractive, and there were still hints of the stunning beauty she must once have been.

"Do you think my husband is right? That I'm old and fat?" She was unbuttoning her blouse. Now her arms were behind her, unfastening the clasp. Then, as Tony watched, she leaned forward. Her bra fell away and her breasts came free. They were beautiful, shapely and full. She lifted her hands up to cup them. Tony's eyes were drawn to the perfect nipples, which were dark brown and erect.

"You're a beautiful woman, senora. Your husband is a fool to neglect you. But I came only for my friend's wallet." Tony glanced back toward the door. Would Mr. Barone be the next person to enter?

"I understand," she said. "But things happen for a reason, don't you agree? Your friend was lucky to have your help and maybe now you'll be lucky, too. Why not take advantage of your good fortune?" Her skirt was already on the floor. She stepped out of her panties, which had magically fallen from her hips. She was now fully naked, standing proudly before a man she expected would soon be her lover. Tony reviewed his options. There was an attractive woman standing naked before him, and she was, to use Frazier's terms, making it easy. But he felt no desire.

"You are very beautiful, Mrs. Barone."

"Thank you, Andre. And please call me Celia. Don't you like what you see?"

"Yes, yes I do. Very much. If circumstances were different . . ."

"If circumstances were different, what?"

"If circumstances were different, I would welcome the chance to be your lover. But right now, I am only here for the wallet."

"If my husband found it, one of us might be dead by now." She pointed her finger and fired a round, then blew the smoke away. "He's crazy. But what about us? What about now?" She glanced downwards. "I can see that part of you wants to stay very badly. To collect your reward." She crawled onto the couch and was soon kneeling, looking back at him over her shoulder. Her eyes were sparkling and her lips pursed. When she was sure he was looking, she shifted her hips and moved her knees apart in an unabashed display.

Tony stared and took a mental photograph. Then he reached across to the desk, snatched the wallet and left. When he got back into his car, he threw it onto the seat next to him. Then he reached into his crotch and pulled out the thick pouch of lock-picking tools. *No Mrs. Barone, it's not that I'm happy to see you. I'm just here to pick your lock.*

That night, when Tony brought Ironman his wallet, he expected a hearty thank you. And at first, Ironman was very grateful. "Oh, man. I knew you could do it. What did you say to her? How did it go?"

Tony told Frazier the whole story, including Mrs. Barone's impressive show. Which is when Ironman went from grateful to jealous. "What kind of a friend are you?" he snapped. "How could you act like that with a friend's girl?"

"You're kidding right?" Tony shot back. "I didn't get it on with her. I told you, all I did was look. And besides, when did she become your fiancée? What would it have meant to you if I had taken her up on her offer? You've known her, what, five minutes?"

"That's not the point," Ironman protested. "You shouldn't have let her do that. It violates the code."

"You can't be serious. What an idiot! Next time you leave your shit somewhere, find someone else to go in and fetch it for you. A blind guy, maybe. Somebody who won't even look. And while you're at it, you can screw yourself and your stupid code."

Frazier looked up. He had examined his wallet. "It's all in there. She didn't take a thing."

Tony harrumphed.

"Ah, shit. You're right. I'm sorry. You saved my butt. Thank you. I am an idiot."

"I think you need a new name. You're not Ironman anymore. From now on, you're Idiot Man."

"I'm really sorry, Tony. Really. I appreciate what you did. And to be honest, you *should* have nailed her. I'm pretty sure I would have. I don't know what I was thinking. Hell, I'll make it up to you. Next time I see her, I'll ask her about a threesome."

Tony shook his head. "If it's all the same to you, I'll settle for a beer."

"That's my short buddy," said Frazier, and he handed Tony a cold one.

# CHAPTER 29

The next day, when Tony arrived at the office, Mr. D'Onofrio was waiting. "Congratulations. The new bug in Allende's phone is working nicely. You did well at the palace."

*More than you know*, Tony wryly observed to himself.

"You've handled your assignments admirably," D'Onofrio said. "I'm impressed."

"Thank you, sir," Tony said.

"You're beginning to resemble an operative. Not quite fully-fledged. At least not yet, anyway. But you're definitely making progress."

"Well thanks, chief. That means a lot, coming from you. So when do I get my secret decoder ring?"

D'Onofrio gave him a look. "That's funny. But don't get too loose. You're working again tonight."

Tony's confidence was at an all time high and he was ready for his next adventure. But he wanted to project maturity. "Good," was all he said.

"What do you know about the casino?" D'Onofrio asked.

There was only one in Chile and Tony knew all about it. It was located in Vina del Mar—a small town on the scenic Pacific coast, a hundred kilometers or so to the northwest of Santiago. The government had built it there to escape the disapproving view of church leaders in the capital. Chile was a predominantly Catholic country, but even a socialist government needed money, and nothing produced cash more effectively than the slot machines and roulette and blackjack tables of the Casino Vina del Mar. Unlike the factories, farms and ranches, which struggled to generate revenue, the casino was wildly productive right from the start. Open 24 hours a day, every day, it featured 1,500 slots and ninety gaming tables. There were three different restaurants on the property, several bars and a hotel. Foreign tourists and well-dressed Chilenos mingled with one thing in common—the way pesos flowed out of their pockets and into the house's cash boxes. The numbers surprised even the casino's operators.

But Tony said only, "I've heard of it." He had been taught to understate his knowledge. One of his instructors at Camp Peary had a plaque on his office wall. It said, "Silence is the only adequate substitute for brains."

D'Onofrio revealed that tonight, Tony's assignment would be to start a fight with a Cuban blowhard named Paco Sanchez, who hung out at the El Rincon nightclub in the Huerfanos district of downtown Santiago. Tony was familiar with them all, the district, the nightclub and the blowhard. The club was owned by a close associate of the Finance Minister himself, which meant that if he called the police, he would likely receive a grand show of support and as many security personnel as they could muster. The tussle had to be dramatic enough to catch the attention of the club's manager, and it needed to last long enough to make sure he called the police. Pushing and shoving until a few tables got turned over and a few bottles broken. Nothing more serious than that. Customers would leave, business would be lost, the manager would get upset, and the police would arrive en masse.

Tony wondered what would happen if he got arrested. "Not to worry," D'Onofrio assured him. "There'll be a guy there to watch your back and get you out before anything like that happens. His name is Eli. And he's as good as there is."

Tony sensed the evening's agenda was bigger than D'Onofrio was suggesting. He had no right to ask, but he craved more detail. No field officer in a clandestine operation is supposed to receive more information than he needs to carry out his particular assignment. That was basic compartmentation theory. But then again, all of the Company's officers had been carefully screened for loyalty and reliability before being hired. They were clever, resourceful, and capable. Such men have confidence in themselves and believe the more they know, the better off they'll be. D'Onofrio had been out there himself and as a result, tended to give his boys as much as he could before sending them on anything dangerous. It might be against the book, but D'Onofrio believed his officers were entitled to information that might help them stay safe, and he took for granted that what he told them would go no further. By the time they got to him, they had been drilled, more times than any of them could count, on the importance of protecting information.

Tony could tell D'Onofrio had read the expression on his face because he continued talking. "Casino Vina del Mar is grossing more than $1 million dollars a month. Not exactly Vegas, but huge by third world standards. And it may be the last government operation that people here still admire. An open and flagrant robbery by an anti-Allende group will rock the people's confidence, which will further dampen their loyalty. Loyalty is a commodity. Smart people know that by backing the winner, they could be set for life. Money, power, anything they want. But if they stick with the loser for too long, they could get swept down the drain right alongside him."

Tony nodded. On his first day, he had read about Kissinger's notion that the people had been fooled into electing a Marxist and would come around gratefully, as soon as they recognized their mistake.

"General Gonzalez is in charge of security and responsible for protecting the cash flow," D'Onofrio continued. "Robbing the casino is such a crazy idea that it would never occur to him and his security police that anyone might try it. And, I can add, I don't think he fully appreciates our imagination. Over the last few weeks, night clubs and restaurants around the city have been targeted for disturbances. Fights and brawls. These incidents became a problem for business owners, who demanded that the government provide more security. As a result, General Gonzalez began re-assigning some of his security police to night spots downtown. Which took them away from their positions on the coast, guarding the casino. Tonight you'll do your part and soon something quite surprising to General Gonzalez will happen. And I know you won't let us down."

"No sir, I won't," Tony said. He knew he was feeling just what D'Onofrio wanted him to feel—patriotism and pride.

"Sometime after ten, Henderson will pick you up and drive you to the Rincon Club where you'll find that Cuban. You won't have trouble picking him out. He'll be the loudest mouth at the bar. Just Hang around until 1:00 AM. Then provoke him. Make it last a while."

D'Onofrio reviewed Sanchez's file with Tony. The man wasn't particularly admirable when he was sober, but he was downright insufferable when he drank. And he loved to drink. More than once, the whole bar had heard him boast about the important people he knew and how much influence he had back in Havana. He claimed he had been sent by Fidel himself to assist Allende, a brother revolutionary. Another favorite subject of his was women. There was a rumor, probably started by Sanchez himself, that he had his way with one of Allende's nieces. It had so irritated the President that he forbade any of his ministers from accepting Sanchez' assistance. And Sanchez had the nerve to boast that his triumph over Allende's niece had been worth his disqualification from some lofty advisory position in the government. That was Allende's loss, as far as Sanchez was concerned.

Sanchez was a big, mean man and people feared him. But Tony wasn't convinced. No doubt he would be just like any other bully—full of bluster until confronted and challenged. Then he'd turn tail and retreat, like bullies do. And it wouldn't be the first time Tony tussled in a bar. He wondered if D'Onofrio knew about the night in O'Brien's when he had taken on big Tim Downing. Probably. He seemed to know about everything. Well, almost everything. Tony was pretty sure he didn't know about Cristina—at least not yet.

"Now go home and get some rest. I need you to be sharp." D'Onofrio ordered. So after his lunch of empanadas con queso and dessert of dulce de leche, Tony left the café and returned to his apartment for a nap.

# CHAPTER 30

El Rincon was a late-night club in the Huerfanos, or orphans, district, a section of town that was home to factories and warehouses during the day and bars and nightclubs at night. El Rincon didn't even open until eight and didn't get busy until midnight. It was dark inside and smoky. There were about twenty tables, served by a couple of friendly and efficient waitresses, and a long bar in the back that was always crowded. The music was good. Sweet love songs and rhythmic dance numbers. It was on the list of bars Tony frequented, keeping his eyes and ears open around the VIPS—politicians, players in Allende's government, high ranking-soldiers and influential businessmen.

When Tony entered the Rincon Club, he saw Paco Sanchez at the bar, then looked around to see who else was there. He was especially interested in faces he didn't recognize. Was anyone likely to defend Sanchez once a fight broke out? Tony needed to consider and account for anyone else that might warrant attention when things got started. And where was the mysterious Eli, the man that had been sent to back him up? He saw the usual faces. Men who were fixtures at the bar. Only one that struck Tony as out of place—a blond man, with a tan, corduroy sport jacket. He looked directly at Tony and raised his glass. Eli.

One of the waitresses, Isabela, came over and greeted him warmly. Her smile was an invitation, no doubt, but she wasn't on Tony's agenda for the night. She was several pounds overweight, and a few years beyond her prime. But she smelled clean and sweet and had beautiful teeth and a great smile. One particular night he had stayed later than he intended and drank more than he needed to. Isabela had taken him home and made him strong coffee. Then she snuggled him to her ample bosom and called him her borachito, her little drunk. And then she reminded him what his manhood was for. A couple of times. It had been fun. As much as Tony had had in Chile. Since then, Isabela was his favorite waitress, and El Club Rincon was his favorite bar.

Tony ordered a tequila and told Isabela he wasn't going to be able to stay long, that he just wanted to stop by to say hello and maybe leave her a big tip. She laughed and told him it was too bad. She had no plans for the morning and could sleep late. Then she smiled again. When he said nothing, she pouted for a moment then sauntered off to get him his drink. Tony watched her hips sway and wished he could take her up on her offer.

He had one drink and nursed it for a long while before ordering another. As Isabela left after serving him the second one, she lifted her tray above her head to squeeze past him, and her breasts pressed momentarily against his back. Tony reached down and tried to touch her leg. But she was not willing to let him show such open familiarity in the club and moved away quickly. What happened after she left work was between her and Tony and no one else's business. Tony liked that about her. She had been wild and lusty in bed, but she was still very much the lady and insisted on being treated like one. He regretted this night was going to end in a fight because customers would leave without paying and Isabela would surely lose money. But more than that, she looked good. He would have enjoyed ending the night in her arms, but that wasn't going to happen.

Tony glanced at Paco Sanchez, who was standing at the bar, telling a story to everyone and no one. It was twelve-thirty, almost time to get the show started. Tony stood up, took his drink in his hand and wove through the crowd over to the bar, where he took a spot near to Sanchez. After a few minutes listening to him tell another offensive story, Tony moved closer. When Sanchez paused to take a breath, Tony told him he was the most entertaining thing in El Rincon, that they should change the name of the place to Paco's. Sanchez let out a laugh which quickly became a deep throaty cough. He's half in the bag already, Tony surmised. This is going to be easier than I thought.

After another few minutes, Tony again checked the time. One o'clock. He ordered another drink for himself and one for Sanchez who wasn't nearly finished with his current one. "What are you trying to do, get me drunk?" asked Sanchez, laughing like he had just told the joke of the year. Nonetheless, he gulped down what remained in his glass and promptly reached for the new one.

"How's it going for you, Paco?" Tony asked, with the sincerest tone he could produce. "You doing all right?"

"Paco Sanchez always does all right," the big man answered. "Why? You want to sell me a new telephone, Senor Chiltelco?" Again, Sanchez followed his statement with a deep, exaggerated laugh.

"No, no," Tony answered. "I was just trying to be friendly." Then he changed the tone of his voice. "Besides, I didn't know that stinking dogs like you even knew how to use a telephone."

For a second, Sanchez had difficulty grasping what he had just heard. The people standing around them were looking at him, like spectators at a sporting event. "You trying to commit suicide, gringo?" he stammered.

"Maybe," Tony smirked. "After all, I am inhaling while I stand next to you."

Sanchez's mind, foggy from alcohol, was still struggling to comprehend what was happening. Also missing was a good way to end what had become a very awkward moment. So he did what he always did when he felt uncomfortable. He laughed. Tentatively at first, but then he graduated to a full, roaring bellow.

"You are funny, gringo," he stammered as his laughing again turned to coughing. "Now go back to your table before I put you over my knee and spank you like a child."

Sanchez looked around and saw that he had scored. People were laughing with him. But Tony was still standing there, his eyes fixed on the man's face, and Tony was not laughing. Sanchez grew silent and so did everyone else at the bar. The big man, bleary eyed, blinked slowly. Then he began turning back toward the bar, and away from Tony, but as he did he reached out a clumsy left hand toward Tony's chest. "Go ahead phone man. Go sit down. You can apologize to me later for trying to be funny."

But Tony stood still and kept his eyes on Sanchez. He wasn't going anywhere. Not until this debate graduated into a brawl. He slapped the bigger man's hand away and told him to eat shit. Then he waited. He knew that a line had been crossed and Sanchez would have to respond and he was right. Sanchez lunged, quite quickly considering his size and the amount of alcohol in him. But Tony had been trained. And he was ready. He moved to the side, like a toreador in the bull ring, and thumped Sanchez square on the back of the neck. Hard, just like Captain Melamud had taught him. But Sanchez didn't go down. He just stumbled forward for a couple of steps and then righted himself. Tony was surprised, and not in a good way. He had made solid contact that would have sent most men sprawling. But there Sanchez stood, turning to face Tony, rubbing his neck and smiling the evil leering smile of the devil. Tony expected he would charge again and adjusted his feet. He wanted to keep his balance so he could deliver the next blow with even more leverage. But Sanchez didn't charge. He just kept smiling. Then he reached inside his jacket. Tony thought, oh, shit. What's he doing now? He hesitated, his muscles in a knot. Don't panic, he told himself. But he didn't know what to do. Should he rush Sanchez, or stand still, or head for the exit? Before he could make up his mind, he saw the flash of lightning and heard the thunder.

The next thing Tony knew, Eli was calling to him from the back door, just a few feet away, but Tony wasn't comprehending the words. He was too stunned by what had just happened. It wasn't at all like the movies, when a fellow takes a .45 slug at point blank range, clutches his belly and keeps walking forward. Paco Sanchez had been lifted completely off the floor and hurled backwards by the shot from Eli's gun. It sounded like a bomb. Sanchez came to rest on the floor, lying flat on his back, with a dime-size reddish black spot in his chest getting bigger by the second.

Eli stepped in close, pointed his pistol down at Sanchez and fired again. This time Sanchez' face exploded, with bits of what had been his forehead splattering across everyone and everything in the vicinity. What was left of Sanchez' head bounced once from the impact and then he was still. The ringing thunderclaps of the shots were echoing in the air. Tony couldn't believe what he had just seen. He stood, eyes wide and mouth open, feeling disconnected from reality, looking at what used to be Paco Sanchez. Eli stooped over Sanchez and slipped his free hand into the jacket to find whatever Sanchez had been reaching for. It was a Smith & Wesson six shot revolver. Sanchez had been armed and had been about to pull the gun on him. Tony gagged at the realization. He felt light headed and dizzy. He watched Eli slip Sanchez' revolver into his pocket, then turn toward Tony. "Okay, time to go. Come with me," Eli said forcefully, but calmly.

Then Eli moved backwards, sweeping the room with his pistol, looking for anyone who might pose a threat. But no one was moving. Paco Sanchez had been alone. Or at least no one was showing any interest in joining his fight. By the time Eli had reached the back door, Tony still hadn't moved. Eli came back for him, gripped his upper arm and pulled him toward the door. "Its time to go now. This way," he said. Tony looked around and saw only disbelief on the faces. He thought, I guess I won't be coming back here anytime soon. He had an urge to call out to Isabela but thought better of it. His legs came under control and he quickly followed Eli out the door.

A Mini Cooper was parked in the alley behind the club. "Get in," said Eli and Tony did as he was told. Before he could catch his breath, Eli had started the ignition, put it in gear and gunned the engine. The car bolted forward and just like that, they were gone.

After several blocks Eli offered Tony his pistol and Sanchez's, and said, "We're coming to the Tortuga bridge. When we get to the top, toss these as far into the river as you can. All right?"

Tony didn't answer. He stared straight ahead, deep in uncomfortable thought.

"Hey, Stephens," Eli said. "You there?"

Tony blinked and looked at Eli. He stared at the guns, but said nothing.

"Listen to me, I need you to get a grip. Can you hear me?"

"Okay," was all Tony could muster. He was fighting his nausea.

"Toss these guns in the river when we get to the top of the bridge. You with me?"

"Why'd you kill him?" Tony asked. He never expected to see such an awful thing and his stomach was struggling with the images.

"What are you, writing a book?" Eli asked. "I did exactly what I needed to do. In case you missed it, you were in over your head back there. So I went to plan B before it was you who ended up bleeding on that floor. And while I was at it, I did a favor for a friend who will be happy that asshole's dead. Hell, I might have just earned myself a big bonus. As far as I'm concerned, it went very well." He shook his head. "So what's the matter with you? You feeling upset?

Wanna cry? Wanna call your mama? Or you gonna' try and act like a grown-up officer and stop your whining?"

The man's belligerence caught Tony off guard. He was embarrassed, but it stabilized him. "No, no, I'll be all right. It's just that everything happened so fast. I didn't expect him to have a gun. I guess I should have. And I wasn't expecting you to blow his face off. Shit . . ." Tony was stuttering. "I never saw anything like that . . ." As he pictured it, he did feel like crying. But he braced himself and took a deep breath.

"Sorry," Eli said. "Next time I'll ask everybody to play nice so they don't upset the new guy. But for now, we need to handle it."

"I'll be fine," Tony said.

"Okay, good," Eli responded, just a bit softer. "We get some surprises out here. You gotta deal with 'em. Which is why these ops are best done by guys with military backgrounds. Guys who've been through some shit. Who've seen things. Not some college boy whose main qualification is he speaks Spanish."

Tony knew it was true. His background couldn't have prepared him for what had just happened. But he didn't like being told he was inadequate and he was determined to step up. He summoned his resolve and put it into the look he was giving Eli. "I told you, I'm fine."

"All right, then," Eli said. "Take the damn guns and throw 'em when I tell you, okay?"

"Yeah," replied Tony, although he still felt weak and queasy and not exactly sure of anything. He took another deep breath and reached for the guns. "Shame to just throw 'em away, though," he said, trying to act nonchalant, like he'd seen people's heads blown off before and was quite used to it. "Why waste 'em?"

Eli looked at him sideways, and with no small amount of contempt. "Just do it. Okay?"

"Just curious why you want to throw away a couple of perfectly good guns. You sure seemed comfortable with yours."

"Listen, rookie. Half the security forces in Chile are on their way to El Rincon right now. And the other half will be swarming all around the city. Soldiers. Police. Right wing paramilitary. Left wing paramilitary. Chances are we may get stopped. Some of them won't have a problem with what I just did. Others will. If they do, you want to have to explain the smoking pistol in my pocket?"

"No sir. I'm sorry, sir," Tony stammered, embarrassed. "I guess I didn't think—"

"Yeah, I guess you didn't," Eli interrupted. "So from here on out, leave the thinking to me. Do as I say and maybe we don't get ourselves killed tonight. Is that all right with you?"

Tony said nothing, but there was a new feeling bubbling in his gut. He didn't care who this guy Eli was—he didn't like being talked to like that. His father would surely want him to fight back. But Eli was not a man to be trifled with. That much had been made quite clear. And he was right. Guns could be replaced. So Tony bit his lip and waited for his steam to cool.

They rode on in silence for another ten minutes. Tony's mind raced. Something about Eli seemed familiar. But if he had seen him before, surely he would have remembered. Maybe it was his voice, or the way he spoke. Tony couldn't place it, but it nagged at him. Who is this guy? And then there was the bigger question. What the hell had he gotten himself into? Tony had expected adventure and excitement working for the CIA, but not cold-blooded murder.

It was nearly 3:00 AM when they passed through the arches marking the entrance to Tony's neighborhood. Just a few blocks to go and he would be home. Eli would drop him off and go on his way. Tony hoped he would never see the man again. They had just turned from Campesino Road onto Montana Boulevard when a black sedan sped past them on the left and then cut sharply in front of them, screeching to a halt. Men in military uniforms poured out of all four doors, fully automatic weapons pointed at the Mini Cooper. Eli spat one word, "mierda" and pulled to the curb.

The men shouted for Eli and Tony to get out of the car but didn't wait for them to obey. Tony was pulled and thrown. Before he could even think of resisting, he was lying face down on the sidewalk with his hands tied behind his back. He turned his head, looking for Eli. He was on his knees, hands behind his back, yelling something about General Fox for the second or two it took for the soldier to deliver a rifle butt to his temple. Eli fell, silent and unconscious. If he did have a plan, he wasn't going to be sharing it with anyone soon.

# CHAPTER 31

Tony woke with a blazing pain in the back of his head. He wanted to reach up and touch it to find out why it hurt so bad. But he couldn't because his arms wouldn't move. He thought his eyes were open, but he wasn't sure. It was pitch-black, so dark he couldn't tell. He made himself blink, slowly, one eye at a time. At least his eyelids felt like they were working, but he still saw nothing. Other than that, he was numb. Then, when his senses started to come back to him slowly, very slowly, he began to take stock. The discomfort in the back of his head seemed to be worsening. He noticed he was sweating profusely, just dripping, yet the room was cool. His shoulders began to register, and they hurt. When he struggled again to bring his arms forward, he couldn't because they were tied behind him. He felt some nausea, just a little, but that too was quickly getting worse. And then he realized he was sitting in a chair. Actually, he was tied to it, with restraints around his wrists keeping his arms angled awkwardly behind his back. The room was quiet and so damn dark. He tasted blood in his mouth. His flight response kicked in, and his brain sent out its most urgent messages. Adrenaline was being dumped by the gallon into his to bloodstream, which was pumping it to the muscles in his legs and his arms. His body wanted to explode and burst free, but nothing was moving; and in that exquisitely terrifying moment, Tony felt desperate fear.

A door opened, letting in some light as two men entered. Then it closed. "Hijo de puta, Americano," someone snarled. Tony's body spasmed, his arms and legs pulling desperately, but the restraints didn't budge. He had to get hold of himself. He'd received some training at Camp Peary in surviving capture and escape. The idea, his instructors had repeatedly urged, was to accept the inevitability of death. Everyone dies. Be at peace with it, like a Viking entering battle while announcing, "Today's a good day to die." One instructor called it Zen Buddhism for warriors. Pain will end the moment it occurs, and then there will be only peace. In the meanwhile, be alert. Your captors might make a mistake. And stay calm. A calm man can think. A thinking man can survive.

So Tony swallowed hard and tried to clear his head.

"Hijo de puta, Americano." This time a different voice. Another person in the same room. But the hissing sound the words made was just about the same. They were cursing him, and they knew he was an American. Or at least they were accusing him.

"No, no," Tony protested. "I am Canadian. Canadian. My name is Andre Stephens." Tony's words came out in a hoarse whisper. It hurt to talk. He struggled to remember his training. Stick with your cover, his instructor was saying somewhere inside his clanging head. "I'm a technician for Chiltelco. I fix telephones. What the hell is going on? This hurts. Can someone please untie me?"

"Shut up, you son of a bitch. We know who the hell you are. You're working for the goddamned MIRistas that robbed the Casino Vina del Mar tonight. And we're going to make sure the general gets his money back. And you're going to help us, communist. Or you will surely die where you sit."

Tony strained again against his restraints and struggled to contain the panic. The words were too real, too strong to ignore. He felt the nausea rising. He tried to control it. He didn't want to vomit. He closed his eyes and searched his mind for an image, something to focus on, something to distract him, to keep his churning gut from erupting. *I must not panic. I will not panic.* And then the image came in, faint at first, but quickly gaining focus. Cristina de la Vega was leading him up the wooden staircase at the rear of the palace. There she stood before him, pouring his coffee. And then, quickly, she was in his arms. He focused on those memories for all he was worth. The fragrant aroma of the coffee. The intoxicating scent of her neck. His mind fled the darkness and the chair and the tight knots binding his wrists, the pain. And the smell of his fear. But a rustling sound coming from his left interrupted the reverie. He heard groans, and the reality of his situation came blasting back like a gust of frigid wind. Another deep groan. He couldn't be sure, but it sounded like Eli.

"Glad you decided to join us," said the voice in charge. "Let's have a look at our sleeping beauty."

A light came on in the corner. Tony winced as its brightness exploded in his eyes. It was a spotlight, and it passed across his face for just a second. Then it was aimed at the figure to his left, which was Eli. He was also tied to a chair, still moaning as he regained consciousness.

"Help him wake up," the voice said. The order was followed closely by the sound of a bucket full of water being flung in Eli's face. He coughed and sputtered and lifted his head.

"Did you have a nice nap, comrade amigo?"

"You're making a big mistake, asshole," Eli said. *The man has nerve*, Tony thought. He expected his colleague's belligerence to bring a swift reprisal. And in fact, the sounds of footsteps signaled the approach of a soldier, no doubt to be followed by the sound of another punishing blow. But before that happened, Eli said forcefully, "You better call General Fox before you make it worse on yourselves."

"Wait," the voice said, and the footsteps stopped. "Okay, hombre, you got my attention. What exactly do you want me to tell the general?"

"Tell him that the honor of his niece has been avenged. Once you do, he's going to tell you to come back here and untie my friend and me and apologize to us and hope we don't hold a grudge. And you better hurry your ass up, too, if you know what's good for you. While I might still be willing to forgive you. And in the meanwhile, I'll thank you to shut off that damned spotlight."

Tony didn't know what Eli was talking about, but the man's tone was so damned confident he started to feel some hope. And again he had the disturbing feeling that he knew him from somewhere. The man in charge told his associate to shut the spotlight, and the room went dark. Tony had not been able to see the men in the room but could sense the uncertainty Eli's words had created in them. Finally, the voice announced that he was going "inside." The door opened, letting in another flash of light as the man stepped through it. Then it closed, and all was dark again.

Less than ten minutes later, the man returned. This time he left the door open. "Untie them," he barked. Then to Eli and Tony, he said, "You are free to go."

It was not quite six in the morning when Tony got in the car with Mike Henderson. "I'll take you home," Henderson said.

"If it's all the same to you, Mike," Tony said, "I'd like to go see Mr. D'Onofrio." He was exhausted but felt too wired to sleep, and wanted to report everything that had just happened while it was still fresh in his mind. And then there were the questions that he wanted answered. What had just happened? And why? And others about right and wrong that went to the center of the debate he was having with himself. Are we really the good guys or are we something else?

When he got to the office, Mr. D'Onofrio brought him right in and offered him a cup of coffee. Tony declined. He just wanted to talk. "Thanks for seeing me, chief."

"My door's always open, Andre."

"Thanks," Tony said. He wasn't fully composed and didn't know where to begin.

"So, what's up?" D'Onofrio asked, as if he hadn't a clue. "I heard you had a little excitement last night."

"You could say that," Tony answered. He tried to smile, but his face wouldn't cooperate. "First, that Cuban guy pulled a gun on me. Then I see him lying on the floor, getting his head blown off. Next I find myself tied to a chair surrounded by guys telling me I'm about to die because I robbed their casino. And then they're wishing me all the best and brushing my shoulders off like a bunch of old tailors admiring the fit of my suit. And I didn't have a score card and I still don't know who's on first. Forgive me, sir, and maybe I'm just overwhelmed, but something doesn't feel right."

"Just another day at the office, really," D'Onofrio chuckled. But he saw that Tony wasn't amused, so he went on. "When Gonzalez heard there was gun play going on at El Rincon, he took the bait in a big way. Sent a small army there, including most of his casino security. So we jumped on it. And as far as Gonzalez is concerned, the MIRistas robbed the casino at Vina del Mar last night and got away with a pile of cash. Not the first time for those boys. They're known for radical fund raising techniques, the dirty thieves. No doubt they'll put the money to good use terrorizing Allende. But that's his problem. To us, what matters is that you did what you were supposed to do at El Rincon. You contributed. And you were lucky enough to get through it in one piece. So all's well that ends well. Right, old sport?"

"I guess so, sir. But can't you give me a little more? Like, who the hell is Eli and when did last night's plan change to an assassination?"

"That's easy. Eli is one of us. And the short answer is the plan was the plan. If anything, it went better than we expected. The leftists are blaming the right wingers and the right wingers are blaming the leftists and everybody is calling Allende pathetic because he couldn't protect the casino. The bottom line is more paranoia across the board.

Pretty soon they'll change their name to the Popular Disunity party, if I can coin a phrase."

"But cold-blooded murder?" Tony persisted. He was still shaken. "Is that the way we accomplish our goals? I mean, what happened to making campaign contributions and letting the locals do the dirty work?" D'Onofrio just looked at him.

Tony continued, "I had reservations about passing out dynamite. But last night I watched a guy lying helpless on the floor get his head blown off. Maybe I missed the lectures about that in my political science classes. Does that really need to be part of our foreign policy?"

"Calm down, Andre," D'Onofrio said. "Last night had to be a shock. I know."

"You think?" Tony said. "Sure as hell went beyond anything I ever anticipated. I still have bits of Sanchez' brain on me." He paused briefly. "And I didn't enjoy being captured and tied up and threatened by angry soldiers with guns." Tony had worked himself up and was almost out of breath. He realized he had been shouting at his station chief. He inhaled deeply and exhaled. When he continued, it was with a more respectful tone. "I don't consider myself a pansy, Mr. D'Onofrio, but I was scared out of my mind last night."

"I understand, Andre. It's a lot to handle so early in a career. If you want a couple of days off, I can arrange it. Send you to Valparaiso or something. Or maybe I need to get you to a counselor. Nothing to be ashamed of. A year ago, you were chasing co-eds on campus and now you're here watching people die. I can arrange for a shrink to come talk with you. Is that what you want?"

Tony was still gathering himself and trying to be calm. "No, chief, I'll be all right. But it would help to know why Eli shot the guy."

"You know the rules. You just don't have a legitimate need to know."

"Was it because he was Cuban?" Tony asked.

"No," said D'Onofrio. "I mean we all hate Fidel, but we don't shoot Cubans just because of that. At least not yet."

"So why then?" Tony asked. "I have no problem using lethal force in self-defense. And I was sure as shit glad that Eli cut Sanchez down before he could use his gun on me. And, by the way, no one said anything about Sanchez having a gun. Was I supposed to expect that? Because I didn't. Maybe somebody should have said something to me beforehand. What about that, chief? Just a little miscalculation? A little oversight that could have gotten me killed?"

"Not true, Tony," D'Onofrio answered curtly. "You weren't in any danger from that weapon. Unless he clubbed you over the head with it."

Tony just looked at him, waiting.

"Sanchez had just gotten that gun back from a local gunsmith he paid to nickel plate it for him. The gunsmith was a friend of ours. That dumb Cuban had no chance to test it before he got to El Rincon for his little tango with you. He had no idea it was loaded with blanks. Which, by the way, is the real reason Eli took it from him and had you toss it in the river. So even if Sanchez got to pull the trigger, which Eli was never going to let happen, nothing would have come out but a loud bang. Only real danger was that you would crap your pants. But you didn't, did you?" D'Onofrio smiled, craning his neck as if to see the back of Tony's pants, but Tony wasn't ready for humor.

"No, sir."

"I am sorry, Andre," D'Onofrio said. "Your mission was supposed to be simple. Get in a bar brawl with a loudmouth. If I'm not mistaken, you've had some experience along those lines. Wrestle around, break a few tables and get the hell out. But someone important had a special beef with Sanchez and that put him on the agenda. Just a little cooperation between allies."

"So you knew all along that he was going to end up, well, . . . like he ended up," Tony mused. "Sanchez wasn't really my target. Any bozo would have been fine for our purposes. He was Eli's target."

"Now you're with me, Andre," D'Onofrio said. "Let's just say Sanchez was picked as your target for a reason. The fact that he got shot after he pulled a gun in a fight, in full view of a bar full of people, all of 'em independent witnesses, well that was just good setup work, actually, eliminating the mystery, as far as anyone might be concerned, about why he died. Asshole was drunk, got in a fight, pulled a gun, got the short end of it. Happens all the time. No reason for anyone to suspect a thing. And as a bonus, a call goes out that there's been a shooting, which sucks the security away from the casino. Damned fine work, if you ask me."

"But why did those soldiers arrest us, threaten to kill us, and then just let us go? Or is that something else I don't need to know?"

"That part wasn't planned. But things happen in the field. The army blamed the robbery on the communists. They've robbed a few banks before. So they grabbed anyone they could find still on the road at that hour and you were in the wrong place at the wrong time. Trust me. We had no idea you'd get picked up. Or that Eli wouldn't have a chance to talk his way out of it before it got as far as it did. But you're okay now and that's what matters, isn't it?"

Tony shook his head slowly back and forth. "So Eli was there to shoot Paco Sanchez no matter what. It was a calculated hit, you just admitted it. Like a gangster on The Untouchables. I'm surprised Elliott Ness didn't walk in afterwards and give a speech about a bad guy getting what he deserved. But aren't we supposed to be the good guys, the Americans, the ones with the moral high ground? Can't we accomplish what we want without killing people?"

"Look, Andre. As much as I would like to debate philosophy with you, we have gotten ahead of ourselves here. We just wanted a ruckus to draw security away from the casino while the MIRistas, or whoever it was, did their thing. The idea to kill Sanchez came from someone else and it had nothing to do with politics. From what I've heard, Sanchez died because he was a piece of shit maggot who beat up women. He's been doing it from the first day he set foot here in Chile and probably before that. Only difference was he finally got around to hurting someone with connections."

The words struck Tony hard and sent a chill down his spine. He added the things that Cristina had told him about Maria to the things Eli had said to the soldiers, and just like two plus two, they were making four. Maria was General Fox' niece. She hadn't taken Frazier's calls because she had been attacked by a creep. And Eli had told the soldiers to tell General Fox that the honor of his niece had been avenged. Now Tony could fill out his own scorecard. Sanchez must have been the creep that raped Maria. He had finally pissed off somebody able to do something about it. General Fox. Suddenly Tony realized why Eli had sounded vaguely familiar to him. Eli was Rubio, the garbled voice on the tape with General Fox. Quite the all purpose problem solver, that Eli. He didn't just trade antique weapons for information, he also provided revenge. *Not a bad bargain, as far as the general was concerned,* Tony thought. And Sanchez had gotten what he deserved.

"Now put it behind you and you'll be all right," D'Onofrio said. "I don't want to lose you. You're green, but you've got potential. You're a smart kid and you've got guts. But if you feel like you're over your head and you can't deal with it, just say the word and I'll send your ass home in a heart beat."

Tony was back on the high school football field. He'd just gotten knocked off his feet and had his bell rung. His coach was asking him straight out, are you man enough to stay in the game? "Screw it, chief," Tony said. "I'll be fine."

"That a boy. Take the rest of the day off. Go home and get some sleep. I bet when you come in tomorrow, you'll be fresh as a daisy."

"You bet, Mr. D'Onofrio. No crap in my pants, sir. Fresh as a daisy."

# CHAPTER 32

Tony hadn't been able to get Cristina out of his mind, even before he and Eli had been captured by Allende's soldiers. And he was all the more anxious to see her once he had been freed. There was such a power in those stolen moments with her, the result, no doubt, of the combination of being unexpected, forbidden and truly dangerous. Her image had transported him during his moments of terror and kept him from falling apart. Now he had to restrain his imagination or his fantasies would surely drive him to distraction. He desperately hoped she hadn't changed her mind about meeting him again. He could not wait to see her.

Wednesday night before their date, Tony had trouble falling asleep. A vague sense of guilt mixed with his excitement. And when he did fall asleep, his dreams were vivid and disturbing. They were full of bad guys, Russians or Germans, from their appearance. They were looking for him with sinister intentions. He had eluded them and was watching them from a distance. Then he was hiding in the bushes alongside a driveway in Carrie Barber's neighborhood. The men were sneaking around the corner of her house, silent and serious. They gestured toward the window on the side where her bedroom was. Tony wanted to shout at them, to confront them, to warn Carrie, to stop them, to protect her. But he couldn't move, and he couldn't get a sound to come out. He was paralyzed and unable to speak as they climbed in her bedroom window. Again he tried to come out from his hiding place and run to her rescue. Again, he could not. His lungs were bursting as he tried to scream, but nothing. The men were entering, and Tony could not stop them. When he awoke, he was sweating and breathing as if he had just run a marathon.

The day passed slowly, and Tony had trouble focusing on anything other than getting himself to the palace and inside the auxiliary kitchen by five thirty. He arrived a few minutes early, taking a seat at one of the tables. He had brought tools and some paperwork to explain his presence, but much to his relief, the place was deserted. Then he smelled her fragrance. Something floral. Very subtle, but unique and unmistakable. There she stood, only a few feet in front of him. "I didn't hear you come in," he said.

"I should not be here. I must be crazy," she said, speaking softly.

"Perhaps it is insanity," Tony replied, "but there's no cure for that, is there?"

She looked taller than he remembered. Her dark brown jacket-style blouse buttoned down the front. The collar was high and made her shoulders look square. Her hair came in waves. Her tan skirt covered her legs to just below the knees. Her high-heeled shoes were black and round at the toe. Tony didn't hide the fact that he was looking her up and down.

"I thought of you when I dressed myself this morning," Christina said in a voice now barely above a whisper. "Do you like?"

"You look spectacular," Tony answered. "More beautiful than ever." His arms wrapped around her, and he pulled her close. They kissed, gently at first and then more forcefully.

"Not here," she said.

Tony heard her but loosened his grip only slightly. "Where, then?" he asked.

She hesitated for a moment, and Tony used it to steal another kiss. Lightning could not match the electricity he felt shooting through his lips into and throughout his body. He was instantly aroused and on fire. He held her tightly, and his pelvis moved against hers. He didn't want to overwhelm and frighten her, but he needn't have worried. She returned his kiss and pressed herself against him. "Do you ordinarily get so excited?" she asked as she moved her hips from side to side, rolling her crotch back and forth against his upright hardness.

Tony dropped his hand into the small of her back to pull her more tightly against him. They stood fixed to one another, their bodies caressing in a slow grind while they kissed. Tony had to stop to take a breath. "There is nothing ordinary about this moment," he said. "And nothing ordinary about you. I haven't been able to think of anything else since the last time we were together."

"That I am here at all," she said, "should show you that I feel the same." Her eyes were moist and deep, reflecting a hint of sadness. "I am already in a relationship and I thought my days of behaving like a schoolgirl were over. I came close to not coming, but here I am."

"I'm so glad," Tony whispered, stroking her cheek with his left hand.

"Please tell me you told no one of this," she said.

"No one," Tony responded. And with that, he moved his lips to hers. They kissed again. Hungrily. Desperately. "I have dreamt of touching you," he said as he reached his hand under her skirt. Cristina felt herself swept up in the excitement. Tony looked into her eyes just as she closed them, and then he closed his. It was too wonderful. He moved his fingers over the silky fabric of her panties and felt her wetness through them. "Wait," she said. "Please wait. We can't do this here. I will take you someplace. A secret place that my father built. But promise you will never tell anyone. Never."

"I promise," Tony replied. He meant it, but then again, he likely would have promised anything.

"Come, let me show you," she said.

She moved to the door and looked out into the hallway. It was empty. She turned back to point at the stepladder leaning against the pantry. "Bring that with you and come quickly." Tony took the ladder and followed Cristina into the hall and down the few feet that separated the dining rooms and kitchen from the Independence Lounge. Just before she opened the door, she turned toward Tony and put her finger up to her lips. Then she opened the door and looked in. The room was empty. She gestured for Tony to enter and pointed to a spot near the corner. "Put it there." As he began to set it up, she closed the door.

Her skirt pulled tight across her buttocks as she climbed the rungs of the ladder. He was staring up at her legs, which looked even longer from that angle, trying to see what she was doing above her, how she gained access to wherever she was taking him. For a second he looked up her skirt and saw her panties. It was intoxicating to watch her then, stretching toward the ceiling.

She deftly pulled a ceiling panel aside and reached into the space above it. A length of cord dropped as Cristina climbed back down the ladder. He tried to kiss her, but she stopped him. "Wait," she said. "Put the ladder back where it was. Hurry."

Tony brought the ladder back into the auxiliary kitchen and returned to the lounge in seconds. By then, Cristina had pulled down an attic ladder. It unfolded on its hinges and extended in two sections of wooden steps, the bottom section reaching the floor. Cristina was at the top. "Quickly," she said, and Tony scampered up behind her. Before he knew it, they were in a dark little room, pulling up the ladder. Cristina reached back through the hatch to slide the ceiling panel into place. Tony realized that from below, no one would know that the attic room existed, much less that two people were in it.

With the hatch closed, the room was completely dark. It smelled musty and dank. Tony heard Christina moving and then the sound of a match being struck. Cristina was lighting a thick white candle. After it took, she placed it on a small wooden stool in the center of the room. In the flickering light, Tony could see a rumpled mattress and a scattering of utensils, pots, cans, newspapers. Rum and tequila bottles.

"This is my father's legacy," Cristina said. "This room. These things. I can't bear to clean them out. He was a master carpenter but he had such a problem with the bottle. Mama found him drunk in the bed of another woman and her heart turned cold. She threw his clothes in the street, and locked him out. He built this hiding place. A place to rest when he was remodeling La Moneda."

Tony did not respond with words. Instead he moved toward her and took her in his arms. He held her tightly and kissed her neck. She shuddered and clutched him.

"I am so grateful to you for sharing this with me," Tony whispered.

"Never tell anyone. Never," she pleaded.

"I promise," Tony answered.

Those were the last words spoken by the pair. Tony undressed her even while she was pulling at his clothes. They rolled across the mattress, naked and on fire. First Tony on top and then Cristina. Tony moved the candle to cast its light across Cristina's body. He drank the images in until he could hold himself back no longer and then he moved into her again. They went through every rhythm that lovers can achieve. Gentle, slow lovemaking, followed by frantic out-of-control thrusting. Tony penetrated deliberately, gradually, a fraction of an inch at a time, letting the ecstasy build. And then he pounded himself into her, pushing her up the bed by their groins. Cristina had never been taken so completely, so perfectly, and she was overwhelmed by her own pleasure. She felt her tears come, and Tony kissed them away, the salt stinging his tongue. And then he used his tongue where the taste was sweet, not salty. He tried to memorize her scent. Then she pushed him back and took him into her mouth, stroking him and moaning along with him. Then she turned away from Tony, and he entered her from behind. Thrusting while he reached around to caress her breasts. And then they turned to join together, face-to-face. Each position sent Cristina to another wave of ecstasy, and she could not keep from crying out. By then, their bodies were coated with sweat, each other's as much as their own, and whenever their mouths met, their lips and tongues fused together like the halves of a ripe fruit. For more than an hour, they consumed each other with a passion that neither had felt before. At the end, when Tony was at the height of his pleasure, Cristina took him into her mouth again. She did not want to leave any evidence and could not risk taking his seed into her womb. But in the attic, there was no place to wash, no way to clean up. So at that critical moment, she kept him there.

# CHAPTER 33

The September morning started with a chill, which was a surprise, because the weather had been warmer all week. But there was a distinct coolness in the city, like the presence of a dark spirit in the air. Tony felt it and pulled the covers up around his shoulders. Officially, today was a holiday, part of Chile's weeklong Independence Day celebration. But plenty of clues suggested something significant was afoot. "Stay home," he had been told, "or at least stay away from downtown." Strikes and rallies and demonstrations occurred frequently throughout the city. Some days the leftists took center stage, and other days right-wingers had the floor. The streets around the palace were known, only half jokingly, as bullhorn alley. It didn't matter which side of the political spectrum a citizen was on. No one was happy. The need to stabilize the country was part of every conversation. Unfortunately, there was very little agreement on what should be done. Not among those that were part of Allende's coalition, and not among those that were opposed to it, either on the right or the left. The military found itself in the middle of an unstable political situation that was rapidly accelerating into frank dysfunction.

The day before, Tony had listened to a riveting conversation between President Allende and his secretary and mistress, Miriam Contreras, widely referred to as La Payita. It was unusual for her voice to be heard on the CIA recordings. The secretarial offices were just down the hall from the president's, and presumably they could always speak in person. But for whatever reason, this time they were on the phone. Tony pictured the president sitting at his desk and La Payita in her office, separated by a few walls. More and more, Allende was meeting personally with his advisors, not calling them. The bugged telephone had turned out to be a disappointment, especially considering how risky it had been to place it. But this one conversation between Allende and his little Payita, someone he clearly trusted, someone to whom he spoke from the heart, was touching.

By now, Allende suspected his government wouldn't survive the burgeoning crisis. And he recognized his own jeopardy. Yet he still believed in and relied on the fundamental patriotism of the military and the loyalty of its officers to the Constitution. He spoke of the early days of his presidency, before the disappointments and betrayals, when the streets of Chile were filled with hope and enthusiasm. In a country where no one now seemed satisfied, those days seemed so far behind them. But it was clear from Allende's comments, uttered softly in the privacy of his office, that he was unwilling to yield to the pressures being exerted on him from friends and foes alike. He was determined to fulfill his constitutional role, in as peaceful and orderly a manner, and for as long as possible, regardless of what it might cost him.

Also clear from the conversation was the genuine respect that existed between the president and his little dove. Her voice was barely above a whisper, and her tone soothing and reassuring. Theirs was a complex relationship, to be sure. Allende was very much the married man and appeared frequently in public with his wife and children. Their residence at Tomas Moro was featured often in the media. Presumably, Salvador Allende loved his wife. Yet his relationship with La Payita was also strong and full of affection. Perhaps it was the Chilean culture, and perhaps it was the nature of the man. But the warmth of their feelings for one another was palpable in their words. "Admiral Merino threatens me that it will come any day, that plans have already been made," the president said. "But I am not so certain. Our revolution has enemies," he went on. "Every revolution does. And I am not so naive as they say. But the generals and admirals will protect their president. It is their duty under the Constitution, and these men take their duty very seriously. But if I am wrong, if the time comes, I can go to Los Cerillos," he had added, referring to the industrial belt town outside Santiago where loyal, heavily armed factory workers could provide refuge and, perhaps, launch a counterattack.

"Why wait for them to attack?" La Payita had asked. "Why not let General Pickering and General Sepulveda and Carlos Prats go on the offensive? They've been waiting for you to order a purge of the disloyal members of parliament. You could reverse this march toward anarchy."

"I won't risk a civil war just to protect myself," Allende had said. "This is not about Salvador Allende. This is about a divided Chile. Families would be split apart. My nephew is with the opposition. Should I direct General Sepulveda to arrest him? To arrest everyone that opposes me? No matter the cost to be paid in blood? Many of our countrymen would surely die. No, little one. I will not be responsible for that."

"Then leave the country, Chicho," she had said. "Let Chile take care of itself for a while. Wait until the hot heads sort out their differences. You will be able to return, one day, to a more peaceful landscape." A silence followed, several seconds that seemed longer. Tony could picture Allende, closing his eyes and letting the thought run wistfully through his mind.

"Ah, my dove," the president had said, "it's too late for that. I wish we could go back to those days, when I first set up my office here in La Moneda. I was filled with such hope, such inspiration. How proud I was of the Unidad Popular. How proud I was of our people. How proud I was to be their new president. Don't you remember?"

"Of course I remember, Chicho."

"I was so excited for our country, for all the good things I could see ahead. I was determined to change everything for the better. To lead my people in the creation of something unique, something beautiful. I could barely sleep. I couldn't wait for each new day to begin. My dreams woke me in the middle of the night, leaving me to wander these halls, so quiet and peaceful, planning the future of Chile. How can I abandon those dreams?"

"Yes, yes, my president. I understand," Miriam had answered. Their melancholy was so strong that Tony had felt it through the headphones.

Then Allende had said, "Do you remember that crazy carpenter? What was his name?"

"De la Vega," had come Miriam's reply.

"Ah, yes, Raul de la Vega. A brilliant carpenter, to be sure. He made such a mess of his life, the way he drank so much. I never told him I knew he slept in that little attic room he built above La Salon de Independencia. He would have been so embarrassed. I liked him. I always hoped he would stop drinking and go back to his family."

Tony had felt his eyebrows rise and his eyes open wide. Allende knew about *el escondido*.

Tony's thoughts were interrupted by the sound of an air force jet streaking overhead. Unusual. Downtown Santiago wasn't in a military fly zone. *I must be dreaming*, he thought. He kept his eyes closed. But then crackling noises came from several different directions, the reports of automatic rifle fire. And then the vibrating bass tones of the tanks joined the chorus. Their engines roared in a deep throaty chant, like a hundred monsters growling in harmony as their treads rumbled across the cobblestone streets. From the sounds of it, they were working their way toward La Moneda. Tony's bed vibrated and shook, and he came fully awake. Then the phone rang.

"Stephens?" It took Tony a second to recognize the voice on the other end: John Colson, the head of Branch 5 operations, which included Uruguay, Paraguay, Argentina, and Chile. Colson ranked above Mr. D'Onofrio and the other station chiefs. Tony had only seen him at a couple of briefings back home and had never spoken to him directly. When Mr. Colson addressed an assembly of field officers, they listened carefully. He gave out information and instructions with particular authority, always concerning especially important or sensitive issues. He didn't repeat himself, and he rarely answered questions. His involvement signaled "priority" with a capital P. Tony knew he was about to receive another varsity assignment.

"Yes, sir. This is Andre A. Stephens." Tony tried to sound alert and ready.

"You going to sleep through this goddamned party, rookie?" Mr. Colson barked.

"No, sir, Mr. Happ." Tony was careful to address Colson by his code name.

"Well then, get in the white Volvo waiting in front of your building. The driver will take you to the palace. You'll be meeting a guy there. Name of Mongoose. Bring your briefcase."

Tony had an official tool kit comprised of a false identification card, some cash, a pack of local cigarettes, and some disguise materials including fake eyeglasses. But the reference to his "briefcase" meant he was to bring his gun. He was not authorized to carry it unless specifically instructed, which hadn't yet occurred. This would be the first time. It was now unmistakable. Something serious was happening.

Tony bounced out of bed and was dressed in an instant. His "briefcase" was always ready, loaded and tucked in its ankle holster. He grabbed it and strapped it on. A glance at his watch told him it was 10:00 AM. He scurried down through the lobby and flew out the front door of the building. The presidential palace was exactly two kilometers to the northwest. Outside, the roar of the tanks was eclipsed only by the occasional sound of an explosion bursting somewhere in the distance, and the sound of small arms fire. The morning sky to the northwest was lit up, as if by lightning, but there were no clouds and no rain, and in between flashes, the sky was blue and clear. It was man-made fire, the kind that accompanied regime change in South America.

Over the last couple of months, Tony had been encouraged to walk to the palace rather than ride, and to take different routes each time. He had wondered the reason, but as with many of the instructions he had been given in Chile, he didn't know what it was. Now the purpose was making itself clear.

He looked into the driver side of the Volvo and saw Steve Frazier, which was a plus. A big plus. Frazier and Tony had been through a lot together and had the kind of trust for each other that only comes after a strong bond has held for years. Tony scooted around to the passenger side and got in quickly.

"What the hell is happening, Murphy?"

"I'm not sure, Andre, but I need to get you to the palace right away. You're supposed to link up with a guy, code-name Mongoose."

"Yeah," Tony said. "Then what?"

"That's all they told me," Frazier replied. "He's supposedly at the top of the Company food chain. He's over there now, waiting to meet someone big in the government, maybe even Allende himself. Apparently he's got authority to deliver a message to the one guy authorized to receive it. They can't close the deal without him. He's in the palace, they're sure of that, but they haven't been able to find him. Apparently, they didn't anticipate this problem. You're the guy that's been in there the most. That makes you important. Someone thinks you know where all the rat holes are, and if he's hiding in one, you need to help them find him. My job is to get you there pronto."

Tony did know a lot about the layout of the palace and was one of few officers that had even set foot on the second floor. He had indeed discovered several little rooms not shown on the palace blueprints or floor plans. Some of the secret places were accessible only through hidden doors in the walls, some required you to lift a rug and climb down through a trapdoor in the floor. Tony had reported each of these secret places and how to access them. Except for one. The one in the attic that required you to climb up through the ceiling in the Independence Lounge. *El Escondido.* Tony knew he had made a mistake when he delayed submitting that report, but how could he describe it, as well hidden as it was, without betraying Cristina? That place belonged to Cristina and her father. And for one magical hour, to him. His feelings were difficult to understand, and he was having trouble sorting them out. She had taken him there at great personal risk, and he wanted so badly to keep the promise of secrecy he had made. He felt foolish holding back, unprofessional, especially once he found out that Allende was aware of it. Yesterday he had assured himself he would write it up at the next opportunity. But he hadn't yet, and now he was in this Volvo on his way to meet a man named Mongoose.

As they neared La Moneda, more than one burnt-out car stood smoking on the road, and craters were increasingly evident in the pavement. Storefronts had been blown out, and several small fires smoldered. The noise, deafening to begin with, had gotten louder. Automatic weapons fire seemed to come from every direction. Tony spotted two bodies on the ground in carabinero uniforms, members of Allende's personal guard, his most loyal soldiers. Tony wanted to ask Frazier to stop for them, but they weren't moving; and even through the smoky haze, Tony could see the pools of blood that surrounded them. Not likely they could be helped now. Besides, Frazier was driving. If he wanted to stop, he could. But he didn't.

As Frazier and Tony turned onto Avenida Del Palacio, something struck the right front headlight, which popped like a flashbulb on a 1950's news photographer's camera. A hole appeared in the Volvo's upper windshield followed closely by a popping noise coming from somewhere down the street. It was surreal as Tony realized that they had taken fire, and the bullets had arrived before their sound. Tony said a silent prayer, hoping Frazier hadn't forgotten the special driver training he had been given. Just then Frazier swerved the car toward the sidewalk on the right. It bounced hard over the broken curb and barreled through a pair of trashcans. Tony watched the old cans, bent and dirty enough to be trash themselves, fly sideways away from the car, their grimy contents spewing out along the way.

Tony knew the street and most of its alleys from walking them to work and back. "There," he shouted. He pointed to the alley that ran right between the tabacalera on one side and the offices of two notarios on the other. Frazier downshifted in time to keep the old Volvo from stalling. He gunned the engine and popped the clutch. The engine shrieked, and the car charged ahead. The alley was narrow. If it was wider than the Volvo, it was barely so, and Frazier wasn't quite able to get all of the Volvo away from all of the wall. He smacked the right headlight, the one that had just been shot out, a glancing but solid blow against the cornerstone of the tobacco shop on the right. The car shuddered hard and rotated clockwise. Tony flew forward and smashed his right forearm hard against the steering wheel, which Frazier was pulling frantically to the left. On the football field, Tony had delivered many a "forearm shiver," as his coach liked to call them, and his arm was thick with hard muscles. The steering wheel bent way back before tearing a deep gouge through the skin. Still, Tony hardly noticed the wound as Frazier straightened out and got the Volvo chugging back up the alley.

Tony ducked low and hoped nobody hostile was close enough to take aim from behind. They would emerge from the alley onto Calle de la Paz, which was almost funny. While on any other day it may have been "Avenue of Peace", today was September 11, 1973, and in Santiago de Chile, the world was exploding.

Frazier paused at the end of the alley. Tony hoped the engine wouldn't quit. A British-made Hawker Hunter jet was screeching overhead and tanks rumbled no more than a block or two away. Judging by the sound of the explosions, some had already reached the palace.

Tony directed Frazier through a series of turns as they made their way to the palace. Twice they had to turn back when damage and debris on the street rendered it impassable. Still, they kept moving. Eventually, though, the Volvo had had enough. It coughed and sputtered, hissed and stalled. Frazier tried to restart it, but the car had taken them as far as it could. The men surveyed their position. By Tony's reckoning, they were only two blocks from the palace. They cautiously climbed out and started toward their destination.

Running as quickly as they could in full crouch, Tony and Frazier soon came to the side of the palace, which took up an entire square block. The sound of gunfire had quieted, and while they could still hear jets screaming low overhead, their passes were no longer followed by the sounds of explosions. Frazier pointed toward the windowless side of a building located across from the palace. Tony saw no movement. "What?" he asked.

"There," Frazier directed and Tony looked closer. At the foot of the wall, in crumpled heaps, were three bodies. Tony could see that their hands were tied behind their backs, and their blindfolds still in place. Bloodstains on the wall corresponded to where they had been standing, probably just minutes before. Tony thought he recognized a security guard he had seen in the palace. And then he saw the lifeless body of Corporal Francisco Garcia, the man who had intercepted him in the hallway outside Allende's office. He felt like throwing up and probably would have except his horror was interrupted by shouts coming from the front of the building. This was no time for paralysis. He crouched down and followed Frazier around the corner. Their mission was to get to the palace and find Mongoose. Tony clung to the notion that it had been secured, and that once inside, they would be safe.

The front of the palace was a beehive of activity. Khaki uniformed officers were shouting orders to dozens of soldiers who were moving from their positions out along the perimeter of the building. Some stood guard over a group of civilians, a few of whom were bleeding noticeably. Tony looked at their faces. He was relieved not to recognize any more of them, but their desperate, fearful expressions would not soon leave his memory. As Tony watched, a soldier led a man in a white shirt out of the palace and down the steps. When they got close to the group, the soldier pushed him roughly to the ground. One of the women went to help the man. The soldier pointed his pistol at them both and shouted. She froze and said something, more of a wail than a statement, then collapsed in tears. Tony could not make out her words. Another soldier holding a rifle said something to the one pointing his handgun, who put the weapon back in its holster. He nodded toward the one with the rifle, then went quickly up the stairs and into the palace.

Frazier grabbed Tony's arm. He had recognized a CIA officer named Bradshaw standing among a group of Chilean military men. Their uniforms displayed enough brass to establish them as leaders of the forces that had engineered the coup. Two more bodies lay on the steps to the palace entrance. Like the dead men he and Frazier had passed on the way, they were wearing the uniforms of Allende's loyal GAP unit. And like those other bodies, no one was paying any attention to them. Anti-Allende soldiers were everywhere. A pair approached the officers standing with Bradshaw and asked for instructions. The officers gave orders, and the soldiers quickly moved off to comply. Tony saw that Bradshaw and the Chilean officers were smiling as they spoke. It gave him a chill.

Bradshaw turned and saw Frazier and Tony approaching. He waved them forward. "Which one of you is the telephone guy?" he asked. Tony raised his hand.

"Good," Bradshaw said. Seeing the tense looks on their faces, he continued. "Relax, fellows, the hard part is over. General Pinochet and his men have the palace under control. Of course, it's still wise to be alert and keep your head down until you get inside. And you, Stephens, I don't recommend you raise your hand again. We've been mopping up the buildings around the plaza, and we think we've gotten all the snipers. But there might be a stubborn one still out there, and your hand in the air might make him think you're important. Of course, with my luck, he'd probably aim at you or one of those guys decked out in ribbons and stars over there and end up hitting me." He laughed, and Tony flinched.

Bradshaw got on his radio. "He's here," was all he said.

Tony and Frazier made their way up the steps. At the massive entrance doors they were met by a trio of heavily armed soldiers. From the looks of them and the gear they were carrying, they were part of a special weapons and tactics unit.

"Which one is Stephens?" one of them asked. He had lieutenant stripes and a big bushy moustache.

"That would be me," Tony responded, careful this time to keep his hands down at his side.

"Come with us," Lieutenant Moustache said. "And keep your eyes open. We just neutralized a few of Allende's personal guards upstairs. That was probably the last of 'em, and everything should be quiet from here on out. But you never know. You'll be all right, especially inside, but it's still heads-up around here."

Tony and Frazier began to step forward. "Just him," the soldier said, dipping the tip of his AK-47 toward Tony.

When Frazier looked like he wanted to protest, Tony told him, "Go home, big guy. I'll be all right." He patted Frazier on the shoulder, though he really felt like hugging him. Frazier was his best friend in the world, and Tony would have liked to have him at his side here in Insanityville. But that wasn't up to him. Tony braced himself and turned back toward the soldier. "Let's go," he said in his best John Wayne.

"Okay, then. Follow me," the moustache directed.

# CHAPTER 34

Tony and the soldier headed to a small room off the main lobby: the mailroom, where incoming correspondence was sorted for delivery to the various offices and outgoing correspondence was prepared for mailing. The lieutenant knocked briskly and stood back. A few tense seconds passed and then the door opened. A man in a tan suit stood on the other side. Mongoose. He looked at Tony, expressionless. "Who are you?" he asked.

"Andre A. Stephens," Tony replied.

"I've been waiting for you," the man said, sounding as calm and unhurried as an undertaker. He dismissed the soldier, who turned briskly and walked away. As soon as the door closed behind him, Mongoose said, "I have something for a government official, and I need to deliver it in person. Kind of like the last step in the process. I guess he's reluctant to meet with anyone right now, so I've got to find him. We're convinced he's in the building. We just don't know where. We've checked all the nooks and crannies in the place, including the hidden ones mentioned in your reports, but no luck. He's in here somewhere, and we need to find him, and we need to do it right away. Understand?"

"Yes, sir," Tony responded.

"Good. Now I want you to search your mind. Something you saw or heard might help me solve this little mystery. It could be the most important thing you'll ever do. So what can you tell me, Mr. Stephens?"

It didn't take Tony long to digest the situation. One secret place hadn't made its way into a report. Cristina's place. He didn't hesitate. "There's somewhere I just discovered yesterday," Tony lied. "I didn't have a chance to report it."

The man looked at Tony but said nothing. Tony felt his brain being x-rayed. He stared back, waiting for the man to say something. Mongoose looked around forty, about six feet tall, with brown hair, graying at the temples. He was tan and thin. In his suit and tie he looked out of place in this war zone—like a mild-mannered diplomat. But a thin scar running vertically from his cheek up to his forehead suggested otherwise. Tony wondered what it was he wanted to deliver and to whom, and why it was so important, but he knew better than to ask questions.

"Sounds like a start," the man finally said. "Are you sure that's the only place that hasn't been reported?"

"I'm sure," Tony answered.

"Okay, then," Mongoose said. "Tell me where it is."

"It's on the second floor," Tony began. "In an attic above the Independence Lounge. There's a trapdoor in the ceiling, hidden above one of the panels in the recessed lighting. You have to climb up and pull it open and then pull down a folding spring ladder attached to the back of it."

"You know how to find it?" Mongoose asked.

"I do," Tony answered.

"Excellent," Mongoose said, "so why don't you show me?"

As they made their way upstairs to the Independence Lounge, Tony's thoughts were of the last time he had been there. How Cristina had directed him to retrieve the stepladder from the auxiliary kitchen and then led him down the same hallway. How she looked as she put her finger up to her lips, telling him to be quiet. Tony didn't know what to expect then, any more than he did now. But the anticipation he felt walking with Cristina was intoxicating and wonderful. What he was feeling right now as he walked with Mongoose was much different. For one desperate moment, Tony prayed that Cristina was safe, somewhere far from this violence.

At end of the hall, a couple of Allende's personal guards were lying in a shared pool of dark blood near the entrance to the Sala Toesca, one of Allende's favorite meeting rooms. Mongoose stopped and whispered, "Those boys took the worst of it in a firefight with the SWAT guys you met on the way in. Nothing to worry about." The place reeked of death. Tony could smell smoke, tear gas, and gunpowder. His throat tightened and his eyes burned. Mongoose pulled a Colt .45 from inside his jacket before continuing, "From here on in, no talking. You point, when you need to, and do your best not to make any sounds. Okay?" He looked at Tony, then casually cocked his pistol.

Tony nodded solemnly. He had been given training in nonverbal communication back at Camp Peary. "Charades class," they had called it. In one exercise, Tony had to go to a department store and pretend to be dumb. His task was to approach a salesperson and purchase a particular brand of lipstick, in a particular shade, without speaking a word. The first time he went in, he made some gestures to indicate that he could not speak. But the clerk simply asked him to write down what he wanted. Tony was pretty sure that wasn't the way he was supposed to handle it, and when he met with his instructor afterward, he learned he was right. The next time he went to the store, he had to convey not only the inability to speak, but also the inability to write in any language familiar to the clerk. He got through it then, but hadn't needed to use those skills since. Until now.

Tony and Mongoose moved slowly past the room called Puccio's Office. Then Tony pointed to the entrance to the Independence Lounge. Mongoose crouched forward and pressed his ear against the door, closing his eyes to concentrate on listening. As he did, his suit jacket opened. Tony could see holsters on both sides. One still held a weapon. A third pistol, a Russian Kalishnekov .9 millimeter, was tucked into his waist. Tony diverted his sight. He didn't want to be caught staring. He had a Walther PPK with him, and this seemed like a good time to be holding it. He withdrew it from the holster on his ankle as quietly as he could.

After a few more seconds, Mongoose straightened up. Then he gripped the door handle and turned it. The latch released, and he gently pushed the door open. He darted his head in and quickly withdrew it. Standard procedure. Officers were trained not to poke their heads into a room to take a leisurely look around. If it turned out that someone hostile was inside aiming at you, you wouldn't have time other than watch him pull the trigger. It was much better to dart in and dart out. You'd still have an instant to see what was inside, and if it were hostile, your face would be a quickly withdrawing target.

But the room was empty. Mongoose stepped in and looked around, then gestured for Tony to follow. Tony pointed to a chair that was sitting in the middle of the room, just beneath the plastic ceiling panels through which he and Cristina had climbed. Then he pointed up to the panels themselves. Mongoose nodded, then pointed at Tony and at the chair. Tony re-holstered his pistol and climbed onto the chair. He reached up to the panel, second from the back and third from the side, and slid it quietly out of the way. Above it, the hinged door in the ceiling came into view. Tony pointed at it, concentrating on not trembling, and Mongoose nodded again. He gestured for Tony to get down off the chair. As soon as he was standing back on the floor, Tony reached down to his ankle and retrieved his gun. He didn't know why, it just made him feel better to be holding it. Then Mongoose gestured for him to follow him out. As they exited, Mongoose turned back to close the door delicately behind them.

Suddenly, Tony heard something stir down the hall. One of the presidential guards that had been lying there "dead" must have come back to life because he was raising his arm. He was covered in blood, but Tony saw only the barrel of the gun he was pointing at him and Mongoose.

"Get out of there," the soldier rasped. He started to say something more, but his words were drowned out by the roar of Tony's pistol followed closely by the rapid-fire explosions coming from Mongoose's weapon. The guard flew backward and landed on top of his dead comrades. Mongoose moved toward him and emptied his gun into the man, who bounced like a puppet with each shot.

"Stupid sons of bitches," he said. "They were supposed to check these bodies. How the hell did they miss Lazarus here?"

Tony stood stiffly but said nothing. He was trying not to shake.

"What the hell," Mongoose continued. "At least now we know we've got the right room. He sure didn't want us in there, did he?" When Tony didn't respond, Mongoose looked closely into his eyes. "What's the matter, Stephens? Don't tell me you never shot anyone before. You all right?"

Tony took a deep breath and let it out through pursed lips. His eyes were moist. He blinked several times. His heart was pounding.

"Hey, you'll be okay," Mongoose said. "Don't pass out on me now. Everything is all right. You did well. What you had to do. Maybe saved my life." Tony inhaled another lungful and let it out slowly. "Hell, rookie, you stepped up. Reacted like an old pro. I'm proud of you," Mongoose said. "This line of work might be just right for you."

Tony wasn't so sure. He could think of a lot of things he'd rather be doing and a lot of places he'd rather be.

Just then, the SWAT guys came running up. Tony jerked. "What the hell was that?" Moustache asked. "I heard shots."

"Not much," Mongoose answered. "Just me and Stephens cleaning up a mess you guys left behind."

"What're you talking about?" Moustache asked.

"Those bodies over there, you know, the ones you were supposed to make sure were dead? Well, one of 'em wasn't, and he decided he didn't want us hanging around this room. He almost got a shot off, too, before Stephens here interrupted him."

"Sorry about that, sir," Moustache offered. "We'll go back and check the rest."

"Yeah, maybe you should do that," Mongoose answered with a laugh. "I don't think Stephens can take any more excitement." Tony couldn't believe how casually the men were talking.

They moved down the hallway, and Mongoose took Tony back the other way. "What happens when I pull open that little trapdoor in the ceiling, Stephens?" he asked.

Tony took a deep breath and concentrated.

"On the other side of that panel, there's a folding ladder with spring hinges. You'll see a short cord. Pull on it, and the stairs will unfold down to the floor. Then you can climb up into that room. It's a little attic. Maybe ten feet by ten feet. Only about four feet high. Not enough to stand," Tony answered.

"What's in the room, son? How is it laid out?" Mongoose asked. He was so calm, it helped Tony focus. He listed everything he could remember. Pots and utensils. Cans of beans. Can opener. Newspapers. Candles. Whiskey bottles. The little wooden table. And then he described the mattress—the one he and Cristina had made love on. He paused for a moment, reflecting. "That's about it, sir," Tony concluded.

"You've been very helpful, Stephens" Mongoose offered.

"Don't mention it," Tony said, trying to act like it was his ordinary routine.

"Now before I let you go, I need to ask one more time," Mongoose said. "Are you sure there aren't any other places in this building where someone could be hiding?"

"That's it, as far as I know, sir," Tony answered.

Mongoose looked Tony right in the eye. "You should have reported this room in the attic right away. You know that. Might have saved me some time and you a trip out here in the middle of these . . . festivities."

Tony cringed. "Yes, sir."

"Okay, that will do, then. If you don't mind, I am going to conduct a private meeting with our friend up there. You should go now. Get yourself a cold beer. Maybe I'll have one with you someday, and you can tell me how you found that trapdoor in the first place."

Tony felt himself tighten but said nothing. The silence was awkward. Tony was sure Mongoose meant it to be.

"All right, Stephens," Mongoose finally said. "Time for you to head out. We'll take it from here." He reached out and shook Tony's hand. Then he pulled out a radio, turned, and began talking into it as he walked away.

Tony didn't waste any time. He headed for the lobby and then the exit. On his way, several more SWAT types hustled past him. Their boots sounded heavy on the palace floor. They were dressed completely in black, and each sporting a full load of equipment, including tear gas, grenades, and gas masks. There could be little doubt about Mongoose's intentions. After all, if he just wanted to tell the guy something or deliver something to him, he could simply announce it into the attic room. No, it was clear Mongoose was anticipating an unpleasant confrontation. And from the look Tony had seen in his eyes, he was looking forward to it.

As Tony emerged from the palace, sweat was dripping down his forehead and into his eyes. He raised his right arm to wipe it and felt a twinge of pain across the forearm. Blood stained his sleeve. He remembered smashing it against the steering wheel in the car. He rubbed it tentatively and decided that no bones were broken. Just a flesh wound, he told himself in the English accent of a Monty Python character. He was starting to feel better but not enough to smile.

As he made his way down the stairs, he looked around. The streets were a bustle of activity, but no explosions and, as far as Tony could hear, no close gunfire. Whatever had taken place was winding down. Any resistance that had been offered by President Allende and his loyal police had been thoroughly suppressed. The military was in full control of the palace and the surrounding buildings. And there was Ironman, standing out in the street next to Bradshaw. He looked up and saw Tony. They nodded to each other. So this is what it's like to serve your country.

Tony looked back at the palace. A part of the roof was missing, and many of the windows were broken out. Several craters had been scorched into the outside walls, which were pockmarked with bullet holes. It didn't appear that anything was still on fire, but smoke hung heavily in the air. People were freely entering and exiting the building. Tony's nostrils, throat, and lungs burned from the smell of cordite. One by one, he negotiated the first few steps down to the street. Suddenly, he was feeling very, very tired. His knees threatened to buckle under him. Frazier sprinted toward him, taking two steps at a time.

"You all right?" Frazier asked.

"Yeah, I guess," Tony responded. "I just shot a guy in there."

"What?" was all Frazier could say.

Tony wanted to act like it was no big deal, like he did it all the time. But he felt like throwing up and crying and screaming and running away, all at the same time. But he was an officer in the CIA, not on some college debate team, and he took a deep breath and then another and gradually reigned in his emotions.

"I don't know what happened. One minute I was showing that Mongoose guy a hiding place I knew about, and the next thing I know this guard, who's supposed to be dead, is aiming his pistol at us. I pointed my gun back at him and started pulling the trigger. I don't even know how many times." Tony lifted his right hand, which still clutched the Walther PPK. "Mongoose fired a bunch of times too.

The guy went down, blood was everywhere, and then SWAT came. Nobody acted like it was any big deal. Then Mongoose told me he would finish his business in there, and that I should leave. Told me to go have a beer."

"Hell, Tony, that sounds like a damned good idea," said Frazier. "Mongoose is my kind of guy." Frazier reached out to slap Tony on the shoulder. "Bradshaw wants me to drive a couple of guys across town to an airstrip on the east side of the city. It's called Pudahuel." He gestured toward a white van parked at the curb. Tony could see two figures through the window. "I was there on a stakeout once. Watched some soldiers off-load a few boxes of guns and dynamite flown in by the Cubans. It happens to be pretty close to that place we like, La Taverna. Whadda ya say we get those guys to their plane and then go get ourselves a pitcher? Maybe a shot or two of tequila to go with it." Tony had to smile. Frazier was still the Ironman. Then Frazier noticed the bloodstain on Tony's forearm. "What's that?" he asked. "You hurt? You want to get that looked at?"

"Nah," Tony said. "It's nothing. I banged it in the car when you were playing demolition derby on the way over. Remind me to sue you when we get home. In the meanwhile, let's get the hell out of here. I can wash up when we get to La Taverna."

Tony and Frazier turned and made their way down the rest of the steps. As they got to the curb, they waited to let a rumbling truck pass, one of those open cattle trucks that the military used to transport troops. As it pulled in front, Tony saw that the truck bed was crammed with unhappy civilians. Their appearances reflected the same pathos Tony had seen on the faces of the captives along the sidewalk when he first arrived. Some were crying. Others just had the eerie vacant stares of zombies. Tony shook his head. None of my business, he said to himself, but he wasn't fully convinced.

The truck grinded noisily to a halt. The Chilean general moved up to the driver's open window. Tony and Frazier started to walk around behind the truck, intent on getting to Colonel Bradshaw, but they could still hear the driver say, "Yes, General, we'll make sure to take good care of them." His grisly meaning was clear. Tony had not forgotten the site where a firing squad had done its dirty work. He passed slowly behind the idling truck, his look fixed on the faces of the prisoners. Until the sight of two of them, huddled together against the wall, hit him like a punch in the gut. Carlos and Diana Gonzalez.

# CHAPTER 35

Carlos was sure he was going to die. Truthfully, he felt resigned to it. His brother had hurt a lot of people and was deeply despised by many. Carlos himself was good-hearted to a fault. But he was not completely naive. He knew that his good life was at least partly the result of his brother's ambition and ruthlessness. Carlos was aware that the violence in the streets, the grassroots retribution and revenge was increasing by the day, and while he tried to put it out of his mind, he recognized that frank revolution might not be far behind. So when the first explosions came, as they had this terrible morning, he understood this could be the day—the one he had anticipated with dread—when life as he and Diana had known it would end. The telephone rang. It was his brother, General Agustin Gonzalez, calling from the palace.

"Gusto," Carlos said, using his brother's nickname, the one by which he had been calling him since they were little boys, "what is happening?"

"Some traitorous sons of bitches in the army have attacked, but the president is secure inside the palace and has taken control of the situation. Even now he is issuing orders and preparing to coordinate a counterattack."

"Are you safe, my brother?" Carlos asked, his anxiety increasing by the second.

"I am fine, Carlos. But you should come to the palace. You and Diana will be safer here." Carlos heard what he took to be stoic resolve in his brother's voice and was comforted. He summoned Diana, and together they got in their car and headed for La Moneda.

What Carlos could not have known was that within moments after the call, an explosion at the main palace entrance rocked the entire building. Smoke was everywhere. General Gonzalez retreated to the GAP security room on the second floor accompanied by what remained of his command—four carabineros. He had lost touch with the president and had no real plan himself. Instead, he was praying, like all within the palace, that something would reverse the assault, that somehow the attacking military would be restored to sanity and this whole episode would reverse itself, just as the Tanquetazo had been quelled. But with each passing minute, with each new detonation, it became more apparent that this time the insurrection would not be stopped. This was a well-coordinated and comprehensive effort that would not end until the president was overthrown. Gonzalez tried to call his brother back to tell him not to come, to go somewhere else, anywhere else. Midway through dialing Carlos's number, the telephone line went dead. He tried another line, but it too was dead. He raised his pistol and charged downstairs to confront the enemies of his president. Before he could make it to the door, a bullet fired by a rifleman on Morande Street whizzed through the window and found his heart.

By the time Carlos and Diana arrived at the palace, it was already under the control of the rebellious forces. They were quickly arrested. People were being rounded up like cattle—shoved and pummeled and thrown to the ground. Or shot. Carlos and Diana were pushed along with several others into the back of a truck. From there they could hear the sounds of chaos. People shouting and crying, and gunfire and bodies thudding to the pavement. Diana screamed and screamed until her voice grew hoarse. Carlos tried to soothe her, to quiet her to avoid angering their captors. More from exhaustion and despair than anything else, she grew silent. She wanted to scream again, to shout this nightmare away, but all she had strength for were sobs and whimpers. Carlos wrapped his arms around her and whispered softly about the child Diana was carrying.

Grief was plain upon their sooty faces when Tony saw them crouched together against the low wooden planks of the truck bed's sidewall. It was unlikely they even saw Tony. But Tony saw them clearly and watched Carlos adjust his arm around Diana's slumping shoulders. Tony could barely make out her face at first until she looked up at Carlos, and then Tony could see her eyes. She looked disoriented and very frightened. Tony could see her expression soften as she took comfort from her husband's protective embrace. Their love for each other broke Tony's heart. He knew he had to do something to save them.

He looked around and quickly surveyed his options. When he saw the white van parked at the curb, the one Frazier was going to be driving to the airstrip, he formed the start of a plan. He turned to Frazier and said, "Ironman, I've got to help a couple of those sorry souls in the back of that truck, and I could use your help. You with me?"

Frazier's eyebrows lifted, he didn't hesitate. "Of course, Tony."

"Thanks, Steve," Tony said. "You get in the driver's seat of that van and start the engine. I'm going to talk to Colonel Bradshaw. Hopefully, he won't have a problem with it and I can get those people off that truck. But even if he does, Ironman, those people are coming with us. And depending on how it goes, we may need to get out of here on the double," Tony said. "You still with me?"

"Always, my short brother," was Frazier's response. "I just hope he doesn't throw any beer cans at us." Tony remembered their adventure in front of Johnny's Tavern. It seemed like a lifetime ago. But this wasn't New Haven and the soldiers around them weren't campus cops. He took a deep breath. The truck engine was rumbling. It was time.

Tony marched toward Colonel Bradshaw. His heart was beating double-time. "Colonel," he said, putting as much urgency into his words as he could muster, "there are two people on that truck that shouldn't be there."

"What are you talking about, son? Those people are in the custody of General Miranda. They're headed to San Sebastiano," Bradshaw snapped.

Tony recognized the name. San Sebastiano was an old prison a few kilometers south of the city. It had a nasty reputation to begin with, and God only knew what was going on there now. Tony's resolve increased. "I can't let that happen, Colonel."

"Listen. What happens to those people is none of our concern. This operation is going quite well, and we don't need to get in General Miranda's way for a couple of unlucky sons of bitches."

"What happens to those two people *is* my problem, Colonel. I'm making it my problem," Tony persisted.

"It's out of my hands," Bradshaw barked with finality. "You're dismissed, Stephens. Now get the f—k out of here and let me finish my work."

"I am not asking you, Colonel," Tony said carefully. "I'm telling you. I just shot a man in there, and I will shoot you where you stand if you don't help me. Those two are getting off that truck and coming with me."

Bradshaw turned toward Tony and could see the pistol in his hand. "Listen carefully, young man. You're upset. You've had a rough morning. You're not thinking straight. What would you do with 'em once you got 'em?" A pause hung in the air. Then Bradshaw added, "Get a grip and wave bye-bye to that truck."

"Colonel, I'm telling you to stop that truck right now," Tony hissed, sounding as cold and mechanical as he had ever sounded. Then he raised his pistol. Bradshaw could see the barrel pointed at him. He also noticed that Tony's hand was as steady as a surgeon's.

"I don't get it, Stephens," Bradshaw said. "You're willing to threaten a superior officer over this? Are you out of your mind?"

"I suggest you don't test me, Colonel. Tell the general over there to let me get those two down from the truck and do it now." Tony's eyes blazed, but the barrel of his gun never moved from its target.

"Okay, kid, take it easy," Bradshaw said. "You can lower your weapon. If you feel that strongly about it, I'll help you. Its your ass." He turned toward General Miranda and the truck driver and shouted, "Wait. I need to take two of your prisoners."

Tony didn't wait for Miranda to respond. He hurried to the back of the truck and pointed at Carlos and Diana. "Those two."

The general saw Carlos and turned back to Colonel Bradshaw. "I can't let you take them, Colonel. That's General Gonzalez's brother."

The words took Tony by surprise and instantly pushed his anxiety meter toward frantic. How was he going to get around this roadblock without somebody getting shot? His heart was pounding so hard it was about to burst out of his chest, and sweat poured off his face. He didn't know what to say so he said nothing. Instead, he begged for help with his eyes, letting the expression on his face show the colonel how important it was.

Bradshaw addressed Miranda. "General, my associate here has a real mean streak, and I believe he's got some special plans for those two, if you know what I mean. I suggest we let him deal with 'em. Save you the trouble."

General Miranda looked at Tony, who readily adopted Bradshaw's approach. He had replaced the pathetic expression on his face—the one he had just shown to the colonel—with his best snarling scowl. And it worked. The general recognized viciousness when he saw it. Tony had the look of a sadistic murderer just before he tore someone's head off so he could pour acid down the hole. Which was all right with Miranda. To him, the late General Gonzalez was a disgrace, a soldier who had traded his military discipline for the soft benefits of serving as Allende's lapdog. Willing to do anything to please the president, regardless of who it hurt. To him, Gonzalez's death represented an appropriate end to a sad tale of a career gone bad. But precautions needed to be taken against anyone who might be interested in revenge. Gonzalez's family, including his brother there in the back of that truck, represented a threat. They needed to be dealt with swiftly and with finality. And General Miranda had a good plan for them, which was to have them "disappear" along with everyone else in the truck. But how they disappeared didn't matter, so if this crazy American wanted to punish Gonzalez's brother beforehand, it was no skin off his nose.

"Whatever you wish, colonel," Miranda said. He shouted for the two soldiers standing at the back of the truck to get Carlos and Diana out. They pulled the tailgate down. One of the soldiers climbed up and roughly grabbed Carlos, who didn't seem to have any idea what was happening but put up a feeble struggle anyway.

Tony stepped up and said, as sternly and with as much authority as he could summon, "Take it easy. I don't want the filthy son of a bitch to die of a heart attack before I can deal with him."

The soldiers looked at Tony with suspicion, but General Miranda was smiling. He had no doubt Tony was going to take care of this business in a most appropriate way. He shouted to his men to be a little more gentle with the prisoners. "Don't worry, boys. He's going to give them what they deserve. Let's not ruin his special plans."

The soldier took hold of Carlos, who was too exhausted to resist any further, and gingerly lowered him to the other soldier waiting below. Carlos gathered himself and looked back as the soldier in the truck took hold of Diana and handed her limp body down to him. She was barely conscious but still had enough spirit to try and push his arms away.

Carlos reassured her. "It's okay, my love. Don't worry. It's going to be all right. We're going to gather flowers for the palace."

"Yes, lady, you are going to pick some flowers. And then you will be pushing up daisies," General Miranda mocked. The soldiers laughed.

Suddenly another prisoner in the truck made his way clumsily toward the back as if he was going to jump out. "Take me too, comrades. I want to pick flowers with you—" His words were interrupted by the thumping sound the rifle stock made as it pounded into the back of his head. He fell silent and collapsed in a heap on top of another man, who roughly pushed him aside.

The soldier in the truck jumped down, and he and the other soldier pushed the tailgate back up into place. General Miranda shouted an instruction to the driver, who shifted into gear and lurched off abruptly. By then, Tony had his mouth close to Carlos's ear. He whispered, "Carlos, it's me. Andre Stephens. From the . . ." Tony caught himself. He was about to say that he was the guy from the telephone company. It might not have mattered considering the circumstances, but he knew he was already in trouble, and revealing his cover could cause more problems. But Carlos, as dazed as he was, had already recognized him, and his eyes were saying "thank you."

"Come, you filthy dog," Tony spat at him with as much contempt as he could. "Get in the van. You and your whore are coming with me." Just talking to these gentle people in such a manner made Tony wince, but he shouted the words forcefully, loud enough for the soldiers to hear. Carlos struggled to get Diana to stand. Together they stumbled toward the van, where Frazier was waiting with the motor running. Tony guided Carlos and Diana in through the open side panel door and then hopped into the front passenger seat. Frazier gunned the engine and they were gone.

# CHAPTER 36

Tony rubbed his eyes. He was beyond weary. He was numb, lost in a place that to him, at least, was overwhelming and out of control. He looked over at Frazier as he drove. There was actually a smile on his friend's face. Damn if Ironman wasn't having a good time. *Son of a gun is nuts*, Tony thought. He's the one suited to this work. He'll make his father proud.

Carlos and Diana were huddled together on the rear bench seat. Diana appeared to be sleeping in Carlos's arms. In the middle seats sat the two men Frazier was bringing to the airport. The one seated behind Tony was looking down. A large baseball cap concealed his face. The one seated against the window, immediately behind Frazier, returned Tony's glance for a moment before looking down again. But Tony knew right away who he was. General Lorenzo Fox. It made perfect sense. Fox had been on the CIA's payroll since being recruited by Rubio. His allegiance to Allende had eroded long ago. But the soldiers swarming the city wouldn't know that. His role had been secret. The coup makers would undoubtedly consider him just another member of the president's inner circle, and therefore a target. He needed to get out of Chile before he too was shot or taken to a place like San Sebastiano for questioning, torture, or death.

The bargain General Fox had made with Washington a year ago was proving a very wise one right now. When the coup erupted, he immediately called Rubio, and now he was being whisked out of Chile by U.S. government services like a prominent statesman. No doubt he would arrive, with a pocketful of money, at a suitable and safe destination—Mexico City, Houston, or Miami. He would have every opportunity for happiness, unlike other Allende supporters who had been left behind to face the harsh music of Pinochet's repressive and vindictive junta.

So if Fox was escaping, where was Cristina? And who was the other man in the van? Tony looked at him again, out of the corner of his eye, and waited. The man was wearing a heavy coat and baggy trousers, and the hat covered his eyes. But something about him was curious and wrong. The way he sat, the way he held his head, the curve of the jaw, the smoothness of his cheek. With another sideways look Tony recognized Cristina, and realized that she had already recognized him. His eyes riveted themselves to her face, and she returned his stare. It was not the same smoky, sensual gaze he had seen the last time they were together, but it communicated just as much. Without so much as a word, they spoke. *You're not who you said you were, are you? You don't really work for the telephone company.* She was frightened and desperate to protect her plan to escape with the general. She needed Tony to say nothing. Tony's eyes responded with their own messages. That he was sorry he had deceived her, but that their moments together had been real. That he was happy she was safe. That he cared for her and about her and would not hurt her. He understood her situation and respected her and would say nothing. But the realization that she was fleeing the country brought him more sadness. Piled on top of everything else, it was almost too much. He was in a cataclysm, everything changing at once, and it had him feeling worn-out and empty. He and Cristina had been so intimate—their time together so exhilarating—that he was sure something special, something lasting would be built on it. They had planned to be together again soon. And now, like so much else in this godforsaken country, it was ending.

But he had no right to claim her and certainly none to betray her. She had warned him, right from the start, that this, whatever this had been, was impossible. So he needed to keep quiet and watch her get on the plane. Maybe someday their paths would cross again and they could talk and he could explain. But for now, she needed to go, and he needed to let her.

Thinking about it later, Tony couldn't really remember how long it had taken to reach the airstrip. But somehow Frazier, with that irrepressible grin on his face, had gotten them there. He had stopped at an open gate long enough to take a look around. "Just where I remembered it was," he said. Then he wrapped his arms over the top of the steering wheel and drove the van through the gates and down the pathway until he stopped alongside the farmhouse. The surrounding fields had already been harvested, judging by their flat, empty surfaces. And there were no signs of activity in the barn and stables, other than a few chickens and a couple of goats. Down a dirt path, at the beginning of an open field, an airplane waited, its twin propellers whirring. The plane and the airstrip had both seen better days, but the engines sounded strong, and there was still enough faded asphalt to qualify it a runway.

Frazier drove slowly along the path until he got about fifty yards from the plane. Then he stopped, dropped the gear shift into neutral and jumped down out of the van. "Wait here," he said without directing his words at anyone in particular. His eyes were on the airplane. But General Fox wasn't taking orders. He jumped down, too, and moved quickly to join Frazier as he advanced toward the open cockpit. Tony thought of saying something to Cristina. But she kept her head down and avoided his eyes. Carlos and Diana were still huddled in their seats together. "It's going to be all right," Tony said. Carlos nodded but stayed quiet.

Fox and Frazier were talking to the pilot, shouting to make themselves heard above the roar of the propellers. Tony jumped down and jogged to them. When he got close enough to see into the cockpit, he saw that sitting in the pilot seat was none other than Captain Jimmy McCluskey, the same Jimmy McCluskey that had driven the step van to the military airlift base at Dover, Delaware, and had stopped somewhere in Jersey to pick up a six-pack and see an old friend. It had only been a year since Mac rescued Tony from his cubicle at the CE plant and the lady with the great legs had joined Tony in the front seat. But it seemed a lot longer.

McCluskey interrupted whatever he was saying to Frazier and Fox and looked at Tony. "Is that who I think it is?" he shouted. He jumped out of his seat and climbed down.

"I can't believe my eyes," Tony said, by then enthusiastically shaking McCluskey's hand. "Captain James Frances McCluskey, as I live and breathe."

"How the hell are you, Tony?" McCluskey offered.

"Hanging in there, Mac. How are you doing?"

"I'm good. It's all takeoffs and landings for me," McCluskey said. But he was interrupted by General Fox, who was impatient to board and wanted to know where to sit. "Wish I had more time to visit," Mac said. "But crossing the Andes is dicey enough in daylight, and it'll be dark in a couple of hours. And your buddy here tells me he wants me to take four passengers, but there's only two listed on my manifest. The extra weight is going to chew up fuel. I'm worried maybe I won't have enough."

"Mac," Tony said, "you've got to take 'em. Things are berserk in Santiago, and the extra two are my friends. It's not safe for them here. Please, I'm begging."

"Well, that leaves me no choice, then does it, pal," McCluskey chuckled. "Me and you, we go way back, don't we?"

"Yeah, Mac, all the way back to New Jersey," Tony replied.

"I guess we're working on story number two then, aren't we?" McCluskey said. "Wait 'til the grandkids hear about this one. All right. I'll take 'em as far as Buenos Aires. Get 'em on board and tell 'em to shake a leg. I may have nerves of steel, but flying over the Andes at night, low on fuel, that'd even make Superman nervous. The quicker we take off, the better our chances of getting there in one piece."

"Thanks, Mac," Tony said. "You're the best." Then he hustled back to the van to help get Carlos and Diana. Cristina had already started walking toward General Fox. Tony hoped she would look back one more time, just so he could see her face. And just before she boarded, she did. Her expression no longer reflected any fear or uncertainty, only courage and determination, and gratitude to Tony for his silence. It reminded him, with a lightning bolt to his heart, of the way Carrie Barber looked when she was conquering a big wave on her surf board or zigzagging gracefully on water skis or galloping on horseback, her blond hair swept back from her beautiful face. Her intrepid look, he called it.

He hugged Carlos and Diana and wished them well. Then he walked toward the van, alone, pinned under the heaviest melancholy.

# CHAPTER 37

Tony got home with just enough energy left to strip off his shirt, splash some water on his face, and wash off his tender forearm. He wasn't sure what day it was, much less what time. He flopped across his bed and was asleep before his head hit the pillow.

In the morning or maybe it was the afternoon or maybe it was the next day after that, Tony awoke. For a few seconds, he wasn't sure about the mad images careening around in his brain. Were they all part of a wild and disturbing dream? He lifted his head and looked around the room. There was his gun and ankle holster. There was his bloody shirt. He felt the ragged laceration on his arm. Reality started coming back to him, or him to it, in reverse chronological order. First he remembered slugging down shots of tequila with Ironman and washing the burn out of his throat with long swigs of lukewarm beer. Then the scene at the airstrip came into focus. Had he just said good-bye forever to Cristina de la Vega? And what about Carlos and Diana? The little clock on the nightstand was showing two o'clock. Assuming it was the afternoon of the day after, the plane would have carried them across the Andes and into Buenos Aires.

Tony dressed slowly and then went out into the street. Things appeared normal, except for the heavily armed soldiers standing on the street corners. Tony stopped at a newsstand and picked up a copy of El Mercurio. The headline screamed, ALLENDE OUT. Reports indicated that Allende had killed himself rather than surrender. A junta of generals, led by Augusto Pinochet, had assumed full authority over the government. The forces of destabilization had won, Tony observed. Allende was dead.

He looked at the photographs accompanying the article. The first showed General Pinochet triumphantly inspecting his troops. But the next one nearly knocked the wind out of him. It showed Salvador Allende in a crumpled heap in the Independence Lounge. He was slumped across a couple of chairs, his head tilted down toward his right shoulder. His face was swollen and unrecognizable. He was wearing dark pants and a pullover with a tweed jacket. Even in the black-and-white of the photograph, the bloodstains were evident. Two soldiers stood stiffly at his side, one of them sporting the distinctive facial hair of Lieutenant Moustache. Alongside his body, next to a steel helmet and a gas mask, was the pistol he had reportedly used to shoot himself. According to the sub caption, the weapon was a Russian antique, a gift from Cuban president Fidel Castro. It's a Russian antique, all right, Tony thought. But I don't think Castro gave it to him. As a matter of fact, it looks exactly like the .9 mm Kaleshnikov I last saw in Mongoose's waistband.

The newspaper made no mention of the trucks loaded with detainees or what was going on at San Sebastiano Prison or at the National Stadium. The mission had succeeded. The communist enemy had been defeated, a president lay dead, and Tony had been a part of it. His days had been filled with alternating moments of terror and exhilaration. How close he had come to real disaster! And what about Cristina? Had she been his victim? By seducing her, the mistress of an important man, he had discovered the hidden attic. And when he needed to, he gave that information to Mongoose, despite his promise. He was a spy. Spies lie to people and betray them all the time. It's in the job description. So why did it hurt so much?

# CHAPTER 38

Six months after Tony got back to America, he called Carrie. Her telephone number hadn't changed and he still remembered it. She answered on the first ring, and for a moment, he didn't know what to say.

"Carrie?"

"Tony?" she answered without hesitation.

"Yes, it's me."

"Where are you?" she asked.

"Back in the States. DC, actually," Tony told her. "I have a few things to finish here, and then I'm thinking maybe of coming to New Haven."

"Oh, really," Carrie answered. "Why's that?" Her reserved tone stung. He wasn't expecting her to be giddy and gleeful at the sound of his voice. Not after the way Tony had ended things. But he hadn't fully considered that she might not care about him anymore, that she had moved on.

"To be honest, well, . . . I really wanted to . . . uh, I guess . . ." Tony was stammering. Finally he got the words out, "I was hoping to see you."

Carrie's aloofness crumbled. She told him how much she had missed him, but that she hadn't forgiven him for leaving. She said that she hadn't really known it or understood it until she was on the telephone with him at this very moment, listening to him say the words she had dreamed he would come back and say, but right now she felt it in every cell of her body: she was still very much in love.

They spoke for almost two hours. They reminisced, they cried, they laughed, and by the end, they were confessing their love. Carrie told him that she regretted making it so easy for him, but she couldn't help it, and then she gave him directions to her new apartment. He promised, with the excitement of the teenage boy he had once been, to drive straight there. She cried some more, and when she couldn't stop, Tony asked her, with heartfelt tenderness, what was wrong. Through her sobs, she told him, "I am so happy. I just can't wait to see you."

They said good-bye and hung up. Before the receiver, which had been pressed so tightly to his ear had a chance to cool, Tony was in his car, racing toward his true love.

The next three days were perhaps the happiest in Tony's life. He spent almost every minute with Carrie, their lovemaking interrupted only for food and sleep. They held each other tightly and made promises, sacred promises, first whispered then shouted, full of words like *forever*. She played their favorite records, and they danced around the bedroom naked until they leapt back into the bed to savor each other again. She served him Campbell's tomato soup and peanut butter and jelly sandwiches and chocolate chip cookies. They loved each other so fervently and with such passion that afterward they passed out in each other's arms. Then they awoke in the middle of the night and made love again. They were making up for all that lost time, all those weeks and months apart. Tony told Carrie that while he was gone he missed her so badly it hurt. That it had been a huge mistake to take the job in the first place, and he had already quit. "I am so sorry I went away, and I will never, ever leave you again." Carrie cried and Tony kissed away her tears.

Then Carrie asked, "Tony, were there other women?"

Tony had known the question might come. And yes, he had wondered whether Carrie herself had been with another. "Do we want to start asking those questions?" he asked. She looked at him. "I loved you every minute I was away," he continued. "No one could ever take your place. And I know that I was away for so long and you would have had every right to . . . to . . ." He choked up to think of Carrie with someone else. "But if you were, I don't want to know. I only want to think about now and tomorrow and all the days after that. I am just so grateful I didn't lose you." Tony's tears came, and now it was Carrie's turn to kiss them away. They embraced again and held each other so tightly they could hardly breathe. Later that day, Tony left Carrie's apartment only long enough to pick up her favorite Chinese food. But it got cold because they made love again before they ate. Then they laughed and then they slept. When they awoke, they kissed and hugged and made their happy plans.

Tony went to the University of Miami School of Law determined to let it refine him. And Tony's experiences in Chile had prepared him well for the process of getting a legal education. Certainly, the stress was mild by comparison. Unlike kids that enrolled right after college, Tony took no offense at the mean-spirited attacks of his professors or the petty competitiveness of his paranoid classmates. These things didn't involve life and death. But there were similarities between clandestine service and law school. Both rewarded the same skills: the ability to identify and prioritize issues—what can control the outcome and what won't matter; staying calm and focused; applying logic to negotiations and problem solving.

Beyond that, Tony had discovered his humanity in Chile. He was not invincible and couldn't overpower everyone. There were people out there that were tougher than him. Ruthless, brutal people. It was foolish and dangerous to try to solve problems with a fist or a gun. There would be no more fighting with strangers. Besides, he didn't want to do anything that might reveal his background or the training he had received. He was determined to keep the pledges of secrecy he had made to the Company when he had quit. Whenever he was asked about the two years he spent between college and law school, he explained that he had been a technical representative for the Continental Electric Company and had provided electrical engineering services, upgrading communications systems pursuant to its contracts with the government. "Too much routine when you're working on a government contract, you know," Tony would mention. "Bureaucracy, no incentives to think outside the box, no way to advance quickly, not a good place for a young person with ambition or initiative. Way too dull." He tried not to lay it on too thick and then he tried not to smile. "A couple of years of boredom was enough," he would add. So he had left CE to become a lawyer. He could recite the story in his sleep. "Always thought about being a lawyer. Took the law boards, did fairly well. Got accepted to Miami . . . blah, blah, blah." No one suspected a thing. Not his classmates, not his parents. Not even Carrie.

Still, a couple of moments did test him. Like the time his Constitutional Law professor broke the class into teams of five students each and tasked them to write a brief on the constitutional right of privacy. The *Roe v. Wade* abortion rights case had just been decided by the Supreme Court, and one of the grounds for its decision was that while it was not specifically identified in the Constitution, the drafters intended it to provide a right of privacy—the right of citizens to be left alone by their government. Tony was grouped with three female students and a good-looking and self-impressed fellow named Rick. In their first meeting, held in a seminar room on the third floor of the Kresse building, Julie Robinson offered to be the group's recording secretary. As the members brainstormed, listing the arguments to be considered on each side of the issue, she took notes. After a couple of hours, the group was tiring. Someone asked Julie to read what she had written. Just a few sentences into it, Rick interrupted. "That's not right," he complained. "You missed the point.

Here, give me your notes." He snatched the notepad out her hands, then started reading out loud, in a mocking tone. "We've been wasting our time for the last two hours because of you," he concluded.

Rick was an arrogant young man from a prominent family, and his high opinion of himself had been apparent from the first day of class. He had been a gymnast in college and still had the broad shoulders and narrow waist of an athlete. He worked out several times a week at the university gym and probably spent as much time admiring himself in the mirror as he did studying. Tony hadn't liked him from the start. When Rick's verbal assault grew even nastier, Tony had had enough. He sprung forward in a lightning quick maneuver that would have made Colonel Melamud proud. Before anyone could blink, Rick found himself lifted off the floor and pinned tightly against the wall by Tony's left forearm, which was securely braced across his Adam's apple. Tony quickly retrieved Julie's notepad from Rick's hand without loosening the grip his forearm had across Rick's throat. Tony thought about delivering a punishing blow, as he had once been trained, but caught himself. The need for such tactics was long gone. Rick was not a hostile paramilitary officer. He was a punk law student whose rudeness had already been punished. And this wasn't revolutionary Chile. It was Coral Gables, Florida, at the University of Miami Law School, for heaven's sake.

Tony looked into Rick's eyes, inches from his own. He could see fear. Rick was frozen, struggling to breathe with Tony's arm across his windpipe. Tony took a second to look around at the rest of the group. Not one of their faces reflected appreciation for the violent turn Tony had taken; in fact, they were terrified and aghast. He saw, with sudden clarity, that his life had changed, and he needed to change too. He wasn't a CIA officer anymore. He was a law student, a civilian, and he had better start acting like one. As his mother and Carrie had both been telling him forever, people cannot earn respect with violence. So Tony calmed himself down, from the inside out. "I know we've been working hard for these last couple of hours, Rick, and we're all tired," he said. "I've reacted badly, and I'm sorry. But I think you need to show a little more respect to Julie and the rest of us." Tony spoke in a voice deliberately made quiet, like the soothing tone a parent might use with a child who already regretted his misbehavior. "Can you do that, Rick?"

Rick nodded quickly. "Good," Tony said. "Then let's get back to work." He let Rick down off the wall and handed the notepad back to Julie. Rick rubbed his throat and coughed a couple of times. Then he took his seat. The group finished its project without further incident. Later, Tony reflected on the episode. He vowed to talk his way through any future confrontations. He was going to achieve his goals with words, not violence. It was time for him to grow up. Two days later, Tony asked Carrie to marry him. The fight with Rick the Dandy had been the catalyst.

When Tony graduated law school, he went to work for the downtown Miami law firm of Ginsberg, Simon, Dunphey, Gamble and Graham. It was one of the oldest and most prestigious firms in the city and had an enviable reputation. The partners didn't know about his background with the CIA, but his engineering degree from Yale and the two years he spent between college and law school working as a field engineer for Continental Electric convinced them he was no dummy. He had done well enough academically at Miami Law, and at his interviews he displayed that same engaging personality. Self-confident but not arrogant. The members of the firm's hiring committee liked him and offered him a position as an associate attorney without hesitation. He fit in right from the start.

Tony came out of law school a new person. He had made friendships there that would last forever. And his relationship with Carrie was better than it had ever been. While he hadn't forgotten Cristina de la Vega, his thirst for adventure, and for affairs with other women, had been quenched. Of course, there were moments when he wondered whether he had given up that life too quickly. When he reflected on the awesome power and authority that working for the CIA had briefly given him and about the exhilaration of completing a secret mission. What other adventures would he have enjoyed had he stayed with the Company? What other people would he have met and what other places would he have seen? But he had made his decision, and despite the occasional questions, he did not regret it.

Those that worked with Anthony Gannon, or against him, could see a strong emotional component in the way he practiced law. Like he was on a mission, one that went beyond making a living. He was devoted to the concept of fairness and didn't like pompous hypocrites who looked down on the rest of the world. He had become a passionate advocate for justice. And a compassionate one who empathized with his clients and worked hard to protect the vulnerable among them. When Tony Gannon went to battle before judge or jury, his heart was invested along with his mind. And once in a while, he let a little of his ardor show as a way of suggesting to his opponents that they should keep their tactics aboveboard because his self-control shouldn't be taken for granted. All things being equal, Anthony Gannon, Esq., was a funny, fun-loving middle-aged lawyer. But when he was braced for battle, there was an unmistakable air of the warrior about him. If you were arrogant or dishonest, you could get him angry. And when Tony Gannon was angry, he could still be genuinely scary.

# CHAPTER 39

"Mr. Gannon?" It was the voice of Tony's secretary, Deborah Thomas. He snapped back to where he was—standing next to her desk in his luxurious Miami offices. "Do you want me to call Ms. Gonzalez back? I can put her in touch with our hiring committee."

"No, thanks, Ms. Thomas. I'll call her." Tony took the message slip back and returned to his private office, closing the door on his way in. The scenes in his head were still swirling like ghosts. He needed to snap out of it before he could call. He sat down, dialed the number, and waited. When she answered, he said, "Ms. Gonzalez?"

"This is she."

"Ms. Gonzalez, this is Anthony Gannon from Ginsberg, Simon. I'm returning your call."

"Oh, thank you so much, Mr. Gannon. My parents, Carlos and Diana Gonzalez, wanted me to give you their regards. Actually, they told me to send you their love."

"How are they doing?"

"Well, they're quite the couple, especially now that my brother and I are out of the nest. Dad's business is doing so well, I think he's going to sell it. They're members of a country club. They play a lot of tennis and golf. I don't know if they're any good, but they really enjoy it."

"I think about them all the time," Tony said. He pictured the Flower Man at a country club. It was a long way from the back of a truck in Santiago to the back nine of an American golf course. *What a country*, he thought. Then he closed his eyes, hard. The emotion was taking hold, and he didn't want Ms. Gonzalez to hear it in his voice. "Tell me about your parents," he managed, and then listened as the young woman told him what had happened to them after Tony had put them on Mac's plane.

Carlos and Diana had come to Miami, where they made a fresh start. They had indeed lost friends and family members in the vindictive, authoritarian rule that took hold under General Pinochet in the weeks and months after Allende fell. Pinochet's political opponents were vigorously persecuted; and hundreds, if not thousands, were kidnapped, imprisoned, tortured, and murdered. Many vanished without a trace. And agents of Pinochet's junta were fully capable of punishing people whose only sin had been their allegiance to Salvador Allende, even those no longer in Chile. Orlando Letelier, Salvador Allende's defense minister, had been assassinated in Washington. General Carlos Prats, the member of the Chilean military most loyal to Allende's democratically elected Popular Unity party, had been blown to bits with his wife in Buenos Aires. Many of the Chilean expatriates that Carlos and Diana befriended in Miami continued to live in terror and pain. But it was not in Carlos' nature to obsess. Sorrow, not a desire for revenge, was the emotional legacy left to Carlos Gonzalez. And hope.

When Diana gave birth to a girl several months after arriving in Miami, Carlos beamed as he bragged to everyone he met about the wonderful mother she had become. And they began selling flowers again, posting hand-written advertisements by the side of the road near the church parking lot where they worked out of a battered van. Carlos devoted himself to building the foundation for their future, choosing not to waste time on things that had occurred before and could not be changed.

After Carlos and Diana's second child was born, a son, the family moved to San Francisco, where Carlos had a cousin. The climate there was more moderate than Miami and reminded him of central Chile. He and Diana had always wanted to go to California, perhaps because they had heard it was the home of "flower power." And indeed there were many lovers of flowers in northern California. Carlos found a neighborhood near Union Square with several grocery stores serving the Hispanic community. He offered them a deal. He could surely sell a lot of flowers from a nice grocery store in exchange for which he would pay them a share of the profits. It presented little risk to the store manager and might just produce a respectable pile of cash at the end of the day. He only had to pitch his plan to a couple of grocers before he found a partner.

Carlos sold a ton of carnations and roses and other pretty blossoms from a Latin supermarket named Alberto's, not far from Fisherman's Wharf. And when Alberto's did well and opened another store in upscale Marin County, Carlos was able to sell more flowers. He was soon able to hire several people to help him. And then another store was opened in South San Francisco. And so on, and so forth, until Alberto's was a huge success in the bay area and Carlos and his many employees were a hugely successful part of it. Carlos bought a lovely home with plenty of rooms and a nice garden in the backyard for Diana.

And then one day when Carlos and Diana were visiting their daughter at law school in Miami, Carlos had read an article about a settlement Anthony Gannon had won for a deserving client; accompanying the article had been a picture of Tony. Carlos recognized his face, and had asked his daughter to call Tony.

"Mr. Gannon?" she said.

"Yes?" Tony said.

"I need to ask you a question, sir. And it might seem silly. I hope you won't mind."

"Of course not," Tony said. "What is it?"

"Well, since we were little, my brother and I have been after our parents to tell us how they chose our names. And whenever we do, they act strangely, like it's a big secret. All they say is that we were both named after the same great man. A Canadian."

"Really?" Tony said.

"And when they told me I should call you, they hinted that you knew the man we were named after and might be able to tell us about him. I don't know why, but they say it has to come from you."

Tony paused. He could feel something weighty coming, something important. "I can try. But you'll need to tell me your first name, and your brother's too."

"Oh, yes. Of course. My name is Andrea. And my brother is Stephens, with an S at the end. Stephens Gonzalez. Unusual, don't you think?"

The information hit Tony hard as the depth of Carlos and Diana's gratitude became plain. They had named their children after him. Or who he had been. Andre A. Stephens. Tears filled his eyes, too many to hold back. They flowed down his cheeks until he wiped them with his hand. He would never again have any trouble answering those questions, the ones he had been asking himself for the last thirty years: Had he done the right thing? And was it worth it?

Get Published, Inc!
Thorofare, NJ 08086
12 March, 2010
BA2010071